Step Alpha

A Wolf Shifter Academy Romance

Wolf Ridge High

Renee Rose

Want FREE Renee Rose books?

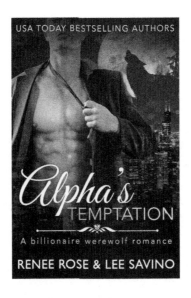

Go to http://subscribepage.com/alphastemp to sign up for Renee Rose's newsletter and receive a free copy of *Alpha's Temptation, Theirs to Protect, Owned by the Marine* and more. In addition to the free stories, you will also get bonus epilogues, special pricing, exclusive previews and news of new releases.

Chapter One

Rayne

There are three things I hate about Wolf Ridge High School: the alpha-holes (the football players who rule our social lives), the volleyball players (think female version of alpha-holes), and the rest of the student body, with the exception of the humans.

So, yeah. That leaves me pretty much with no one.

Which, as the pack runt, is where I've been from the beginning, so it's nothing new.

At the moment, it's the volleyball players who I most despise. Mainly, Casey Muchmore.

"Runt!" she yells at my back as I try to fast-walk it around the school. "Runt! Don't make me chase you."

Casey is the alpha she-wolf of the school, nearly as mean as her brother Cole was when he ruled these hallways two years ago.

Crap.

I stop my fast-walking but don't give her the satisfaction of turning around. She catches my shoulder to spin me to

1

face her then plows me against the brick wall where I hit my head.

"I don't heal like you," I say quickly. It's a warning for both our sakes. I might be the daughter of a shifter–maybe two, my mom would never say–but I'm not like the rest of them. My cells don't regenerate as fast as theirs. Meaning, if she hurts me, it will leave marks. There will be evidence of her torture that I could use against her.

Not that I would. I'm not stupid.

"Then you'd better listen," she growls.

"I don't need to hear it."

"Well, you're going to."

"*Casey*," I interrupt. "I don't care who you make out with. Or what you do. I don't judge, and it's not my business."

"Damn straight." She's lost a little of her fire. I think she thought I would cower and squirm and promise to keep my mouth shut.

In my quest to find a place alone to eat lunch, I just stumbled across her kissing River, one of the cheerleaders. It shouldn't be a big deal. In this day of inclusion, being gay isn't a stigma for teenagers anymore. At least not at human high schools.

But this is Wolf Ridge. Shifters are nothing if not extremely gendered. It's part of wolf culture. Considering how ostracized I am in this pack over being small and never hitting transition, I can't imagine how they would shun a gay wolf.

"You know what I'd be asking myself, if I were you?"

"What?" She seems surprised to hear the confidence in my tone. Yeah, I may be small, but I'm not a coward. Plus, I've been kicked around by these kids since preschool, so I've developed quite a bit of resiliency.

"How River feels about you hiding your affection."

Casey's brows draw together.

"But like I said. Not my business. Your secret's safe with me." I don't look her straight in the eye. I show my throat to offer my submission, but I also say, "I'm sorry you're not comfortable being yourself at the school you practically run."

I definitely went too far. Her eyes narrow, and she gets right up in my grill. "I'm sorry your mom fucked a mouse to get pregnant with you."

"Nice one," I say drily.

"But I guess her whole status finally changed, didn't it? How's your new step daddy? Did he take you into the family, too, or did he build you a doghouse out back? I mean a mouse-house?"

"Does it make you feel better?"

"What?"

"Being cruel to me? Does that help you feel better about your own inner trauma?"

Casey releases me as if my skin burns her. "Back off, Runt."

I let out a dry chuckle. "I'm the one with her back smashed against the wall, here, Casey." I dare to meet her eye for a moment, and I see the pain behind her gaze.

Apparently, getting real with Casey worked because she abruptly turns on her heel and stalks away, her long, thick ponytail swinging behind her.

I sag against the bricks in relief.

Looks like I get to live another day. Getting beat up at school would be just another point against me at home.

A reminder that when Logan Woodward, a member of Wolf Ridge pack royalty, married my mom three weeks ago, he took on the biggest loser in the pack as his new stepdaughter.

Something for which I'm quite certain his son, Wilde, former team captain of WRH, will never, ever forgive him.

Something for which I'm sure my new stepbrother will make me pay dearly.

* * *

Wilde

Our hotel room's popping, party vibe on full blast.

The smell of humans is thick in here. I'm used to the stench, but I still hate it. It's in the locker rooms, the hallways at school. In the frat house where I live with my so-called buddies from the team. It's a dull, sickly scent.

Or maybe it's just that my senses have dulled from living amongst humans.

All I know is, most days, I'm crawling out of my skin pretending to be one of them. At the moment, there are far too many packed in one place.

Duke just crushed Clemson, so my teammates are celebrating their asses off. Cheerleaders from both teams circulate in skimpy clothing. It's funny to me that the Clemson girls would come. I guess they have no loyalty to their own kind. Humans are weird like that.

I'm not surprised they were invited. A lot of my teammates have a thing about conquering the other team's women. Some primal shit, I guess. Honestly, I was going to try to cheer myself up with a tall, leggy fake blonde, but something has my wolf on edge.

Some prickling. Some awareness that I need to keep my wits about me. Pay attention. Which is why I'm the only sober one here. Not that it's really possible for a wolf shifter to get wasted. We metabolize way too fast. Everyone's doing lines because we just got drug-tested yesterday, which means we're safe to sample for a few more weeks.

Our quarterback and my roommate, Ryan, went out to buy more beer, which we definitely don't need, considering how much Big C we have. Ryan is a senior, and I'm a sophomore, but we're the star players, so I rank high enough socially on the team to be his roommate. Either that or I'm the only guy he trusts not to steal the very large amount of snow he bought before the game to sell when we get back.

We already got thrown out of the pool area and the bar. That's how things ended up here, in our room. The manager asked us to keep it down about twenty minutes ago, but we didn't pay much attention.

I walk to the window and look out, rubbing the back of my neck. My wolf must have drawn me there because I see two cop cars below.

Fuck. This must be why I had no urge to join the party.

"Everybody out. Cops are here. *Now*, people." I use some alpha command into my voice, even though they're humans. Sometimes they'll respond to it, depending on how sensitive they are to energy.

Most of these people are too fucked up to notice.

I put my fingers to my lips and whistle then hit the lights on and off. "I said, everybody out. The cops are on the premises. Party's over."

There are groans, but my teammates put a little hustle into it, knowing if we get busted Coach Granview will kick our asses. The cheerleaders grab their discarded clothing. The guys claim their women for the night.

The cops arrive as the last people walk out the door.

And...there's white powdery probable cause all over the dresser.

I would've been better off letting the party be broken up by the cops because now there's a whole lot of coke and just one guy.

Me.

I literally just set myself up to be the lone guy taking the fall for Ryan and the rest of the dickheads on my team.

For some reason, I get nothing from my wolf. No guidance whatsoever. And he's the dickwad who warned me. So that must mean...he wanted me to get caught.

And then I get it. This is revenge on my dad.

I fuck up my football career, his pride suffers.

It's payback for what he did to my rep the day he decided to marry that defective little runt's mom.

The day he made Rayne the Runt my new stepsister.

And that's why I say and do nothing when they handcuff me, read me my rights, and take me to jail.

* * *

Rayne

I strut around my new bedroom—the space still very much inhabited by the energy of my dickwad stepbrother—in a brand-new pair of Manolo Blahnik stilettos.

I'm barely five feet tall in a pair of thick-soled sneakers, but I know how to walk in heels. Not because there's ever an opportunity for a seventeen-year-old outcast in a small Arizona town to dress up and go out.

Nope. This is an at-home-only activity. Supposedly, there's only one way out of Wolf Ridge after high school, and that's a sports scholarship. Considering I'm the runt of the pack with no athletic abilities whatsoever, I had to find a different way.

Academic scholarships are out. No one from Wolf Ridge High ever gets much of a merit-based scholarship because our school sucks. I mean, my human friend Bailey got one, but she also transferred into WRH her senior year, so she had all kinds of AP classes and accolades before she ever moved here.

I make a circuit around the room and survey my image on the computer screen. I'm in a black lacy bra and panty set with an unbuttoned flannel shirt thrown over the top to keep me warm. The shoes are shiny black patent leather. They pinch my toes, but I look amazing in them if I do say so myself.

No, I'm not joining a beauty pageant.

I'm selling videos of my feet on the internet. Men who are into feet pay for videos like this. One such man bought these shoes for me. I have five other pairs hidden in my closet. All I have to do is make a video every day to post to the viewers on my OnlyFans and Patreon accounts, and the money pours in.

Lots of money. I made two thousand dollars last month, and I've only been at this since July.

Yes, I know it might be illegal. I'm not entirely sure. I'm under eighteen, so it might be considered child pornography. Then again, it's just feet. So...? I think it's fine. Obviously, I don't want anyone who knows me to find out, but it's definitely a risk worth taking.

If I can increase my income to three or four thousand a month, I'll have enough to go to ASU next fall. I've already been accepted and offered a partial tuition scholarship. Don't be impressed–they have to accept any Arizona student with a 3.0 or better GPA, and the scholarships are automatic based on GPA. Even so, the room and board costs a fortune–way more than my mom could ever afford. Plus, I have a C in Calculus right now, which if I don't fix, could ruin everything.

And there's no chance I would ask or expect Logan, my new stepdad, to pay my way.

He probably could afford it, but I think we're already supposed to be grateful that he even agreed to marry my mom after he found out he knocked her up.

I angle the laptop screen down, so it only shows me from the waist down and hit record. Then I strut back and forth in the shoes. "What do you think of my new shoes, gentlemen?" I ask in my most sultry voice. "Are these sexy? If you want to see something different, just send me the shoes in a size 6 to the post office box address at the bottom of the page."

I stop and pose. Do my awkward version of sexy legs, sliding one toe up behind my calf and down again. Posing with one foot out to the side. Turning around and taking a wide stance then bending over with my hands sliding down my thighs.

My dark blonde hair falls over my shoulders.

I stopped bleaching it to platinum and have grown it out into soft layers that fall to my shoulders. Not for the videos–I never show my face or hair. My mom asked me to. I guess we're supposed to look more presentable as new members of the Woodward family.

As if anything could ever change our status in the pack.

But since my defective genes make me the primary cause of our low status, I could hardly refuse. I mean, I want to refuse. I want to rebel and tell the whole town to fuck off. But my unborn sibling deserves to have his or her father around. My mom deserves to not be a single parent this time around.

So sacrifices had to be made.

I grudgingly made myself more presentable. We moved into Logan Woodward's house. That would've been okay. He's a pompous dick but not unkind to me. It would've been fine if it wasn't for his son Wilde—one of the biggest alpha-holes Wolf Ridge High has ever seen.

Fortunately, he's off playing football on scholarship at Duke.

Which doesn't mean he won't make my life miserable the second he's back in town. I mean, *I moved into his bedroom.*

That's gotta be like a bone in the throat to him. The school's biggest loser is now his stepsister, living under his dad's roof, sleeping *in his bed.*

I was too scared to change a single thing. His dad emptied the dresser and closet for me, but most of my stuff is still in bins stacked against the wall. I don't want to take down his school letters or football pennants, but I did tack flowy scarves over the disgusting pin-ups he has on the wall.

I continue to twirl and pose, then come closer to the camera and turn one knee in. "Do you want to see me *out* of these shoes?"

I make it sound like I'm stepping out of panties, but to the people—men, mostly—who are into feet, that's what it's like.

"Hmm?" I purr. "Is that what you want? Remember, you can always book a private session with me and ask for everything your dirty heart desires."

I step out of the shoes to give them some naked foot time. I raise one heel to demi-pointe and turn it right and left like I'm putting out a cigarette on the floor.

I ripple my toes like I'm playing piano with them—something that drives them wild.

"Do you want to suck these toes? You want me to walk all over you with them? Hmm?"

I turn around and rub my toes up the back of my leg in what I hope is a coquettish move.

"Who wants to give me a foot massage? That would get me so hot." My voice is coated with honey.

I put some lotion on my feet and then rub it around without my hands–using my toes only. They go absolutely wild for that.

I finish up and end the recording then upload it.

Fuck–I'm running out of time. My mom and Logan will be home any minute, and I'm supposed to have dinner ready.

That's me–Cinderella.

It's not Logan who ordered the chore, it's my mom. She's trying very hard to make this work. To show what a helpful, grateful teenager I am. I feel like an unwelcome guest in this house, to say the least.

I yank a pair of shorts over my lace panties and button up the flannel then put the Manolos back in their shoebox and hide them in the closet.

Out in the kitchen, I throw open the refrigerator and pull out yesterday's roast chicken, along with onion, celery, grapes, pecans and mayo. I chop the chicken, onion, and celery and slice the grapes in half.

I hear Logan's Tahoe pull up as I'm dumping it all in a bowl. Crap. I rush through spooning mayonnaise and dumping curry powder in and stir quickly.

He and my mom both work at the brewery. My mom has a low-paying job on the production floor. He is one of the upper echelons, not an executive, but upper management. He's not pack royalty, but he thinks he is. Or at least his son certainly thinks he is.

I hear him shouting before they even come to the door. Not at my mom, I don't think. It sounds like he's on the phone with someone.

Oh.

"I do not understand how a son of mine could possibly have fucked up this badly. This better be a fucking joke. A bad fucking joke."

Uh-oh. I'm only a tiny bit gleeful that it sounds like Wilde's in trouble.

Logan throws open the door and stomps inside the house. He walks to my side and peers in the bowl of curry chicken salad then recoils like I'm cooking caterpillars or something.

"If you think I'm going to post bail to get you out of there, you are dead wrong. You've embarrassed yourself, me, and this pack. What do you think Coach Jamison would say? After all he did for you to get you on that team? This is the way you repay him? This is the way you repay all of us for the investment we made in you?"

I may not be able to shift into wolf form, but I do have shifter hearing, so I hear Wilde's muttered response, which is just "I know, Dad. Sorry."

Maybe I'm hearing it with my own bias, but he doesn't sound all that sorry to me. It sounds a little more rehearsed than I would expect from someone who is obviously in jail, off the Duke football team, and getting shamed hard by his dad.

"I wouldn't be surprised if Alpha Green booted you out of the pack. You know what happened with Trey and Garrett, don't you?"

"Yes, sir," Wilde answers.

Logan's referring to the alpha's son and his best friend,

who were both thrown out of the pack for marijuana use just out of high school.

I steal a furtive glance at my mom who stands in the doorway of the kitchen, one hand on her swollen belly, her worried gaze on her new husband.

And yes, it's *husband*, not *mate*. They married at a courthouse three weeks ago after Logan discovered he'd knocked her up during a full moon run a few months back. Just another reason for the pack to hate us. Everyone thinks she trapped him in an effort to raise her status.

As if Logan Woodward farts rainbows, and he's that much of a catch.

"Well, you can sit your ass in jail and think about how you just threw your entire life away. You won't be getting help from me." Logan ends the call. "What is that?" He points at the chicken salad as if nothing just happened.

"Curried chicken salad."

"I need more meat than that," he grumbles.

"It's literally a meat salad."

"Rayne." My mom opens her eyes wide in a warning.

"Sorry, but am I wrong?"

"Heat up some hot dogs, too, honey." My mom tries to fix it.

I whirl to the fridge and pull out the hotdogs, biting my lips to avoid saying anything snarky. In fairness, he probably does need a ton more meat than I do. Fate knows my mom's been eating twice what she used to now that she's pregnant.

"What happened, Logan?" my mom asks softly.

"Don't pretend you didn't hear. He was arrested in a hotel in Greenville for possession of cocaine with the intent to sell."

I literally hear his teeth grind.

I turn to face the cabinets as I rip open the package of

hotdogs and dump them in a frying pan with a little water. I wouldn't want my mom or stepfather to see how satisfying I find the scandal.

King Wilde, former WRH Football Team Captain and all-star alpha-hole, was knocked down from this throne.

I'm not sad for him.

At all.

Especially not if it means he will never return to Wolf Ridge.

Wilde

In the end, it's Ryan who shows up for the arraignment and pays my bail. He should–he fucking owes me.

I don't know whether the cash was his or he borrowed it. I don't ask.

He has both our overnight bags with him–the ones from the hotel. The rest of the team will be gone by now on this morning's flight back to Durham.

He gets behind the wheel of what must be a rental car but doesn't start it up. Both his hands are on the wheel, and he looks straight ahead. I swear he's tenser than I am. "Listen, we'll get you a good lawyer. Get the charges dropped. You'll be back on the team by next season."

I nod, numbly. He wants me to keep my mouth shut. Keep him and his side hustle of selling snow out of my court case.

"I, uh, I don't know what to say–"

"Don't say anything," I interrupt. "It is what it is."

He gives me a searching look.

I shrug, shoving back the disgust that crawls up my throat every time I think about that phone call from my dad.

Not the one I had from jail. The one that came a few weeks ago. The one where he told me he married Rayne the Runt's mom and moved them into our house.

"Well...I'm sorry. I really am, man."

I shake my head. "We're cool," I say, even though we've never actually been cool. Because these guys aren't my real friends. I'm just playing a role here. "Thanks for bailing me out."

He starts the car and drives to the airport where we return the rental and head to the ticket counter. "I got both our tickets changed," he says.

I stare up at the board showing all the departing flights. There's one going to Phoenix in an hour.

For the second time in twenty-four hours I make a life-changing and probably stupid decision. "Listen, Ryan. Can you spot me another five hundred bucks? I'm gonna fly home instead."

"Yeah?"

I nod. "I have no reason to go back to school if I'm suspended from the team."

"What about your classes?"

The classes I'm failing out of? "Fuck 'em."

Ryan shakes his head like he can't understand me, but he pulls out a credit card. "Then let's get you home."

I guess the bastard must really feel bad about fucking me over because he books me a first-class flight home. And no, they didn't ask for identification before they served me that gin and tonic.

Maybe I'm nuts to go back to Wolf Ridge. I certainly could go and stay with my mom. She'd be overjoyed to have me. But she moved back to her home pack in Ohio after she left my dad. That's not my home.

Of course, my dad was right—the entire town of Wolf

Ridge will be ashamed of me. I might get kicked out of the pack.

But I guess that's kind of the point.

My dad's the one who made a mockery of us by marrying the runt's mom. So I guess I don't mind sticking it to him. He wants me to stay away? He wants to talk about bad choices?

Fuck him.

He's the one who couldn't keep his dick to himself. My mom divorced him two years ago for his propensity to fuck every female with a white tail during the full moon runs.

So now it finally bit him in the ass, and he had to do the honorable thing and marry the she-wolf he knocked up. But, fates, is his taste in females really that bad? He had to pick the lowest female in the entire pack to pin down and make happy out in the forest?

Christ, the woman can't be younger than forty-five. And the last wolf she gave birth to isn't even a wolf. Rayne the Runt can't shift to save her life. She's been an outcast since before puberty, and it only got worse when what we all suspected was confirmed.

She's probably half-human. No one knows who sired her.

No, my dad's the one who has lowered our family's status by marrying into *that*. By letting them move into our house. Take our name.

And if I just added a little more ruin to it, well then, that's icing on the cake.

I recline the wide chair back and close my eyes.

Wolf Ridge, here I come.

Little stepsister, prepare to suffer.

I'm going to make your life a living hell.

Chapter Two

Rayne

R In bed that night, I toss the covers off. Lately, I've been getting sweaty at night, like I'm having hot flashes. Or like I'm the one who's pregnant. Only I'm obviously not since I'm a virgin *and* on the pill because my period went haywire this year.

I've also been more emotional, physically sensitive, and smells bother me. All things that go with pregnancy. I think I'm having an empathic reaction to my mom's situation.

Who knows what's going on with my hormones? I'm the freak, right? Nothing works right in my body.

I hid in my–er, Wilde's–room to eat my dinner and hadn't really ventured out since. My mom has been trying to get us to do sit-down dinners together as a get-to-know-each-other kind of thing, but there was no way I was going to hang around tonight.

Not with the mood dear old dad was in.

Honestly, he terrifies me.

Not because he's been mean to me. He hasn't. But he's pretty much a stranger and as of three weeks ago, we're

17

suddenly living in his house, under his rules. And he's your typical male wolf with strong alpha tendencies. He was captain of the football team, just like his son. He married one of the cheerleaders. Screwed the rest of them, I'm sure because I think the guy gets around.

I'm surprised Wilde was his only pup until now.

His wife–again, *wife*, not *fated mate*–left him the moment Wilde graduated high school. It was the classic "staying together for the kids" marriage. I guess she moved back to her home pack in Ohio.

I didn't expect him to marry my mom. I thought maybe he'd throw her some child support. Make sure she had everything she needed, that kind of thing. But I guess he thought that was dishonorable. He wanted to do the right thing by his pup.

So here we are. Moved into his house. He's already converted the spare room into a nursery, which is why I'm in Wilde's bedroom.

I tried to convince my mom to let me stay alone in our place, but of course, she wouldn't go for it. It was a long shot, for sure.

Outside, I hear the loud rumble of Cole Muchmore's restored 1950's Ford Truck outside.

For one brief second, I get excited, thinking maybe Cole and Bailey have come up from Tempe for a visit. And then I realize there's only one reason Cole would be pulling up to Wilde's house at midnight. It's not for a visit.

It's to drop off Wilde.

Fuck. Me.

I sit up in bed and peek out the window. I'm in nothing but a tank top and panties because I am getting so hot at night. The moment I confirm my worst suspicion, the heat in my body turns to chills.

Wilde jumps down from the truck, murmuring "thanks, bruh," and clomps to the front door.

He turns the knob, and it catches on the lock my mom insists on setting. I doubt any other shifter in Wolf Ridge ever uses a lock, especially not when they're in the house. If any human intruder came in, the shifter could easily overpower them, and if it was a shifter breaking in—well, then, a lock wouldn't keep them out. They could just break down the door.

But my mom has always worried for my safety. Like I'm some delicate flower without the ability to fight who might get snatched from my bed in the middle of the night. So even now, living with Logan, she locks the door, much to his annoyance.

Wilde grunts and throws his shoulder into it.

Not wanting the door to break and my mom to get blamed, I fly out of bed and dash for the door, unlocking it in time to throw it open before he slams his body against it again.

Wilde stumbles through the opening, knocking me backward. His hand shoots out to grab my forearm to keep me from landing on my ass, and he stares at me with a mixture of shock and disgust.

He doesn't release my arm from his bruising grip. Of course, he can see in the dark far better than I can. I flush, realizing what he sees.

Short little me, standing in nothing but the black lace panties I was wearing for the video and a tiny tank top.

His nostrils flare as he takes in my scent, and for a moment, I see the green flash of his wolf eyes. His upper lip lifts in a snarl.

I attempt to take a step back, but he doesn't let go. Not that distance would help me if he decided to lunge. He's practically twice my size and ten times as fast and strong as I am.

"Rayne." He says it like a curse. Like I'm the bane of his existence. His large fingers make my forearm look like a twig between them, but they send sparks of awareness racing across my skin.

The cold flash turns to heat once more. A feverish burn that starts in my core and pools there, flowing down the insides of my legs. Am I...*turned on* by him? Or is it just the awareness that I'm standing here in a pair of panties?

"Wilde."

He's still as jock-gorgeous as ever. If you think jocks are gorgeous, which I don't. But Wilde is a perfect specimen of male physique. Tan. Bulging muscles. Square jaw with a cleft chin. Dark, curling lashes that frame a pair of hazel eyes.

"What the fuck is this?" Logan's heavy footsteps stomp down the hallway.

Wilde finally drops my arm, choosing to ignore his dad as he heads toward his bedroom.

My bedroom. Fuck.

My stomach draws up into a tight knot under my ribs.

"That's Rayne's room now." Logan says it as a challenge. As a punishment.

It's enough to make Wilde stop in his tracks and swivel to face not his father but me.

The look he gives me could freeze water in the desert. *"Is that right?"* There's a threat in his words like he's daring me to confirm the fact.

For some reason, it makes my nipples hard.

Fate help me, Wilde's gaze drops to the front of my tented tank top.

His dad says, "Your workout room is now a nursery. Looks like you'll have to find somewhere else to crash."

"Logan, no," my mother entreats. She stands just outside the master bedroom in a short bathrobe that swells at the belly. It's apparent she was sleeping in the nude.

Ugh. Not something I want to think about.

"Wilde belongs here, no matter what happened in South Carolina. *Especially* if he's in trouble."

Logan's teeth grind.

"I'll sleep on the couch," I offer, even though it's the last thing I want to do. I already feel so out of place here.

"*No.*" Logan gives his son a death stare. "Wilde will sleep on the couch. He can put his things in the nursery for now."

"Naw, I'm good." Wilde drops a single duffel bag onto the floor by the couch, toes off his sneakers, and stretches his giant form out on the sofa. He's too big for it. His feet hang off one edge, his arm drops onto the floor.

"I'll get a pillow," I say.

Logan seems to see me for the first time. "Put some clothes on first, for fuck's sake," he mutters.

I scurry to the room—Wilde's room—and pull on a pair of pajama pants. When I return with the pillow, Logan and my mom have gone back to their room. It's just me and Wilde.

I swear to fate, it's like walking into a forcefield of hate. Like my body slows down when I get close to him, reluctant to even enter his sphere of anger. But there's also heat. An inferno of heat that licks through my core and limbs.

I take the memo and stop to toss the pillow at him.

He refuses to catch it, letting it hit his body and drop to the floor then staring at it. "Pick it up, Runt." His eyes glint with green again, like just the sight of me makes him angry enough to shift.

My belly flip flops.

To say I'm scared is an understatement. I'm terrified of him. Of what he might do to me the moment he gets a chance.

But I don't show it. "Pick it up, yourself, jackass." I toss my hair as I turn on my heel and strut back to the bedroom like I'm a spoiled princess, and he's the serf instead of the other way around.

His growl seems to surround me, to enter me. To turn my blood to molten lava.

I gasp as I throw open the door to the bedroom and close it behind me, leaning against it as if I expect him to come and beat it down any moment.

When my heart stops racing, I strip out of the pajama pants and crawl under the covers. I lie there for a long time, but sleep completely eludes me. For some reason, I'm feverish again, a slow pulsing heat starting up between my legs. I've never been one to masturbate, but I bring my fingers there, surprised by how sensitive I am. The barest brush makes me shiver and clench.

I keep touching, to take the edge off, but sleep still eludes me. All night long, I'm tossing and turning and squeezing my legs together with no relief.

Finally, at dawn, I slip into a fitful dream about meeting Wilde in his wolf form out on the mesa. He's hunting me, a huge black wolf, walking slowly on enormous paws, toying with his prey. I run and run until I crash into Bailey, who hands me a shotgun. *Silver bullets*, she says. *It's the only way to kill them.*

I aim the shotgun right at his chest but find it impossible to pull the trigger.

I can't kill Wilde, I tell her frantically. *He's my step-brother now.*

Do it, she urges. *Or you'll never sleep in peace again.*

Wilde leaps with a snarl. Now is the moment. It's either kill or be killed. But I don't do it. Instead, I allow Wilde to tackle me to the ground and eat me whole.

* * *

Wilde

I can't sleep on a fucking couch. I don't even fit on the damn thing. The indignity of it rankles me to my core. But it's not the couch that really gets under my skin.

It's the damn runt. Her scent is still on my palm.

Rayne.

I can't believe she's sleeping in my room, in my bed, right now. It's about as wrong as things could get.

What's more...what was up with her coming to the door in her panties?

It can only be because I spent a night in jail not sure if I'd ever see freedom again that my cock got hard when I saw her.

I reach down and arrange my junk. I'm still sporting a semi, which pisses me off. I don't find Rayne even the slightest bit attractive.

She's defective. Probably not even full shifter. My wolf would never want to mate with someone like her.

Still, I have to admit she looks better than when I saw her last. She still has that nose piercing, but her hair is a normal color and not punked out in all directions anymore. It actually looked...well, I wouldn't say pretty, but decent.

Pretty if you didn't know she was defective. The heart-shaped face. The big blue eyes. Bowtie mouth.

And those legs...

For someone so short, she has long legs. She definitely knows how to use them. The way she strutted out of this room could slay a room full of human males. She also has decent tits. She's the right proportions. At least she has that going for her. Did her nipples get hard for me?

No, I must have imagined that.

But I can't stand that her scent is all over me now. Curling up in my nostrils, infuriating me with each breath. It makes my wolf snarly and aggressive.

Fuck, what if my new sibling is just like her? Defective and weak. Small and helpless, like a human?

I turn over angrily, adjusting the pillow beneath my neck. My cock twitches, like it's still interested in knowing what's under those panties Rayne was wearing.

I refuse to touch it. There's no way in hell I will stroke myself off thinking about Rayne the Runt.

I'd rather die.

Chapter Three

Rayne

I wake up from my dream just before Wilde tackles me. I'm covered in sweat, my heart racing, and my mouth wet with saliva. The skin around my nose ring itches. I throw off the covers, yank on my pajama pants and creep out to the shower. It's a school day, which means I have to be ready early, so my mom can drive me to school on her way to work.

Like the homes of all the wealthier citizens of Wolf Ridge, Logan's house is up on the mountain at the edge of the forest. It's not on the school bus route, and I don't have my driver's license yet–a fact that's been a constant source of tension since we moved in.

I shower quickly, worried the whole time that Wilde will have to use the bathroom and be pissed that I'm in it.

But I shouldn't have to live with this much anxiety.

Fuck Wilde.

Screw Logan, for that matter.

But, of course, the moment I step out of the bathroom

with the towel wrapped under my armpits, I slam into a wall of solid muscles.

I thought the senior football players at Wolf Ridge High were muscular, but they are *nothing* compared to Wilde. He's a sculpted *god*. He would win any body building competition he entered and then some.

I bite back the instinct to apologize. I belong here, too, dammit.

"Watch it, Runt," Wilde growls.

"Watch it, yourself, Wilde," I dare. Because what is he going to do? He can't very well hurt me or say anything while the parents are in the house–they will hear everything.

He shows me his bared teeth as he turns sideways to get through the door to the bathroom. I notice he's still in the same clothes he came in wearing last night like he slept all night in them. I get a whiff of his leather and toffee musk, and my knees go weak. The brush against his hard abs sends quivers down my inner thighs, even though I'd never be interested in a guy like him.

I mean, I guess my body is interested, but my brain sure isn't.

I ignore the stab of guilt I have about taking his room.

It's not my problem. He brought all of this on himself.

I get dressed and comb through my wet hair. I have to use some rubbing alcohol around my nose ring. I swear, lately, it feels like the hole is closing, which doesn't make sense because I've had the piercing since Freshman year.

I put on a touch of makeup. I used to go for the heavy black eyeliner punk-emo look, but I've lightened up over the past couple of years. After I befriended Bailey, a human senior and similar outcast, my sophomore year, I had a good nine months of hanging out with the in-crowd–

Wilde included. It was amazing to have a social life for once.

Bailey ended up paired with the star quarterback in the shifter world's most unlikely match ever, and she pulled me into their sphere with her. But then they all went to college.

Still, things softened for me. Shifter kids weren't as outwardly mean to me anymore. I was more familiar. I didn't seem as out of place in a crowd. But I did stop going to social events. I just didn't feel comfortable without Cole Muchmore–Bailey's boyfriend–having my back. No one would bother me when I was under his protection.

I'm still in my room when I hear Logan's deep voice in the kitchen. "You're going to go down to talk to Coach Jamison today," he tells Wilde. "You better tell him what you've done and beg him to let you train with the team."

"I'm not training with high school students." Scorn laces Wilde's retort.

I hear a heavy thud of a body being thrown up against a wall. Even though I know this is normal–that shifters show dominance with physicality because no one can truly be harmed–my heart bangs in my chest. I didn't grow up this way. I haven't been around a parent who gets physical.

I very much don't like it.

"*Logan.*" Apparently, my mom doesn't like it, either.

"You will get on that field and train every goddamn day if you're in Wolf Ridge. And you'll be taking your sister to school from now on."

"My *sister?*"

Oh no. *Oh, fates no.* This is bad. Awful, even.

I want to run out and say it's not necessary, but I already know I won't win the argument. Plus, I'm intimidated by Logan.

"Logan, no. I can take her," my mom says. "Don't make

it a punishment, or they'll never get along."

"He needs to pull his weight around here if he's going to stay."

No part of me wants to emerge from the bedroom, but I can't hide in here forever. I pull open the door and go to the kitchen like there's not a full-scale war going on. I pull out a bowl and pour myself cereal.

"You need to find a job, stay in football shape, keep up with your classes, and take over driving Rayne. Better yet, teach her how to drive, so she can take that burden off everyone."

Burden. Ouch.

I knew that's what I was, but it still hurts to hear it spoken out loud.

I hide my face over the bowl of cereal, keeping my back turned to all of them. Instead of sitting at the table, I stand at the counter and look out the window at the incredible view of the mountains.

"My Jeep is still in Durham," Wilde mutters.

Logan is silent for a moment. "Leslie, give him the keys to your Subaru," he says. "We'll talk more when I get home."

Now I turn to see what my mom will do.

She pauses a moment, shooting me a worried glance, but she's too dedicated to making this thing with Logan work out. She leaves the kitchen and returns with the keys to her car.

Fuck.

Just when I thought things couldn't get worse, they did.

* * *

Wilde

28

For someone so little, Rayne is full of sass. Not with my dad–she's not stupid. But with me.

When it's time to go to school, she comes and kicks my shoe. "Let's go."

No *please*. No meekness. I don't even scent fear on her. She's in baggy shorts and a loose t-shirt, which I hate. She could look so much better. I've seen her body. It's decent. There's no need to downplay it the way she does.

Her scent invades my senses. I don't mind it. It's infinitely better than the scent of a human, even if she is defective. I actually find it pleasant.

I also don't mind the attitude. I'd probably feel a smidge of remorse if she were a cowering sheep. I like that she gives it back to me. It solidifies my decision to make her life miserable.

Because at some point, I need everyone in this house to realize what a colossal mistake this blended family thing is. I want Rayne and Leslie to go back to their side of town with the new baby.

Except that doesn't feel right. That kid will be my sibling. It will be my duty to protect him or her, same as it's my father's duty to provide for and protect both the pup and its mother.

Fuck.

If only Rayne wasn't part of this package.

But I shouldn't get my shorts in a wad over the runt, though. She's nothing. A nobody.

Once she's out of high school, she'll hopefully move out.

It's just that my name will forever be linked with hers.

Fates, my dad called her my *sister*.

As *if*.

Behind all this giant wall of resentment is the knowledge that I really shouldn't care about any of it. I should be back at Duke on my football scholarship–the one I will certainly lose now–living my best life.

I'm one of the few who got out of Wolf Ridge. Someone who had the potential of really making something of himself. I could've been very rich. NFL scouts were already eyeing me. I was literally groomed for that life.

But I flushed that all down the toilet when I took the fall for Ryan and the team.

The heaviness of it makes it hard to walk out to the Subaru wagon. To open the door. Get behind the wheel and move the seat back as far as it goes to make room for my long legs.

I thought coming back to Wolf Ridge would be a relief, but it's almost worse than being at Duke. I don't belong here, either. I feel like I'm having some kind of out-of-body experience. I'm looking down at myself, going through the motions of starting up a car and driving the all-too-familiar route to the high school where I was on top of the world, but I'm a stranger to it all.

I say nothing to Rayne, and she doesn't try to talk to me, either. She just scrolls on her phone, her body hugging the passenger door. Her scent fills the car. There's something intriguing in it, but I can't figure out what. A note that tugs at my senses, like a memory I haven't yet had.

I cut through the back parking lot that faces the football field, which is the least convenient entrance for Rayne. I barely bring the car to a stop before she throws open the door and drops lightly onto her small feet.

"Thanks," she mutters.

I don't reply, but my brain is occupied far too long on the drive home wondering why she bothered to thank me.

Whether it was reflexive, or if she's actually the thankful sort.

For some reason, I'm dying to know what it would be like to have her really, truly thankful. To have those big blue eyes trained on my face like I'm her master, and she's my humble slave.

She'd be on her knees. Naked, of course. Or–*fuck*– maybe in those black lace panties she had on last night. She'd stare up at me with adoration and a longing to please, her tiny body vibrating with the urge to do my bidding.

And now I have a semi.

That's just crazy town. I am not even attracted to the little runt.

It's more just that I want to have power over her. I want to put an end to those haughty tosses of her hair and lifts of her dimpled chin. I want to show her who's boss and have her accept it with every bit of her being.

Now my dick's fully hard. I'm definitely going in the wrong direction with these thoughts.

* * *

After jerking off, going for a run in wolf form and taking a second shower, I obey my dad's orders and text Coach Jamison to tell him I'm in town and need to talk.

He replies immediately and offers to take me to lunch.

I feel like a total asshole accepting, especially because I know he's going to be pissed he's paying when he finds out what I've done, but I don't have any cash myself. I had a full ride to Duke, and they treated us like royalty when we were on the road, staying at the nicest hotels and paying for our meals, but I didn't have spending cash, and I didn't have time to work. That was why Ryan was selling. He was using his fame and popularity and the position as the party-man to generate cash.

Between the frat parties and practice, I had no time for studies.

I show up at the New Moon Diner with nothing but a sack full of burdens and the knowledge that it's time to finally unload some of them.

* * *

Matt Jamison is the guy who has always been in my corner. Not that my dad hasn't been. I know he wanted what was best for me, too, but Coach Jamison knew us inside and out. Better than our own parents. Almost as well as our best friends.

Sitting across the table from him is almost painful because I know he'll see through all my bullshit and call me on every ounce of it.

"It's in the news today," he says flatly, the moment he slides into the booth.

Good. That saves me the trouble of explaining why I'm here.

Except he says, "Care to explain?"

I try to swallow and fail. I know a simple, "No, sir," won't fly.

I shake my head weakly. "I don't know…"

He cocks his head, brows raised but says nothing.

I almost wish for him to berate me the way my dad did, but he waits.

"I didn't like living among humans."

There it is. The real crux of the issue. Why I made the choice I did. On some level, I wanted to be kicked out of school and sent home to Wolf Ridge. Except now that I'm here, it's even worse.

Coach absorbs that for a moment without comment.

The waitress, a middle-aged wolf shifter with a kid on the football team, stops by our table. "Coach. Wilde. What can I get you, boys?"

I appreciate that she doesn't ask what I'm doing in Arizona. I imagine word has already traveled to every citizen of this small town.

"Three hamburgers and a plate of fries," I order. "And a chocolate shake."

"Same for me but iced tea instead of the shake," Coach orders. When she leaves, he says, "Duke was too far from home."

Fuck, I must be the biggest pansy on Earth because something shifts in my chest, almost breaking me.

I expected a rebuke. Understanding is almost too hard to bear.

"We should have worked to get you connected with a pack out there."

I shake my head. I know why that didn't happen. My glory was supposed to be for this pack. Alpha Green, Coach Jamison, and my father didn't want another pack to try to claim my success. To get me to mate one of their she-wolves and settle there. I was supposed to be moving on to the NFL, getting rich, and infusing that money back into Wolf Ridge.

"You were homesick, so you purposely fucked up."

"I wouldn't say purposely."

"You subconsciously sabotaged yourself, then."

I lift my shoulders in misery. "I guess."

"So. What are your options now?"

I'm stunned. I kind of can't believe he's not going to read me the riot act. He can be tough on his players, holding us to a higher standard than most anyone else in our lives. The fact that he's skipping the big shaming and going straight to a solution makes it easier for me to breathe.

I lift my heavy head to look him in the eye. "I don't want to go back, Coach."

"Valid." He surprises me a second time. "Clearly you were miserable, or you wouldn't have fucked yourself this badly."

Now, perhaps because he didn't shame me, actual regret soaks through to the bone. I didn't need to cock things up so horribly. To ruin my reputation and risk prison-time in the process. I didn't need to bring shame on my father's head.

Pain makes it hard to speak. I settle for bobbing my head in agreement.

"So let's look at how to get you out of this mess for now. You don't have to go back. You don't have to play football. Wilde, I think the hardest thing for a young alpha wolf to arrive at is knowing the balance between what's good for you and what's good for the pack."

The waitress brings our food, and I pick up the first hamburger, demolishing it in four bites.

"We're warriors. We're wired to sacrifice ourselves for the greater good. You've always been that guy. That's why I made you captain of the team. You understand teamwork, you understand taking one for the team. You understand that it's not all about you."

My eyes get hot. With his praise comes the sharper knowledge of how this drug charge affects the pack. For a guy who prided himself on team before individual, I made a strange choice. Of course, I did actually choose for my team. Just the wrong one. The human one.

"Garrett Green's wife is a lawyer. Obviously, she's not licensed to practice in South Carolina, but I thought you could call her for advice today."

Garrett Green is the alpha's son. He was banished from Wolf Ridge for marijuana use when he was eighteen, but he's now alpha of a growing pack in Tucson. His wife is human, but they say she's special. She has some psychic abilities, I guess.

I nod as I pick up the second burger. "Do you have her number?"

"No, and I'm not going to get it for you. You're going to figure out who you need to call to get it."

Ah, there's the coach I know. Tough love all the way.

"You're smart and resourceful. I'm sure you can figure it out."

I scoff lightly around a mouthful of burger, and he cocks a brow. "What?"

I swallow down the food. "I'm not that smart. I was barely getting C's in my classes, and even those might have been because the coaches put pressure on the professors to keep me passing." Another bite and I've finished the second burger.

"Duke is a tough school. Wolf Ridge High didn't prepare you properly. I also suspect you had very little time to study, am I right?"

I shrug. "We had no time at all."

"So it had nothing to do with how smart you are. Let it go. Can you drop out of your classes this semester before you fail them or finish online?"

I shrug.

"Find out."

There's alpha command in his words. He must be annoyed with my shrugs. I feel it like a blast to the chest, freezing me in place. When it passes, I straighten in my booth seat. "Yes, sir."

"What else?"

I stop with the third burger halfway to my mouth. "What do you mean?"

"What else are you going to do to get on top of this situation?"

I think of my dad's dictates and set the hamburger back down on the plate. I don't want to go back to Wolf Ridge high to train with children. Seriously, I'd rather punch my own face in. But I guess I should stay in shape to keep my options open.

"I, uh...what would you think about..."

Fuck.

Coach Jamison doesn't help me out. He just chews his final hamburger and watches me, waiting.

"My dad wants me to ask you if I can train with the team."

"What do you want?"

"Nobody cares what I want."

"Ah."

I finish my third hamburger and start in on the fries. I guess I thought Coach would say something more, but he doesn't. Nor does he answer my question about training with the team.

"So can I?"

"No."

"No?"

I'm surprised. I mean, I guess I thought this conversation was going pretty well up until now. He'd seemed supportive. Sympathetic, even.

He throws a fifty-dollar bill down on the table and wipes his mouth with his napkin. "Think about why I said no. When you have the answer, come see me."

Chapter Four

Rayne

Everybody's talking about Wilde at school. He's still Wolf Ridge famous, having only graduated two years ago, and I guess the Tiktok of him being taken out of the hotel in handcuffs went viral, at least in Wolf Ridge, this morning. In my Calculus class, the teacher had to step out of the classroom, and suddenly it was a *What's the Scoop with Wilde Woodward?* fest.

Do you think he'll keep playing football?

Will they even let him?

What will his dad say?

Is he still in jail?

"He's home." I don't know what possesses me to speak. I'm certainly not trying to claim any kind of relationship with the guy.

But suddenly, everyone turns to me.

Suddenly, I'm not invisible.

"Oh right. You're his new stepsister." Casey Muchmore eyes me with interest. "So what's the scoop?"

"He's back while things get sorted out." I shrug.

"But what happened?" Abe presses.

Damn. It's tempting to spill everything I know about the situation. To have people interested in what I have to say. To be able to offer them this currency of information in exchange for a few moments of their attention and appreciation.

But I, of all people, know what it's like to have the entire town gossiping about you. It sucks. And even though I don't owe Wilde anything–unless you count the ride to school he gave me this morning under his father's orders–I'm not quite willing to dish out his pain for everyone to examine.

"It's his story to tell, not mine."

Everyone stares at me, some with surprise, some with outright resentment. Like they can't believe my audacity to not feed them everything they crave.

"Oh, please, Runt." Scorn accents Abe Oakley's words. He used to be semi-decent. Earnest, even. But now he's an outright dick. Rather than following in his brother Austin's footsteps and becoming class president, he took Cole Muchmore's gloried position as the school's biggest alpha-hole. His word is the law around here. "Don't pretend you and Wilde even exist in the same reality. He wouldn't claim you as his stepsister if you were the only family he had left."

That shouldn't hurt. I've heard every derisive comment imaginable from the kids in this school, but it lands like a spear straight through my chest. Maybe because I know exactly how true it is.

My upper lip lifts in a snarl, surprising everyone, including myself. I don't have wolfish tendencies since I don't shift. My eyes don't change color. I don't growl. The hairs at the back of my neck rarely stand on end.

I'm saved from any kind of stand-off by the teacher returning to the room. "In your seats," Ms. Landon, our math teacher, snaps. She's a wolf, so her authority has a particular ring to it that makes us all respond.

Her nostrils flare as she takes in the scents of the room, and for some reason her gaze lands on me. I don't know what she scents. My fear?

I didn't feel afraid, though. Hurt, yes. Definitely defensive. But those scents are more subtle, especially in a crowded room of shifters.

We sit through a lesson on derivatives, and then she passes out a worksheet for us to practice problems. I can't focus. I'm still hot under the collar from the offense Abe gave me, which isn't like me.

Usually, I ignore all the bullshit. I've been dealing with it my whole life. I don't know why this would bother me so much, but it does.

I have the dark urge to challenge Abe, which of course, would be suicide.

I want to get him back for poking my sore spot. But I guess the real question is why that spot is so sore? Nothing he said was wrong.

Wilde does hate me. He hates me being his sister. He probably will never accept me as being family.

When I walk out of class, Lincoln, a new human kid, falls into step with me. "Hey."

I look over at him. It's not the first time he's tried to strike up a conversation. I rebuffed his overtures at friendship because, well, I have enough trouble as it is. I don't want to get a reputation for being a human magnet. Besides, he has a twin here at school. A sister. It's not like he's alone.

With Bailey, it was different. She was cool, older, and worth the friendship, even though it meant disobeying Cole Muchmore's nasty dictate that no one was allowed to talk to her.

But I'm not going to go out on a limb a second time with a human. That would make it a pattern and be the kiss of death for any hopes I have of ever being included again. Those hopes are pretty slim as it is.

"That was mean what Abe said to you," Lincoln says.

Fates.

He has no idea that everyone in this hallway can hear him, including Abe, if he's around. The last thing I need is to be responsible for the human getting the shit kicked out of him by Abe and his buddies.

They're not supposed to fight humans—Coach Jamison forbids it—but that won't stop them from throwing their weight around to prove their dicks are longer. They can't help it. It's a male shifter's instinct to establish dominance everywhere he can.

"Whatever."

"No, really. That sucked. Why do you let them talk to you like that?"

Kids in the hallway give me dark looks. Warning looks. Like after Lincoln gets his ass kicked, I'm going to be the one hanging by my panties on the fence outside school.

"What's your deal, anyway, Lincoln?" I ask to change the topic.

He follows me to my locker and waits while I spin the dial. "What do you mean?"

"Why did you come to Wolf Ridge High? Aren't your parents rich?" Everyone here knows the twins live in the brand new, eight-million dollar home at the top of the bluff. The one that makes the locals snarl because it's owned by a human.

"Parent. Singular."

His words tweak my interest against my better judgment.

I look around my locker door as I shove my notebooks into my backpack. "Which parent?"

"Our dad."

Lincoln is good-looking for a human. Dark auburn curly hair. Brown eyes. A dimple on one cheek. His twin sister is stunning, too. Their clothes are expensive but not preppy. Lincoln dresses more like a rock star. His sister Lauren has that slouchy chic thing going on.

"So, what's the deal? Can't he afford to send you to a private school? Or at least to Cave Hills?" I reference the snobby public school down the mountain from Wolf Ridge. Cave Hills has more wealth than Scottsdale, and its public schools reflect it. We don't compare as far as academics go, but we love to trounce them in every sport.

"We don't like to leave him."

That gets my attention even more. Dammit. I don't want to take an interest in this human. "Why not?" I shut my locker and throw my backpack over one shoulder.

Lincoln shrugs. "He's depressed. Our mom died of cancer last year, and he's having a hard time."

"And he decided to move *here*?" I ask incredulously. Because who in their right mind would choose Wolf Ridge as their refuge when depressed?

"He built the house for her. She loved Arizona. So...yeah."

"Fuck. I'm so sorry."

"Yeah, so the school we go to is the least of our concerns."

"I get that." I don't mean to, but somehow, I've fallen into step with Lincoln as we walk out of the school.

"I have to run, or I'll miss the bus," I tell him. Since my mom works until six, I have to take the school bus to my old neighborhood, then a city bus up the hill, then walk a half

41

an hour. It pretty much sucks. Especially since having pretty feet is a requirement for my college hustle.

"We can take you home," he offers. He hasn't even stopped at his locker to get his books or anything, he's just been at my side since we got out of class. "I mean, if you want."

Gah. Do I want them to? On one hand, it will completely fuck my already fucked reputation. On the other, the hour-and-a-half commute is a pain in my ass and feet.

"Um, yes. Sure. Thanks."

He points toward the east parking lot, and we veer off in that direction, walking down the sidewalk.

Everyone's looking.

I hear snickers and muttered comments about Rayne the Runt loving humans.

I hate everyone at this school. I really do.

I hold my head high and walk toward Lincoln's car. As I do, my hands start sweating although I'm not sure what I'm afraid of. Leading him on? Making a new friend?

I've had such a pathetic social life that I don't know how to handle the simplest of situations. But that's not true. Making friends with Bailey was easy. I guess this is about Lincoln being a guy. Wondering if he wants to date me. What I'll do or say if he does.

And then my already frazzled nervous system gets a jolt of electricity zapping through it when a loud, long honk to our right pulls our attention.

Oh, fuck.

What the...?

Wilde is sitting behind the wheel of my mom's Subaru wagon. His eyes glow green, like he's pissed as hell. For some annoying reason, it makes him even more attractive. I wonder what color his wolf is. How those green eyes look when framed by fur.

Well, screw him. I don't need this kind of scene at school. I get enough negative attention as it is. Now I have him proving out Abe's words.

I frown and shake my head. I never said I needed a ride home. He shouldn't be here, anyway.

"Who's that?" Lincoln asks.

"My stepbrother."

Wilde throws the door open and storms out of the vehicle.

Crap.

"Uh, on second thought, I guess I'm catching a ride with Wilde," I rush to say. I need to head him off before he gets over here and smells Lincoln.

Of course, he's probably already put it together. I mean, if he doesn't know Lincoln from pack life, he'd have to assume he's a human.

And then it pisses me off that I have to even worry about what Wilde thinks or says.

"Thanks for the offer. I'll catch you tomorrow." I peel off from Lincoln to walk swiftly toward Wilde.

"Hang on." He grabs my arm.

I whirl and shake off his hold. I'm not sure what he sees in my face–fear? Anger? Whatever it is, he recoils slightly. "I just want to make sure you're okay. I mean–is he safe?"

"Rayne." There's something dangerous in Wilde's voice. Deadly, even. "Get in the car. Now."

"Yeah, I'm fine." My voice sounds breathless to my own ears. I'm sure he doesn't buy it. "Thanks, Lincoln. See you tomorrow."

Wilde doesn't look at me when I get to him. He's

squared off toward Lincoln, who eyes him back with a sour look.

Oh, fuck.

I jog for the Subaru wagon which Wilde left running and jump in. The driver-side door stands ajar. Wilde is still fronting Lincoln, who finally shakes his head and walks off.

I lay on the horn, now, returning the favor.

Wilde turns, eyes glowing.

I try to pretend I'm not scared.

I'm not.

Still, when Wilde gets in the car and lunges in my direction to wrap his hand around my throat, I have words ready to throw in his face.

"You hurt me, you'll leave marks," I warn him. Meaning his father will see. There would be hell to pay. "I don't heal like you."

He pulls back before he ever squeezed. It worked.

"You stay away from that human, Rayne."

"Why?" I challenge.

"Because if you don't...I will beat him to a pulp."

I let out a shocked scoff. "Spoken like a true bully. It doesn't make you a tough guy to pick on people who weigh half what you do and don't have shifter strength."

Wilde blinks a few times like he's getting his wolf under control. The green fades from his eyes, and they're back to a golden brown. He smirks. "No, but you're worried now."

I hate that he can tell. Shifters sense far too much with their noses.

"Why do you care, anyway?"

Wilde peels out, which is pretty humorous considering the extremely uncool vehicle he's driving. "You're defective, Rayne, but you're not a human."

"Your point is?"

44

He squeezes the steering wheel so hard it cracks. "It's bad enough my name is tied to yours, Runt. I don't need your reputation to tank even further."

I don't care that I just had the same thought. It pisses me off hearing it from Wilde. Pisses me off enough to vow to make Lincoln my new best friend just to piss him off.

"You're not in charge of me, dickwad."

Wilde stomps on the gas, swerving around the line of cars exiting the school to race up the narrow shoulder of the road. "Think again, Rayne. You're living in my house now. I can make your life a living hell."

You already do.

I don't say it out loud. I wouldn't give him that satisfaction.

* * *

Wilde

It takes me a solid fifteen minutes to let go of the rage that came on seeing Rayne with that human.

I wanted to tear him apart. Pick him up and throw him up on the roof of the school to show off my shifter strength. Make him wet his pants in fear. I don't want him anywhere near Rayne.

The level of anger it elicited seems a little irrational, but I'll chalk it up to the fucked up situation I'm in.

My dad letting me know over a fucking phone call that he'd married the runt's mom. Sleeping on the fucking couch. The court case hanging over my head.

After lunch, I was a good boy and did what I was told. I got Garrett Green's number from Bo, and he had his wife call me to talk through legal options. She recommends I plead not guilty. I'm not so sure. She's looking into finding me a lawyer in Greenville.

Then, I dutifully came to pick up the runt. Now, I'm going to teach her to drive. My goal is to have her ready for her test in three days. Because I sure as hell am not going to be her goddamn chauffeur.

I drive up toward the mesa where the roads are dirt, and there's no traffic.

Rayne, who already nearly peed her pants when she saw my wolf-eyes earlier, is still nervous. For some reason, my wolf doesn't like the scent of her fear. Like he doesn't want her afraid of me.

Rankled is fine. Irritated is a must. Furious would be perfect.

But not scared.

I don't like her scent when she's scared.

Her scent isn't horrible under normal circumstances. She has a fresh, spring aroma, like creosote and juniper. Maybe that's why her mom named her Rayne. It's stronger than I remember, but then, I never lived with her before. Never had to associate with her. I find it...

Annoying.

As annoying as I find her new look.

I'm especially irritated that she's pretty enough to have human boys trying to drive her home.

The steering wheel cracks under my grip again.

Fuck. I'm going to pay for that, too.

It seems I'm destined for punishment for everything I do these days.

"Where are we going?"

"You're getting a driving lesson."

"Now?"

I don't bother answering a dumb question.

"With you?"

Again, not worth answering.

"I-I can't do it today."

"Why not?"

"I have homework," she says hurriedly. "And...yeah, homework."

"Well, you'll have to do your homework later. You're going to spend the next ninety minutes driving this car."

"Why? I mean, why does it have to be today? I can't do it today."

She's lying. I don't know why she's so worried, though.

"Because I'm not going to be your goddamn Uber, Runt. You're going to be driving by the end of the week, so we can move past this bullshit."

"I've never even been behind the wheel!" she wails.

"But you have a permit?"

She nods, miserably. "Yeah. My mom made me get one last year."

I reach for the door handle and throw the door open. "Then the time has come." I climb out of the car and walk around.

When Rayne doesn't get out, I yank her door open. "Let's go, Rayne."

She lets out a little whimper but doesn't move. "I really...I don't want to."

I cock my head. "Are you scared?"

She sits perfectly still, staring straight forward as if she can pretend I'm not standing here.

"What are you scared of?" I don't know what possesses me, but I take her hand like I'm a gentleman, and we're on a date. I tug gently to urge her out of her seat and put her fake Converse high tops on the ground.

When she looks up at me uncertainly, I know I was right.

"There's nothing to it, Rayne. It's super easy."

"Super easy for you," she mutters. "I'm defective, remember?"

I snort. "Your genes have nothing to do with your driving ability." Why on earth would she think that had anything to do with it? Every human drives. It's not like you need special abilities.

She takes a step then stops. "I don't even know if my feet reach the pedals."

This time I laugh for real.

"You're not that short, Runt. I think you're functioning from a warped sense of self here."

As I say the words, an uneasy feeling shifts through my chest. Something slightly guilty.

I suppose this whole town, including me, has made Rayne feel like she's less than human, even.

The urge to shake that feeling right out of her comes over me, so I pick her up by the waist, which is easy because she weighs nothing. I walk a few steps around the car then drop her back on her feet and smack her ass. "You're little, Rayne, but you're not incapable of driving."

I'm slightly disconcerted by how pleasant it was to hold her light weight with one arm. To have her clean spring scent tickling my nose up close.

She whirls and glares at me. "What kind of Neanderthal are you?" she snaps. "You can't just go around smacking girls' asses."

She's right, of course. And I'm usually respectful as hell with women, probably because Coach Jamison drilled a sense of chivalry into us from Freshman year.

I cock my head. "You're not a girl, you're a runt. And

my *stepsister*. So unless you want me to spank you for real, you'd better get behind that wheel right now."

She flushes, a blotchy pink that travels across her chest and up her neck. Again, unease shifts in my chest.

She climbs into the driver's seat but can barely reach the wheel. I see panic on her face, like she thinks this is the position she'll have to be in to drive.

"For fuck's sake, Rayne. You literally know nothing about driving a car, do you?" I reach across her to pull the lever below the seat and slide it forward.

"Oh," she says.

"Stop making this so hard." I stomp around and get into the passenger side, sliding the seat all the way back.

Rayne hasn't moved since I adjusted her seat. She's just sitting there, both hands on the wheel, staring through the windshield with big bug eyes.

I let out an exasperated sigh. "Right pedal is the gas. Left is the brake. You use the same foot for both."

"Which foot?"

I raise my brows in a *how-can-you-be-this-dumb* look, and she flushes some more. "The right foot, Rayne."

"Okay." She looks down at the pedals and puts her right foot on the gas. The engine revs.

"Yep. That's the gas. Now press the brake and hold it while you shift into drive."

Instead of doing what I say, she turns the key. Since the car was already running, it screams at her. She screams back and releases both hands, holding them in the air like she just got burned.

"Fuck," she mutters. She doesn't look at me. She's staring through the windshield, breathing hard, like she's an out of shape human who just ran up three flights of stairs.

"Look at me, Rayne."

She doesn't look.

"Chill the fuck out. You're making this too hard. Look at me."

She turns her head and literally flinches when she sees my face, even though I thought my expression was pretty neutral. "What?"

"You can do this. Humans learn to drive every day, and you're better than a human."

Inexplicably, tears fill her eyes.

First instinct–they anger me. Enrage me, almost. Like I want to shift and tear her apart.

No. Not her.

Whatever made her cry.

Which, of course, is me.

In the next breath, I experience a massive subduing of my aggression, like a lead blanket got thrown across me to calm me down. Both impulses were powerful, and the ricochet between them leaves me lightheaded.

"Knock it off, Rayne," I manage to say gruffly. I flick my fingers toward the windshield. "Press the brake and hold it."

For once, she does as she's told.

I take her hand and tug it to the gear shift, molding mine over the top to guide her to depress the button at the side and slowly slide it into drive. The gears engage, and the car tenses, ready to move forward.

"Slowly let off the brake."

She obeys. We roll forward. She whimpers, steering too sharply right and left, like a little kid pretending to drive.

I bite my tongue to keep from giving her further instruction. Some things you just have to figure out by feel.

"Now give it a little gas."

We lurch forward. She screams and presses the brake.

"You've got it," I murmur. I'm surprised to hear anything encouraging come out of my mouth, but there it is.

She darts a worried glance my way.

"Keep your eyes on the road, Runt. Don't worry about me. If you drive off a cliff, I'm indestructible."

That forces a humorless chuff out of her.

"It just takes practice. Drive up to the mesa and turn around and then drive back down this hill."

She sucks in a long breath then bobs her head. "Okay."

She white-knuckles the wheel but makes it up to the mesa and manages to turn around. I make her practice K-turns a half dozen times before instructing her to drive us back down the hill. When we get to the end of the dirt road, she pulls over.

"What are you doing?"

"Getting out so you can drive." She throws open her door.

"No, you're not. You're driving us home."

Her eyes fly wide. "Hell, no. That's a hard no. Absolutely not."

I debate whether to go savage or soft on her. I don't know why, but I choose soft. "You're doing great, Rayne. The only way you get comfortable driving is driving. Now put it back in drive, and let's go."

I expect arguments, but she must be feeling slightly more confident because she closes her door, slowly slides the gear shift into drive and gives it too much gas, sending us jerking forward.

I hold back criticism. We make it to the first stop sign, where she stops and looks both ways four times before slowly rolling forward, even though there's no one there.

"Were you waiting for the ghost cars to pass?"

"Shut up, Wilde."

51

I smirk. Better. She's got the fight back in her again.

By the time we make it home, she's got quite a bit more starch in her backbone, and the attitude is fully in place.

She parks in the center of the driveway, which will make it impossible for my dad to get his truck in, but I don't make her move it. I let her get out and escape to the house before I repark and saunter into the house.

Except we're not alone. The entire firing squad is here.

My dad, the pack alpha, and several members of the council stand in the living room, arms folded across their chests.

Chapter Five

Rayne

I go to my bedroom to give them privacy although I'll be able to hear everything through the walls. I may not be a shifter, but my hearing is still better than a human's.

"Have a seat, Wilde," Alpha Green instructs.

I hear the scrape of chairs from the dining table and imagine the council members forming a semicircle around Wilde, interview style.

Or maybe I should say interrogation style.

I don't know why my own stomach is tied up in knots over Wilde's situation. I have nothing invested in his situation. I don't even know what exactly happened. I don't know what he did or didn't do, other than land in jail on drug trafficking charges. I don't know whether he has an excuse or reason for it.

"So. What happened?" Alpha Green directs the conversation.

Wilde doesn't answer for a moment, at least not that I

can hear, and it leaves me holding my breath, my fingers closed into tight, clammy balls.

"We won the game against Clemson. The guys were partying in our room. We'd just been drug-tested pre-game, which meant it was safe to use."

"You use drugs." That accusation, laced with enough condemnation to sink a battleship, comes from Logan. He doesn't wait for an answer. "Why would you even bother? How fast does it metabolize in your system?"

I hear no reply until Logan snaps again, "Answer me, Wilde!"

"I wasn't sure if those were rhetorical questions."

"Don't get smart."

"Are you using drugs, son?" Alpha Green's voice is mild, like he's cueing Logan to bring down the tension.

"I'm trying to fit in with humans on a tight-knit team. It's not easy." I hear genuine frustration and distress in Wilde's voice and try to resist the sympathy that comes creeping in at the edges.

Wilde is an arrogant prick who surely deserved whatever went down.

If he felt out of place with the humans, then he just got a taste of how it feels to be me every day of my life in this town.

"So you chose to break the law and risk your entire career to fit in." The voice belongs to one of the pack elders.

"I'm a pack animal." Wilde's words fall like heavy stones. There's defeat in them. Resignation. Like he knew he was doing the wrong thing but didn't see a way around it.

"You're a goddamn leader. You were *captain* of the Wolf Ridge football team. You don't follow bad examples. You lead with better ones." Logan's still pissed. I can't imagine there's anything Wilde can say that's going to get him over it any time soon.

"So what happened? How did the police get involved?" Alpha Green asks.

"The party was getting too loud. I don't know. Instead of hotel security, cops were at the door. And they had probable cause to search the room. They found the coke and arrested me. End of story."

"Who else was in the room?"

"It doesn't matter," Wilde says. "I'm the one who got caught."

I hear footsteps, like one of the men got up to pace. "And who bailed you out?" It's Alpha Green again.

"One of my teammates."

"Were you supposed to leave town?"

"I just have to be back for the trial date in a couple of months. I talked to Amber Green. She might be able to represent me."

Amber is Alpha Green's daughter-in-law, a lawyer in Tucson.

"Wilde, I'm not sensing much remorse from you," Alpha Green says.

There's a silence. "I'm sorry I disappointed all of you."

"Oh, we're more than disappointed," the alpha says. "You made some poor choices. Your behavior is a disgrace to the Wolf Ridge High football team, this town and this pack."

"Yes, Alpha."

"What troubles me most is my sense that you really don't care all that much. Am I right?"

A prickle runs across my skin because I know Alpha Green is right. It's what made me feel like Wilde is getting what he deserves.

But why doesn't he care that much? When he was in high school, he gave everything he had to football. It seems strange he would risk sacrificing it now and not seem to mind at all.

"No, Alpha."

"Don't lie to me, Wilde."

I swear, I feel the tension in the silence that follows seep through the walls of the living room and straight into my chest.

What is Wilde supposed to say? The truth will also damn him.

He says nothing at all.

"Well, let's see if this motivates you. I want this situation resolved and you back on that team at Duke, or you're out of this pack. Understand?"

"Yes, Alpha."

"You can stay here while you figure it out You are *going to* figure it out. No failure. No conviction. Back on the team with the scholarship. And if you fuck up like this again, you are permanently banned. Understood?"

"Yes, Alpha."

Even though I personally can't wait to leave Wolf Ridge and get the hell away from this town and pack, my eyes fill with tears for Wilde.

Pack is everything to a shifter. We're communal. We function for the good of all and draw support from each other. If you're banned from a pack, you're cursed to live among humans because most other decent packs will also refuse to take you in.

For a young wolf Wilde's age, with no way to support himself and no community, he'll probably go mad. Of course, Garrett Green down in Tucson might take him in. He knows what it's like to be banned from Wolf Ridge.

I stay in the bedroom until I hear everyone leave and Logan and my mom talking softly from their room. Only then do I come out. The living room smells like misery. I look around for Wilde, but he's not there.

I head into the kitchen to make dinner, and I see a pile of clothes by the back door. My head snaps up, staring out the window. There, disappearing up the side of the mountain, is a black wolf. He's massive, displaying sheer beauty and power as he eats up space with long, powerful galloping strides.

A black wolf with green eyes. I should have known Wilde Woodward would be nothing short of spectacular in his four-legged form.

* * *

Wilde

"Bruh, that's harsh," Cole says a few hours later. He, Bo, and Austin drove up from ASU to lend their support. We're up on the mesa now, with our buddy Slade.

Considering the dressing-down I just took, I'm grateful to be with friends.

I shifted and ran after the council left, unable to even sit in my own skin for another moment, and I stayed out until long past darkness.

When I got back, I found the runt had left a plate piled high with barbecued drumsticks and a bowl full of broccoli with lemon butter out for me. I think it's kind of shitty that it's her chore to feed us. I mean, it would be one thing if she liked cooking, but I don't think that's the case. I think she's doing what she's told.

After I plowed through every last morsel of food she'd

left, I found the guys had been blowing up my phone about coming up.

They showed up at the door without waiting for the official invite and told me to get in the car.

Now, we're sitting around a fire, drinking beer like old times.

Bo and Cole both play football for ASU. Austin goes there, too, although his dad wouldn't let him play. He's supposed to become a doctor, like his dad.

I was the asshole who got chosen by the pack and Coach Jamison to go to a prestigious school and shine while my best friends got to hang out together.

Of course, it could be worse. Poor Slade got stuck in Wolf Ridge, like most of the rest of the boneheads from high school. He works at the brewery on the production floor.

I just gave them the run-down on what Alpha Green told me before dinner.

"So how are you going to get the charges dropped?" Bo asks.

I shrug. "I dunno. I guess I have to find a lawyer."

"So...when do you go back?" Cole breaks a dead tree branch over his knee. Shifters don't need axes. Not when we can snap thick branches with our bare hands or a stomp of one foot.

The sense of stubborn resistance that's been in me since the minute my dad said he married Leslie rises up. I toss a branch onto the fire. "I'm not going back."

"What?" All four guys' heads snap up to stare at me.

I shrug. "I mean, what's the point if I can't play ball?"

"What about your classes?" Austin asks.

"I'll drop them." I hold one end of a branch and catch the top of it on fire, then lift it in the air like a torch.

"Won't that make it harder when you eventually get

back on the team?" Again, Austin's trying to be the voice of Good Student Reason.

"It's already hard, dude," I snarl. "And the only reason I was doing it was for football. For the team."

I think about my teammates, and a queasy feeling comes over me. How many of those so-called friends have I even heard from since Ryan put me on that plane? My coach left me three messages, but I haven't heard a peep from any of my teammates.

None. Not even Ryan, whose ass I saved.

Those are the guys I would've sacrificed anything for.

Hell, I already sacrificed *everything* for them.

But they're human. They understand the concept of team, but not the way these guys–my true packmates–do. This was what was missing for me there.

Except these guys have their own lives now. We're not in high school anymore. Two of them are mated. All four are in the next chapter of their lives. We're not the band of alpha-holes ruling the halls of Wolf Ridge High. I can't have those days back.

I dip the tip of the branch into the fire again. "I guess I need to go pack up my shit and drive the Jeep back."

Of course, I have no money for that.

Bo seems to guess at my dilemma because he immediately offers. "I'll spot you the cash for a plane ticket if you need it." He and his car-jacking girlfriend Sloane came into some money last year, which is the only reason he got to go to college.

My shoulders sag with relief. From the safety of knowing your friends really and truly have your back. "Thanks, man. I do need it. My dad isn't going to help with anything at all."

Bo pulls his phone out and starts scrolling like he's going

to book me a ticket right this moment. "My Uncle Greg would probably give you a job at the auto shop if you need it."

I don't know that much about cars. Not like Cole and Bo, who worked at the shop all through high school. But I've hung around them enough to feel like I could figure it out. "Thanks. Yeah. I'll stop by and talk to him."

"And I can book a one-way to Durham tomorrow morning. That work? You can stay with us in Tempe tonight, and I'll drive you to the airport."

Another sliver of relief filters into the darkness that has made up my solid chest. Or maybe it's gratitude. "Thanks, man. It's really good to be here with you guys right now."

They exchange a look, like they don't necessarily agree that these are the best of times. When they look at me, it's with what appears to be some form of sympathy and doubt. Like they can't believe how badly I fucked up. Or understand why.

I don't even understand why.

I guess that is the worst of it.

Like Alpha Green said—I'm not sorry. I don't care.

I could give zero shits over the supposed tragedy that is my life. All I feel is this mean, stubborn need to hunker down here in Wolf Ridge. In my dad's house. Making him and Rayne the Runt—*especially her*—as miserable as I am.

Chapter Six

Rayne

      I'm already having a shit-tastic day.

      It's my eighteenth birthday, and my mom forgot. I get it–she has baby brain. Her entire body is focused on growing a pup. She's also living in a new house with a new husband who is grumpy over his son's career tank. There's a lot on her mind.

I'm trying not to let it get to me. I'm not the kid who ever had a birthday party or did much, but my mom usually tried to make it special. Like pancakes for breakfast and going out for dinner. And a present or two.

But this morning–nothing.

Now I've made the mistake of agreeing to join Lincoln and his twin Lauren in the cafeteria–I don't know what possessed me–because it seemed to enrage the alpha-holes. Abe, Markley, and J.J. purposely plop down beside us.

"Look at that. The runt finally made another friend," Abe jeers.

"Two," J.J. says. "Or do two losers only add up to one?"

Abe scoots closer to Lauren, causing her to send him a look of utter disgust, which makes him grin.

I ignore them. What else can you do? They're looking for a reaction.

"I'll bet they go to homecoming as a threesome. That would be cute, right?" Markley suggests it, but Abe's expression goes black as if the idea makes him want to smash the table in half.

"As long as we're all there to watch you get crowned king, right?" I shouldn't engage, but I can't help myself.

The ballots went out today for the nominations for homecoming royalty, even though there's no question who will win–Abe Oakley and Casey Muchmore. They're the most alpha. The students at Wolf Ridge are practically biologically *required* to vote for them.

"You know what would be funny?" Abe's gaze is on Lauren, not me.

"What?" J.J. asks.

"To put these losers on the ballot."

"Why?" Markley clearly doesn't see the humor.

Neither do I.

Abe's lips curl into a cruel smile. "Make it happen," he says, and just like that, I know it will go down. Because Abe rules every kid's social life. His attention makes or breaks students' entire school existence. If he tells everyone to nominate us, it will be done.

"You know what would be even funnier?" I give him my sweetest smile.

He ignores me.

"Watching you lose to an outsider." I say *outsider* instead of *human* but they all know what I mean.

"In your dreams, Runt." Abe's smirk is firmly back in place. He gets up, and his entourage follows him away.

"That was literally the dumbest interaction I've ever had the misfortune of witnessing. How are these idiots popular?" Lauren asks, her gaze on Abe's muscled shoulders.

"No idea," I mutter.

My day gets even worse in sixth period when Ms. Landon passes the Calculus tests back. I needed to snag an A on this one to bring up my grade, but I already knew of a few problems I got wrong.

I was just hoping for a high B at this point. Anything that won't further solidify my C.

Kringle-crap! I got a 76. Another C.

This bites.

I was thinking about asking Bailey if she could tutor me, maybe over Zoom or something, but I know she's busy with her college classes. I don't want to be a burden.

"Congratulations to Lincoln, who got the highest grade in the class on the test. The rest of you need to review a little more before the midterm in two weeks," Ms. Landon says.

I look over at Lincoln, who appears nonplussed by the praise. Huh. Didn't know he was a brainiac. But he probably went to a much better school before he moved here.

Maybe...

No. It's a bad idea. And not because Wilde told me not to hang out with him. I don't care about Wilde. In fact, that might be the exact reason I should make time to hang out with Lincoln. Show my infuriating *stepbrother* that he's not in charge of me.

Also, I really need help. I don't want to stay in Wolf Ridge after graduation. I *have* to get out of here.

"Hey, Lincoln." I fall into step with the much taller student as we head out of the classroom.

"Hey."

"I...by any chance do you tutor? I mean, would you be willing to go over my test with me and show me what I did wrong?"

Okay, that's stupid. The teacher literally just said she would do that for us if we came in before school. But I can't come in early because of my whole ride situation.

Wilde has been gone for the last four days, which has been a relief. After the pack elders read him the riot act, he flew to Durham to pack up his bedroom at the frat house and drive back in his Jeep.

"Sure." Lincoln snatches my test from my hand and gives it a quick scan. "Do you want to go over it now? We could go to the library. Or my place, if you want." He raises a brow. "Or would your stepbrother kick my ass?" He doesn't sound the least bit scared by that prospect. More like he's trying to figure out what the deal is.

"Yeah, he's a little...overprotective." I let out a shaky laugh. "And kind of a dick." And then, because it's important to me to prove I'm not being bullied by my stepbrother, I say, "Your house sounds great."

Of course, the moment I do, I realize at least ten people around us have turned their heads to look. They all heard the whole damn conversation.

I have no doubt Wilde will hear about this the moment he gets back into town.

Well, good.

That will show him he can't run my life.

I stop at my locker and grab my backpack and books then walk out to the parking lot with Lincoln. His sister Lauren is already sitting in the passenger seat. He—or they, I don't know—drive a Tesla, which is a seriously sweet ride.

"Rayne's coming home with us. We're going over the Calculus test."

"Oh, cool. Yeah, Lincoln has a great math brain. Me, not so much. I'm in Advanced Algebra."

"So, how come he gets to drive?" I demand as Lincoln starts the car.

"He doesn't. I mean, we take turns," she says.

"Cool."

I imagine what it would be like to have some brotherly cooperation from Wilde. Like if we'd become siblings a little younger.

No, it would never happen. There's nothing brotherly about Wilde. Including the way my body reacts to him.

"Can you drive me home when we're done?" I ask, suddenly realizing there's no way in hell I want Logan to catch wind of this friendship, either. I'm sure Wilde gets his biases from his dad. Human friendships are frowned on.

"Yeah. Of course." Lincoln drives easily. Without thought. Like he's been doing it for a million years, not one or two.

I guess Wilde was right. Humans can do it without any problem. I was making driving a much harder thing than I needed to. Even though he was a total asshole about it, I'm sort of grateful he just forced me to give it a go. Now that I've broken the seal on it, I'm not so scared or intimidated by it.

Lincoln and Lauren's house is a stunning mansion nestled into a steep mountain bank with wall-to-wall windows that look out over the city. I gape as we drive up. It has a three-car garage with doors that automatically open as he pulls in.

"What does your dad do?" I ask.

"He was an investment broker," Lincoln says. "I mean,

he still is, but from home now instead of the Manhattan office."

"You're from New York?"

"Yep."

"No accent, though."

He grins. "What kind of accent did you think I'd have?"

I shrug. "I don't know. East coast."

"Do you think you have an accent?"

"Of course not." I smile.

Their dad isn't around to greet us—I assume he's in his office working.

There are three guitars standing on end beside an amp in the living room. One acoustic, one electric, and one bass. "Who plays guitar?" I ask.

"I do," Lincoln says casually. "Lauren plays piano." He lifts his chin toward the grand piano in the corner.

"Cool."

Lincoln and I sit at the dining room table, which is positioned in front of giant sliding glass doors that lead out to a covered deck on the side of the house. The studying takes half an hour. Lincoln's a good teacher, and it suddenly all makes sense. I think I just missed a few concepts at the beginning of the year because my mind was occupied with my mom's pregnancy dilemma and then sudden marriage, followed by our change of homes.

My stomach growls loudly as we finish. "Oops. For some reason, I can't seem to eat enough food lately."

"Sorry, I should have offered you a snack." Lincoln gets up and walks to a pantry packed with fancy gourmet and European-looking foods. "Help yourself. Protein bar, maybe?" He pulls a couple out of a box, hands me one, and rips one open for himself. It's chocolate and caramel and has 20 grams of protein. I have to work not to shove the whole thing in my mouth at once.

"I was like that when I hit my growth spurt. I'd get so hangry by the time school was over, we'd have to stop immediately for a meal. Not just a snack–a full meal. Like a pre-dinner." He chuckles.

"Sadly, I don't think I'll be having a growth spurt. I've always been small. But at least the extra calories don't seem to be going to my waist."

We eat our protein bars and take fancy bottled blood orange sodas out to the deck where we stand at the deck railing and look down at Wolf Ridge. Lauren joins us.

"I can't wait to get out of this town," I mutter.

"Same," Lauren says. "I've been to snobby schools, but this one's just plain weird. Redneck snobby or something. No offense."

"None taken."

"What's with that guy Abe?"

I look over. "Eh. He's the alpha-hole extraordinaire. Captain of the football team. Pretty much runs the school. His dad is a doctor in town. His brother Austin graduated a couple of years ago. He's actually not that bad. He was always class president. Definitely more friendly than Abe."

"He's my lab partner in chemistry," Lauren says. "He's horrible."

"Agreed. Guys like him are one of the perils of a small town. They think they're practically gods here."

"The thing that's weird is that Wolf Ridge functions like a small town. I mean, isn't it just a suburb of Scottsdale?"

"Mmm." I proceed with caution. I can't exactly explain that most everyone who lives here is a different species. "Well, Wolf Ridge was actually here long before Scottsdale or Cave Hills. It was settled around when Arizona became a U.S. territory. The mountains served to keep it separated from the suburban sprawl down there, and the brewery provided the economic industry."

"Huh. I guess that makes sense," Lauren says.

"It would be weird to grow up in a small town," Lincoln observes. "To me, it's kind of fascinating." He shrugs. "You know, from an anthropological point of view. The workings of small town social life. There's no diversity. Super rigid thoughts about how things are supposed to work."

I laugh. "You must be horrified if you're seeing all that."

"Not horrified. I mean, I'm not trying to fit in, so I could care less about the social dynamics. I'm just trying to crack the code." He looks over at me. "I'm curious about why some kids seem different. What sets apart the outcasts from the in-crowd? It's not money, right? It's more like... athletic ability?" His expression is one of doubt like he can't believe that could be it.

Of course, he's right, in a way.

It's gene-based. So those with the best genetics would be the best at sports.

I look back over the town. "Wolf Ridge is all about its sports, so yeah. You nailed it."

He's scrutinizing me. "And you're not sporty."

"Not at all. You got me. I mean, I go to the games, but I don't play anything."

I have half a mind to ask them both to go to this week's football game with me, but I hold back. Wilde will surely be there. I wouldn't want another confrontation.

"So you don't hate it here?"

He looks back out. "No. Our mom loved this place. She thought Arizona was beautiful, even though all I see is brown and rocks. But now that I'm here, I try to see it through her eyes. Once you're used to the brown, you can see the pops of color. It's slow and understimulating. Is that a word? I like that I hear birds in the morning." He says it like it's a unique thing. I guess in New York City, he wouldn't hear birdsong.

"Yeah, that part is nice. But I still hate it," Lauren says.

"I hear there are wolves here," Lincoln says.

"Oh yeah." I bob my head, trying to sound perfectly casual. "Definitely. There's a whole pack in these hills."

"Have you seen them?"

"Yeah. A few times."

Like every day at school.

Or if we're talking wolf form, every full moon. Not that I go to pack runs. I've been avoiding the pack meetings since puberty when it became painfully obvious that I would never shift. That I am, in fact, as defective as everyone suspected, given my small size.

"Hey, I should get home," I say abruptly. "Thanks so much for the help."

"No problem. We could make it a regular thing if you want." He shrugs. "Or not. Whatever's clever."

"Yeah, I'd like that. Thanks."

Lincoln drives me home, and my stomach drops when we pull up to the house.

Wilde's Jeep is sitting in the driveway.

That's cool. Maybe he won't see me come home. I throw open the door and slide out, trying to make this the fastest drop-off ever. And then I see Wilde, standing at the picture window.

Doublety-fuck.

"Thanks, Lincoln–bye!" I call, shutting the door to the Tesla. I meet Wilde's eye through the window and give my hair a haughty toss.

Eat me, Wilde. I flounce through the door and shut it behind me, not even bothering to greet my bad-boy brother.

He catches my nape and turns me to face him. "What did I tell you about hanging out with that human, Rayne?" His voice is soft and dangerous, and his eyes glow green with anger. There's a possessive edge to the way he holds me.

No, that doesn't make sense.

He's just mad.

Despite the fact that he can snap me like a twig, I lift my chin. "You're not in charge of me, Wilde."

In a flash, he pins me up against the wall by the throat, his other hand holding me up...*oh fates.* His other hand is between my legs.

I'm dangling above the floor *with his fingers cupped around my lady parts.*

Chapter Seven

ilde

W Okay, I didn't think this through. Well, maybe I did. Subconsciously, I'm sure I was trying to protect Rayne from actually choking from my grip on her throat, so I chose to hold her weight up from the other end.

The other end happens to be her hot core.

I don't even know why I'm manhandling her. It's beyond inappropriate, same as smacking her ass when I was teaching her to drive, but something about her brings out a feral aggression in me.

When I saw her with that human again, my wolf went nuts.

For a second, I think we're going to move past this grope and pretend it's not happening. I'll just lower her slowly, and she'll–

Fuck. Me.

The flesh between her legs squeezes. *I can feel it under my fingers.* Fates, is she getting wet?

Her legs clamp together around my hand.

My breath hisses out as I ease her down the wall and onto her feet.

And then I can't stop myself. It's wrong–so wrong. But I move my fingers between her legs. I ripple them against her hot little pussy, giving her a little feedback. Maybe I'm testing for wetness. Maybe I'm trying to turn her on. I don't really know.

All I know is that a shudder runs through her.

Did she just come?

My dick punches out against the zipper of my jeans.

Her lips part and blue eyes go wide. That little heart-shaped face of hers wears a stunned expression.

The scent of her arousal makes me do it again. One more subtle movement of my fingers between her legs.

Another shudder.

I don't want to stop. I don't want to let her go. I want to own this little shrimp of a shifter until she falls down on her knees and begs my forgiveness for letting that human drive her home.

It's that thought that spurs me on. The scent of him still clings lightly to her clothes. Not that I think he touched her–it's not that strong. But her juniper and creosote scent is muted by his.

"*You're* in big trouble," I growl and loop an arm around her waist to carry her into my bedroom.

And *damn.* Carrying her is so fucking satisfying.

I sit on the bed and fold her over my knee like I'm her 1950's husband and start spanking her ass. Hard.

She freaks out, squirming and flailing, her hand flying back to cover her small perfect butt.

I light it on fire, knowing I'm way out of line. Beyond out of line. But I was already teetering on getting kicked out of this house and my pack. So what the hell? All I've ever done was try to live up to their standards. I might as well do what I want for a change.

And right now, I want to turn Rayne the Runt's ass pink.

The scent of her arousal grows even stronger as I spank her, which riles my wolf up, making me hold her even tighter and spank her even harder. My dick presses painfully against my zipper.

It's satisfying as hell—on every level. Feeling her squirm and resist. Loving how easily I overpower her. The sound of her squeaks and squeals. The impact of my palm on her springy flesh.

Knowing she's not made like a normal shifter and will feel pain longer, I force myself to stop. Instead, I squeeze her ass roughly and slide my fingers between her legs again.

"You don't date humans," I growl. "You don't date anyone without my permission." My fingertips seek the damp spot in her shorts, and I rub there.

She bucks in another spectacular little orgasm.

The rush of power it gives me nearly makes me jizz.

"I'm not dating him! He was helping me with calculus. If I don't get my grade up, I'll lose my scholarship."

I want to keep her over my knee, rubbing that incredible spot between her legs that gives her pleasure, but her words snag my attention.

Rayne has a scholarship.

I don't know why it surprises me to hear she has ambitions of leaving. It makes perfect sense. Why would she want to stick around a pack where she's treated like dog shit? I also hate it.

Like she's not allowed to make plans without informing me.

I lift her to her feet, keeping one hand molded around her cute ass. "What scholarship?"

Her face is red, her gaze furious. I sense her legs trembling. "To ASU. I have to maintain all A's if I want the three-quarter scholarship."

All A's.

So Rayne's smart.

I didn't know that, either. It seems there's a fuck-ton I don't know about this girl, and I suddenly make it my business to know everything.

"I still don't want you seeing him," I grouse.

She throws her hands in the air with exasperation. "I'm not seeing him! He's literally a kid at school who is good at math and helped me go over the problems on the test I just choked on."

"Next time bring him here, so I can supervise."

She cocks her head, her upper lip lifting in scorn. "You are not my chaperone, Wilde. You're not my anything."

I squeeze her buttcheek and shake. "Oh, but I am, Runt. I'm your everything. Now, get out to my Jeep. It's time for your driving lesson."

Her jaw drops. "I'm not driving with you! I'm not doing anything with you, Wilde Woodward. You just assaulted me in my own room. I don't feel safe with you."

I stand, towering over her. I lower my face to hers until we're nose to nose. "First of all, it's not your room. It's mine. And you're not safe with me, Rayne. Not unless you learn to obey. The sooner you accept that, the easier it's going to go between us."

* * *

Rayne

74

In the next moment, Wilde tosses me over his shoulder, his hand somehow still firmly on my tingling ass, and walks me out to his Jeep.

I'm the definition of hot mess. I mean, my ass is burning, my pride is in tatters, and I just orgasmed three times on Wilde's fingers!

For all the porn research I've done to become a foot fetish goddess, I've been more or less asexual during my teen years.

I swear, I never even thought about having sex until that first night Wilde showed up in the house and saw me in my underwear. Now, I'm feverish. All I can think about is him touching me there again.

I mean—did that actually happen? Was it a mistake?

No. He knew what he was doing. Maybe not consciously when he pinned me up on the wall, but after he let me down, when he started moving his fingers to get me off—that was intentional.

Did he know what it did to me?

Gah. Of course, he did! He can probably smell the fluids that leaked from me when he stimulated me.

He opens the Jeep door and drops me into the driver's seat then fastens my seatbelt across my lap. Which is weirdly pleasurable. So is him adjusting the seat forward.

It's almost like...he cares.

I hate the riot of sensation that thought produces. Like a tingle just below my skin all over my entire body.

"Rayne." Wilde's in the open doorway, looking down at me.

I don't look over. I can't. I'm way too raw and horribly confused about the nature of our relationship. I mean... doesn't he hate me?

Is he interested sexually?

What in the fuck is going on?

And even just that notion of him being interested sexually sends fresh flames licking through my core.

I fantasize about him reaching between my legs to rub there again. Want his thick, warm digits in my most sensitive place.

"Rayne-bow."

I look over, surprised at the name. Bailey's mate Cole used to call me that, but he did it in a derisive way. Even so, I liked the nickname enough that I've come to use it in my head when I speak to myself.

"I wouldn't actually hurt you."

Holy. Shit.

Is he actually feeling remorseful for what he just said?

"I know you're fragile, Runt."

Fragile. Right.

Another dig at my defective genes.

I snap my gaze straight ahead again. "Fuck off, Wilde."

He chuckles as he swings the door shut and walks around. After he climbs into the passenger side, he leans across me to put the key in. "You can start it this time," he says, reminding me of my stupid mistake last time, of trying to start a running car.

I reach for the brake pedal, depress it, and turn the key. It starts up. I blow out a breath and put the car in drive.

As I start to take my foot off the brake, Wilde's hand drops over mine. "Hold up."

"What?" I can't help sounding defensive. Like I said, my pride is in tatters.

"Are you going forward or backward?"

Oh.

Well, fudge.

I shift into reverse. Wilde keeps his hand over mine the

whole time, which sends spasmodic quivers through my belly. Not just butterflies, but seismic shifts. Knots that tighten and loosen at the same time.

I start to press the gas, and he squeezes my hand. "Hang on, Runt."

For fates' sake. What am I doing wrong now?

"Can you even see in that rearview mirror?"

Rearview mirror. Right. I reach up and adjust it, so I can see behind me. "I guess that would be helpful," I snark.

To my utter shock, when I steal a glance at Wilde, his lips are curved in the faintest of smiles.

Maybe I'm starting to grow on him.

Maybe...

Gawd, no. I can't think about Wilde and drive a moving vehicle at the same time. I turn my focus onto driving, slowly backing into the street, turning the wheel and putting it into drive then rolling forward.

"Speed limit's twenty-five," Wilde observes.

I look at the speedometer. I'm going fifteen. I give it a little more gas, and we lurch forward. Out of my periphery, I think I see Wilde smile again.

But that can't be right.

I find myself driving the route to school since that's a familiar path. Once there, I circle around it. Wilde stares at the football field where the team is still practicing.

"Did you decide not to train with them?" I ask, even though I know he's going to bite my head off.

He doesn't, though. He just lets out a disgruntled sigh. "Coach said no."

"Oh." I steal a glance at Wilde and am disconcerted by the haunted expression on his face. Like he's come unmoored from his life and doesn't know how to get it back. "Why?"

He shrugs. "Dunno. He said when I figured out why I could come and talk to him again. A fucking riddle."

"Huh." I mull that over, and I drive away from the school and that particular source of his pain. I don't know Coach Jamison personally. I mean, of course, I know him. He's a freaking legend in Wolf Ridge. But we've never spoken in my life. "What was the conversation exactly?"

Wilde shifts restlessly in his seat. He points down the road. "Drive down to Cave Hills. That's where the DMV is. We can practice the driving test."

Ack. The roads will be way busier in Cave Hills. My hands get clammy, but I do what he says. I figure it will be his fault if I get in an accident, right?

No, scratch that. I would die. Logan would be ashamed of me–again–and I'd rather jump off a cliff that give him another major reason to think I'm a fuck-up.

"Basically, I asked if I could train with the team, and he said no."

"That was it?"

Wilde rubs a thumb across his lower lip, looking out the window. "I told him my dad wanted me to train with the team. He asked what I wanted."

"And what did you say?"

"I said, *nobody cares what I want.* Then he said no."

"Well, there's your answer."

Wilde looks over at me. I come to a major stoplight and brake. Wilde shoos me forward because I'm hanging too far behind the other car. "What's the answer, Runt?"

"He asked what you wanted."

Wilde stares at me. "Explain."

"He doesn't want you there if you don't want to be there. Why would he? He's not going to waste his time on someone who hates football."

Wilde's body tenses. He scrubs a hand across his face. "I don't–" his voice sounds strangled. "I don't hate football. Why in the fuck would you say that? I was playing for the top college football team in the nation. NFL scouts were crawling up my ass."

"Then why sabotage it?"

I catch a whiff of anguish in Wilde's scent. I don't know how I can tell. My sense of smell has never been that refined. It's way better than a human's but before today, I couldn't pick up emotions and subtle shifts the way normal shifters can.

For the first time since he's returned, I actually have some sympathy for his situation.

Because my assessment–the one I just threw out there without any prior thought–was right.

Wilde sabotaged his own success. For whatever reason, he couldn't take it.

My chest cinches up for him.

Wilde doesn't answer, and I don't push. I just follow the hill down to the busy northern suburb of Phoenix. When Wilde doesn't give me instructions on where to go, I just start taking turns–mostly right-hand ones.

Eventually, Wilde's focus comes back to my driving, and he directs me to the DMV. "The route they take you on is right here. You come out of their parking lot there and follow this street down to the stop sign."

I follow his directions. We do a long loop around several city blocks and end up back at the DMV.

"Now they will ask you to park in one of those spots and then to back up and do a K-turn like we practiced on the mesa."

I go through the motions. It's getting easier. Every minute that passes I get a little more comfortable with driving. The movements become more automatic. My reactions adjust to the Jeep's controls to modulate speed and braking and turns.

"That's it, Runt. That's the test. You passed with flying colors. Tomorrow I'll take you down, and you can get your license."

Right. Of course. The whole reason he's doing this is to get driving me off his chore list. Lift the burden from him and the whole family.

Because that's clearly what I am.

"I don't know if I've had the permit long enough," I say, even though it's not true. I don't know what possesses me to even say it. It can't be that I want more time being driven around by Wilde.

In fact, freedom from him–being able to drive–is exactly what I need.

"Let me see it." He digs through my purse. "Where's your wallet?"

"I don't have one. It's in my phone pocket."

He slides the permit out and examines it. Then he turns to me, his upper lip curled in a snarl. "Today is your birthday?"

Chapter Eight

Wilde

My hand closes into a fist around Rayne's permit. It breaks into a half dozen pieces. One of them digs into my palm gouging it. The rest fall into the center console.

Rayne stares at me with big bug eyes and starts to drift off the road. I reach across her to steady the wheel.

"Eyes on the road," I growl.

I have to hand it to her, though. Even when she is scared, she gives it back to me. "What's your problem?" she snaps.

I don't even know. At least, it takes me a second to realize why I'm so pissed.

"Where's the fucking party?" I demand as if she's having a birthday bash and failed to invite me. But that's not it, of course. I already know there's no party, and that's why I'm furious.

Her mom didn't say a word to her this morning about her birthday. Rayne didn't remind anyone. I don't know why I even care, but it seriously pisses me off.

"Seriously. *What's. Your. Problem?*"

"I just want to know why I haven't heard a word about it."

"Why would you?" She's pissed too. Her eyes flash, glinting in the sunlight through the windshield.

"Because I'm living in the same house as you, that's why. Your mom didn't say anything to you this morning."

"Yeah, well, she has a lot on her mind," Rayne says, but I see her lips trembling.

I have to suppress the urge to smash the window beside me.

Her nostrils flare in a distinctly wolf-like manner. "Are you bleeding?"

I don't say anything else. My head is telling me this is none of my business. I shouldn't give a shit anyway. But for some reason, my body is still a riot of rage and firing impulses. Although what they're firing to do, I'm not sure.

When we drive past a grocery store, I point across Rayne. "Pull in there," I order.

Miraculously, Rayne obeys without giving me back talk.

"Park."

She does.

I throw open the door and hop out. "Let's go, Runt."

She drops lightly to her feet and follows me through the parking lot and through the front doors. "I *really* don't know what your problem is, Wilde."

"Okay." I swing on her. "I'd like to know what your fucking problem is."

She draws back like I've slapped her. Her forehead wrinkles in confusion. "I don't know what you're talking about." She throws her hands out.

"When are you going to start taking up a little space, Runt?"

Her face flushes a deep red. "Shut up, Wilde. You're such a–" She bites off the words and whirls to march down a grocery aisle away from me.

I catch her elbow, and she rubberbands back. "Such a what?" I lower my voice because we're making a scene. And because her anger somehow calms mine. This is what I needed from her. Some kind of righteous indignation.

"Cocksucking bastard."

I grin.

Probably the wrong reaction, but for some reason, I love when she gets feisty with me.

"There you go."

Her eyes narrow as she searches my face. "What in the fuck do you want from me?"

"I want you to take up some goddamn space. Stop tiptoeing around the house like you don't belong. Speak up when it's your fucking birthday."

Incredulity scrawls across her expression as she stares back at me. Our gazes are locked in some kind of battle of wills although I'm not sure what we're even battling about.

Apparently, I win because her big baby blues suddenly swim with tears.

I've never hated winning more.

But I keep holding her gaze and just shake my head slowly. "No tears, Runt. This is your day."

One of her tears escapes the confines of her lower lid and skates down her cheek.

I grip her face in both hands, too roughly.

She gasps and stumbles forward, her body colliding into mine. I mop the tear with my thumb.

"I said no tears, Runt." There's intensity in my whisper. Threat. Danger.

She blinks rapidly, like she's trying to obey me, so I release her and tip my head toward the bakery.

"Come on. Let's go get you a cake."

More tears fall down her cheeks as we walk, but I ignore them, and she quickly brushes them away. When we get to the bakery counter, I drop my hand on her nape, squeezing and releasing. Massaging out the tight knot of muscles at the base of her neck.

"What kind do you want?"

She sniffs. "Oreo."

I lift my chin at the bakery attendant, and she comes over. She's a pack member. No one important. I forget her name. "Wilde Woodward. I thought you were at Duke." Yeah, right. As if she hasn't already heard what happened.

"Not at the moment." It's the best answer I can come up with. I know I'm going to need a better answer because everyone in this town and pack are going to try to find out what my deal is. I point to the Oreo cake in the case. "I need that cake. It's Rayne's birthday."

The attendant looks at Rayne as if seeing her for the first time. "Oh right. Your new stepsister." She says it like it's a joke. Like she's commiserating with me. I want to take every cake in that cabinet and smash them into her smug face.

I don't take my hand from Rayne's neck, squeezing again. Her scent fills my nostrils. Sends a jolt of relief through my system after enduring the salt of her tears.

I guess I haven't been around that many females crying before. I know male wolves are strongly affected by a female's tears, but I thought it was just their mate's. I guess it's any female's.

It makes sense, evolutionarily. A built-in protection for she-wolves when a male gets too rough. The scent will either trigger his protective instinct to solve whatever her problem is or a calming reflex to drop his aggression level.

The bakery attendant pulls out the cake and starts to box it up.

"Aren't you going to write on it?"

The bitchy attendant glances at Rayne again, like she's not worth the bother. "Oh. I didn't know you wanted that."

"Yeah. It's her birthday." I'm starting to fume again.

"So...*Happy Birthday, Rayne?*" She wrinkles her nose like it's a distasteful thing to write.

"Now, please." I must accidentally put a little alpha command in my voice because she draws back, and her eyes widen, then she scurries to comply.

The whole time I stand there with my hand on Rayne's nape.

Seriously. She's my little sister now. If anyone in this town thinks they can belittle or fuck with her, I will be taking names and delivering ass-kickings.

I ignore the fact that my feelings aren't all brotherly.

They certainly weren't when I spanked her ass this afternoon.

Not when I felt that hot core clenching under my fingertips.

But I don't even know what to think about that. I'm not going to think about it because I can't find anywhere to jam it in my mind that fits.

We get the cake, and I pay for it with the few dollars of cash I have in my wallet. It's dark already when we get out to the Jeep.

"Will you drive? I don't feel comfortable driving at night."

I know I should just make her do it. If she's going to get her license tomorrow, she needs to be able to drive at night.

But I must be feeling guilty over making her cry because I take the keys from her hand, push the seat back, and slide behind the wheel. Her scent is all over the seat and steering wheel, and I draw it in through my nostrils as she walks around the Jeep to get in on the passenger side.

My dick swells against my zipper. Fates, what brought that on? Her scent?

The moment I open the door to that thought, the memory of spanking her comes back. I want to do it again.

Badly.

Badly enough that I might make it my ongoing job to discipline my baby sister.

I'll protect her from the asshole town, but she'll have to do everything I say. Obey my every word. Be a good little runt for me.

That idea satisfies me so much, my dick strains painfully between my legs. I have to rearrange it after I hand her the cake to hold in her lap.

Rayne stares down at it, head lowered, her hair falling across her face.

"Happy birthday, Runt," I find myself saying.

* * *

Rayne

I'm a little trembly on the ride home. Everything's tender: my pride, my emotions. I feel sort of hot and bothered being around Wilde–but not in the way I used to.

Not like I want to escape him.

More like there's something I need from him. Some itch I want to scratch. Want *him* to scratch. He got me all turned on with his hand between my legs today in his grossly inappropriate touching, and now I want more.

86

Or maybe I just want more of his hand on my neck. That steadying, calming, protective presence he lent me when we were in the grocery store. Of course, he's the one who upset me in the first place, so it makes no sense that I'd crave his comfort afterward.

It also makes very little sense to me that he bought me a cake.

I mean, this guy is a constant dick to me. He resents my presence in his house then tells me to stop tiptoeing around.

I sort of feel like I'm losing my mind.

Am I losing my mind?

It's long past the time I should've made dinner, and Logan's Tahoe is in the driveway when we get home.

My mom and Logan are sitting down at the kitchen table eating pizza straight from a box.

"Where in the hell have you two been?" Logan demands. He looks at me, making his tone slightly more polite. "Rayne, if you're not going to be able to make dinner you need to give your mom a heads up. She was starving by the time I got some pizza into her."

"It's okay. Rayne, honey, where were you?" My mom barely stops stuffing the pizza in her mouth to speak. Then she catches sight of the bakery box in my hands.

I watch as her eyes widen. She freezes like she's figuring out what the date is. "Oh fates, Rayne! It's your birthday! Oh, honey." She leaps up from the table and comes rushing over to me.

She's obviously distraught. So distraught that I feel it necessary to comfort her. "It's okay, Mom." She takes the cake box and slides it on the table and then crushes me in a hug. Her baby bump grinds against my ribs.

My mom bursts into tears, which makes Logan leap up from the table like he's going to rescue her from something.

"It's fine, Mom." I give her an awkward pat on the back. "Wilde bought me a cake after giving me a driving lesson." I want to be sure he gets points for doing what he's supposed to be doing.

I can't stand living with the toxicity between him and Logan.

"Oh. Thank you, Wilde." She throws herself at him, now, making him freeze under her crushing, watery embrace.

"She's not usually like this." I feel like I have to explain my mother's bizarre behavior. I'm not sure whether I'm offering the excuse up to Wilde or his dad or both. "It's the pregnancy. She's usually very chill."

My mom releases Wilde and returns to me. "Rayne, honey. I'm so sorry I forgot. I mean, I knew it was coming up, I just forgot that today was the day. I have your present. I just need to wrap it."

"You don't have to wrap it."

"Let her wrap it," Wilde grumbles behind me.

I shrug. "I mean...you could throw it in a bag or something."

My mom disappears, and Logan and Wilde both stand awkwardly.

"I...didn't even know when your birthday was," Logan offers.

Not sure if that really helps, but *thanks, Logan. Really.*

Wilde walks over to the pizza boxes and picks up the one on top. There's only one slice left in it. He passes it to me.

My stomach rumbles, but the sugary scent of chocolate and Oreos has been filling my nostrils since we left the grocery store. "I think...I'm just going to have my cake."

It feels very selfish. My mom would disapprove—she's

always trying to push more protein on me. But Wilde just told me to take up more space, and it makes me feel a bit rebellious and daring.

Makes me want to sit down and eat my cake all by myself. Not even offer anyone a slice until I'm done.

"Do it." Wilde, king of rebellion himself, flicks a brow as if to dare me.

I grab a fork and a knife and sit down at the table, flattening the bakery box down to expose the cake.

As my mom sails back in the room with a little wrapped box, I slice myself a giant piece of cake and eat it right there from the carton.

It tastes good. Not just the cake.

The moment. I'm the center of attention, indulging myself with a giant piece of my favorite cake. The one my wicked stepbrother bought me after yelling at me to take up more space.

It's not the birthday I imagined. It sucked in many ways, but I actually don't hate it.

I also don't hate the Apple watch my mom and Logan bought me, either. Something my mom couldn't have afforded on her own.

I don't even hate the way Wilde watches me as I eat. Like he has plans for me.

Wicked, terrible plans. Plans I definitely *will* hate.

Chapter Nine

W*ilde*

After checking in with my professors about doing my work remotely while my legal problems are sorted out, I go to the auto shop and talk to Bo's great-uncle about a job. He's either desperate for help now that Bo and Cole have moved away, or he feels sorry for me because he pretty much says I can work there any time, on my own schedule. I work the entire school day, and then I go to see Coach Jamison the next day right when school gets out. In addition to being the football coach, he's also the PE teacher, so I find him in his office.

"Wilde. What can I do for you?"

"You, ah, asked if working out with the team was what I wanted."

"I did."

"It is."

Coach cocks his head. "Not sure I believe you, Wilde."

I know why he says it. Because I'm only fifty percent on board with the plan. Part of me thinks it would be humiliating to return to train with a bunch of high school kids.

The other part craves the familiarity of it. Being on a team with my pack brothers, who I would kill or die for. Being coached by an alpha wolf who would have my back no matter what went down.

This was what I missed at Duke. I had teammates, but they were human. I was an imposter, trying to fit in. Hiding what I really am. They liked me. I had buddies. But I could never be myself. I was always on guard to not let my secret out.

It fucking sucked.

I shove my hands in my jeans pocket. "I want to work with you." That's the first honest thing I've said.

Jamison's expression softens. "I'd be honored to work with you, Wilde."

Guilt twists in my solar plexus at that. I definitely don't deserve that kind of response from him. Not after I took his gift of football and wiped my ass with it.

"Yeah?" My throat closes around the word.

"I'll tell you what. I could use an assistant coach. You had leadership skills when you were team captain. Skills that you seem to have squandered. I'd like to see them return."

"Fuck, Coach, really?"

His look hardens. "Language, Woodward."

"Sorry, Coach."

"You're going to have to pull your head out of your ass, though."

"Yes, sir."

"I won't have you on the field if you're not pulling your weight. That means if you do anything at all to drag down the morale or honor of this team, you're banished. Got it?"

"Yes, sir."

"Are you using drugs, Wilde?"

I grind my teeth. It's a valid question, considering the circumstances. I could be using drugs. A shifter would always pass a drug test because we metabolize so quickly.

"No, sir."

"Do you have any in your possession–I don't just mean on your person, I mean anywhere here in Wolf Ridge?"

"No, sir."

"And you'll keep it that way."

"Yes, sir."

"Good. Did you bring a change of clothes?"

I nod. I have a gym bag in the Jeep.

"Get changed. See you out on the field."

"Thanks, Coach."

"Don't let me down, Woodward."

"I won't, sir."

The bell rings as I'm walking out. I find Rayne slouched against the Jeep, looking uncomfortable.

It bothers the fuck out of me. Maybe that's why I'm a dick to her. I want to see more of that fire and less of the fading flower.

"I'm staying for practice. Looks like I can't take you to get your driver's license until Saturday. And you'll have to wait for your ride, Runt."

She pushes off from the Jeep. "I guess it worked out with Coach Jamison?"

I should thank her. She's the one who helped me crack the riddle. But I'm feeling dickish, so I just frown at her. "It worked. Sit here in the Jeep and wait." I unlock the door.

"For two hours? No, thank you. I'll find another way home."

All I can think of is that human bastard, Lincoln. I grab her elbow and yank her back to face me. "The hell you will," I growl, lowering my head to get eye-to-eye with her.

"I told you to get in the Jeep and wait for me. Now, do as you're told."

She draws her hand up between us and slowly unfurls her middle finger. "And I say, *fuck. You.*"

"The runt has a death wish," Abe Oakley scoffs, walking past us.

I drop Rayne's elbow like it's a lump of hot coal. It's one thing to manhandle her at home. Here at school, I'm setting a standard for how she can be treated. I'm a mentor now, as Coach just pointed out.

"Get your ass out on the field, Oakley," I snarl.

Abe's head jerks up in surprise at my tone. He's known me his entire life. His brother is one of my best friends, so I'm sure he thinks he gets special treatment from me.

He looks like he's about to argue, but then thinks better of it. "All right." He shrugs and jogs away.

"You call her *runt* again, and I'll smash your fucking face in," I say to his retreating back. Shifters hear everything, so I know he didn't miss it.

"Oh that's ripe," Rayne mutters, rolling her eyes.

"And you get your ass in the Jeep."

I don't know why I'm insisting. I just sort of love the idea of making her wait for me for hours like a good little runt. I also don't mind the idea of her watching me out on that field. Or rubbing those tasty thighs over the seats to fill my Jeep with her clean spring scent.

But she's back to her defiant self. She lifts that little chin at me, eyes flashing. "Didn't you hear? I said, *go fuck yourself.*" She whirls on her heel and walks away.

This time, I let her go, a half-smile lifting one corner of my mouth. "Actually, I think you just said, *fuck you.*"

She lifts her middle finger over her shoulder without looking back.

"You ride home with a human, and there will be consequences." I keep my voice low in case there are any humans within hearing distance.

"I'm catching the bus, dickwad!" she shouts over her shoulder.

Kids in the parking lot are listening. Basically all of them. We're quite the subject of interest. I sort of like the attention, despite my initial rage over the two of us being forever linked in the minds of Wolf Ridge residents.

I like everyone seeing how I get under her skin.

I also don't mind them seeing how she gives it back to me.

Almost as if I'm proud of her for standing up to me. Like I'm helping her prove to the world she's not as weak as everyone thinks she is.

And if that isn't the most insane form of thinking, I don't know what is.

Oh yeah, maybe giving up an entire professional football career for no reason.

That might be it.

Rayne

Thank fates. Now that Wilde's living here, having the house to myself is a rare thing, which gives me no time to make my foot porn videos.

I revel in being alone. First things first–a snack. I'm so damn hungry.

I swear, I must be channeling my mom. Just so long as I don't grow a big baby belly, too, I guess I'll survive it. I devour an entire box of graham crackers smeared with peanut butter.

Then I head into my bedroom to strip down to my panties and put on some sexy shoes. I set the laptop up on the shelf above the bed for a top angle of my legs and feet. Since I may only have limited time, I record two half-hour-long segments (changing into another pair of shoes and different panties for the second one).

I upload them to drop to my OnlyFans and Patreon accounts, then see what private messages I have in there.

I book private, thirty-minute sessions for five hundred dollars a slot, usually getting a couple a week. The trouble is if anyone else is in the house, I can't do them. Shifter hearing sucks for family members who want privacy.

I had to cancel a couple of appointments since Wilde showed up. Maybe now that he's training with the football team, I can fill my schedule again.

I message a couple of my regulars and say my appointment calendar is open again.

One guy immediately books in for this afternoon.

Well, that works. I have to use my time to make money when I have it. I bill him and send a video link. The moment the money hits my account—the one I set up with an online bank by forging my mom's signature—I place the laptop on the floor, so only my feet are in the picture and then open the video chat.

The guy's screen name is Footlover352. Not super original, but they're not here to entertain me, of course.

"Hey Footlover," I purr. I'm sitting on the edge of the bed, giving him a view of my calves and the strappy stilettos I wore for the second video. "How are you today?"

He makes a sound in his throat. His camera is on, so I can see him. He's in a windbreaker with a t-shirt on underneath. His face is round with extra weight, and he's slightly balding. This guy is weird. Sometimes they're perfectly normal-sounding. Sometimes a little nervous. This one is not a normal guy with a quirk. He's a social misfit.

Not that I'm one to talk.

"Take the shoes off, Rainbow."

I slowly reach down, taking my time, stroking my finger along the strap across my ankle before I unbuckle it. I slide my foot out of the sandal and spread my toes like I'm preening for the camera.

"Come closer. Can you please come closer?"

I shift my bare foot closer to the screen, twirling my toes. "What would you want me to do with these feet if we were in person? Walk on your face?"

"I'm going to oil them up," he says. "With massage oil. For the best massage of your life."

"Oh yeah? How would you rub my feet?"

"I'd get between each of those little toes. I'd fuck those toes with my fingers and the oil."

"Uh-huh. What else?"

"I'd put them in my mouth. Suck them hard."

"Mmm, I'd like that. I would like that so much," I purr. "I would love to stroke your face all over with my toes. It would feel so good."

The session goes on, and I cut it off right at the thirty-minute mark, despite his offer to pay me for another thirty minutes.

It's not hard work, but it still exhausts me.

"How much for the shoes?" he pleads as I'm about to turn off the video chat.

"I'll auction them on my site."

"No! I want them. I'll buy them. I need the shoes."

I'm getting creeped out by the desperation in his voice. "They'll be up for auction. See you next time!" I hit the end button and breathe out a sigh.

Time to make dinner. I hide the shoes in the closet and yank on a pair of shorts, then start the upload on the first video to my page. It takes forever because my computer is old, so I leave it to run while I head into the kitchen.

With Wilde in the house, I stick to basic meat. I start the grill up. There's a twelve-pack of frozen burger meat I took out of the freezer this morning to thaw. I pull them out of the refrigerator now and pry them apart to lay on a plate. I sprinkle them with seasoned salt and Worcestershire sauce and pull out the condiments and buns then make a huge salad–the kind with shredded cheddar on top to weigh it down.

Clogged arteries will never be an issue in this house.

As soon as I hear the car pull up, I take the plate of burgers outside and put them on the grill, like a good little girl.

Dinner waiting when the parents get home. I'm earning my keep.

My mom doesn't come out to kiss me, which bothers me a little, but I finish up and bring the pile of steaming meat inside.

Except it wasn't my mom and Logan pulling up.

It was Wilde. And he's been in my room.

In fact, he's standing in the kitchen holding up my laptop.

"Care to explain?"

Wilde

I'm not sure I believed what I saw on Rayne's laptop.

Foot porn?

I think that's what it was. A video Rayne made of

herself walking around and rubbing her legs together. Stroking her own feet.

I saw flashes of her panty-clad ass which made my dick painfully hard and made me want to smash the computer right there on the spot, so no one else ever sees that video.

The runt turns pale now, her azure eyes huge in her heart-shaped face. "What are you doing with that?" she snaps. She tries to reach for it, but I hold it up high, making her jump.

Despite the bravado, I scent her panic.

I shift it low, high, behind my back. I'm faster than her, and over a foot taller. She will never get this laptop from me. I make my voice extra casual. "I needed a change of clothes, and seeing how it's my room, I went in."

"Your clothes aren't in there anymore. They're in bins in the garage." She's speaking quickly, still lunging right and left to get at the laptop.

"Are you making foot porn, Rayne?"

"No. It's, uh, a video for class. Art class. About perspective."

I laugh. "That lie is not even plausible."

"Truth is stranger than fiction."

"Tell me or explain it to my dad when he gets here."

She stops trying to reach behind my back, going still. She's out of breath with high spots of color on her cheeks. The fact that I know what color panties she has on under those shorts makes it hard not to undress her in my mind.

I can see why she might be good at foot porn if that's what this is. She has shapely legs. Tiny geisha feet. They're bare right now, and I look at them with a new perspective. Yeah, they're cute. She definitely looked hot as hell strutting around my bedroom in high heels.

"Explain it to me, Rayne."

My dad's car pulls up in the driveway. Rayne's panicked gaze darts toward the garage.

"You're almost out of time."

Another glance. "Okay, fine." She starts talking fast. "It's foot porn. It pays really well, and I'm saving for college. Otherwise, there's no way I'd make it, even with the partial scholarship." She reaches out her hand. "Now give it here."

The door from the garage opens.

Please, she mouths, her eyes wide and desperate.

I make her suffer for three more seconds then finally hand over the laptop. She lets out a sigh of relief as she snatches it from me and runs to her bedroom.

"Hi, hon," Leslie, Rayne's mom, chirps when they come in. "Oh, hi, Wilde. How was your day?"

My dad gives me his now customary glower.

I'm still in the dog house with him. Unless I figure out how to get back onto the Duke football team or in the NFL, I probably will be until the day I die.

"Good. I got a job at the auto shop, and I'm assisting Coach Jamison with the team."

"That's great!" Leslie says. I have to say, she's really not bad. She has a kind presence, similar to Rayne's. I don't hate her living here with my dad. He needs someone like her to smooth his rough edges.

Rayne reemerges from her room and moves around, pulling out plates from the cupboard and placing them on the table.

She's like a little mouse, scurrying quietly around, afraid of making waves.

I both love and hate it. I want her that way for me. I don't like that she shrinks around my dad. I want her to give him the same lip she gives me, even though disrespect to

100

elders isn't part of our culture. There's pack order, and adults are alpha until they're challenged.

I remember too well how hard that was for Cole when his dad became an abusive asshole, and he finally had to decide to change the order. But thank fuck he did because his dad cleaned himself up. He even has a job at the brewery now. Not his old job, but something that pays the bills.

"You don't need to be Assistant Coach. You need to keep in top shape for Duke."

"Dad, I'm a wolf on a team of humans. I don't get out of shape. But yeah, I'll work out with the team. I'm doing what you asked."

"I think it's great. You have a lot to offer those kids now that you've played college ball," Leslie says.

Do I? Somehow I feel more like the loser bringing everyone down, but her words make me think about what I learned at Duke. Yeah, maybe a few interesting strategies.

My dad gives me a sour nod and sits down at the table. "Rayne, thanks for cooking burgers. I'll try not to eat them all." Despite his words, he piles a plate with three burgers for Leslie. I swear for a moment, his gaze goes soft when he looks at her.

It surprises me. I definitely thought this marriage was born of duty, not affection. But Leslie blushes and gives him a special smile when he hands her the plate, and I'm suddenly not sure at all what's going on between them.

They're not fated mates. Obviously. If they were, he would've mated her the moment they scented each other at puberty. They're both from this pack. There's only a small percentage of shifters who actually find their fated mate. Maybe fifteen percent of shifters worldwide.

Cole was lucky enough–although Bailey's a human, so

maybe unlucky is the better word choice. But he's happy, and I guess that's all that matters.

No, it seems my dad and Leslie may have found the more human reason for marriage—love.

My dad takes three hamburgers, and I take four. That leaves two for Rayne, which seems adequate since she's a runt. She plows through both of hers pretty quickly, though. I see her licking her fingertips out of the corner of my eye, and it makes my dick swell against my zipper.

"Wow. You have an appetite today," Leslie remarks like it's unusual for Rayne to eat two hamburgers.

I pick up my last hamburger, holding her gaze as I eat it as if to prove my dominance. Pack order around here: I eat first. But as my teeth sink into the meat, it turns rancid in my mouth.

"Yeah. I think your hormones are affecting me, too," Rayne says.

"I don't think it works that way," my dad says.

I set my burger down. Fuck.

What if she's so tiny because she never got enough food? I know that's irrational. I'm sure her mother fed her growing up, but some weird protective instinct rears in me, and I find myself picking up a butter knife and slicing my burger in half. I pick up the unbitten half and toss it lightly on her plate. "Eat up, Runt. Maybe you'll actually grow someday."

"Maybe you'll actually get a personality," she fires back as she picks it up then seems to remember she's afraid of my dad and immediately ducks her head, flushing.

Both my dad and Leslie choose to ignore the exchange, which is good, because Rayne waits until the moment passes before she eats the hamburger, and it drives my wolf nuts having it sit there uneaten. Not because I wanted to take it back.

Because I wanted to feed it to her.

And that doesn't make sense at all.

And I still can't stop thinking about her in those high heels. A flood of dirty thoughts run through my head. Like forcing her to put them on for me and giving me the whole performance.

And that's when it really sinks in.

I can.

I basically own the runt now. If she doesn't want me to tell our parents what she's up to in that bedroom, she'll have to do everything I tell her to.

Every. Single. Thing.

Chapter Ten

Rayne

My mom and Logan go to bed early. And yeah, despite the music they put on to muffle their activities, we can hear them.

Gross.

I do my homework in my room and go to brush my teeth fully clothed.

I can't believe Wilde saw what was on the laptop.

I kind of also can't believe he didn't rat me out. He also gave me half his hamburger, which seemed extremely out of character. I don't know what to make of it. Is he just super grateful I helped him figure out what to say to Coach Jamison to give him the Assistant Coach position. I sort of hate his dad for not throwing him a bone.

I mean, I get that he hasn't forgiven Wilde for drug dealing, or whatever it was that happened in South Carolina, and I also think Wilde can be a Class A asshole, but he is, actually, doing everything his dad asked of him. Taking me to school. Teaching me to drive. Working out with the WRH football team.

The fake diamond chip I wear on one nostril is annoying me. Lately, the piercing feels stuck. Too tight. I constantly have to twirl it to try to get it to loosen up.

After I brush my teeth, I decide to take it out. My mom had asked me to six weeks ago when Logan sniffed out the fact that she was four months pregnant and started coming around our house. Back when she pressured me to change my look and basically clean up to make us Logan-worthy.

I'd refused at the time. It was enough to change my hairstyle and stop with the heavy eyeliner. The nose ring felt like part of my emo identity.

But now it itches and pinches and is driving me crazy. So I'm doing it for me, not for Logan. Or my mom.

I have a hard time taking it out like the flesh doesn't want to release the little stud. It takes me a solid five minutes. I take it with me to the bedroom where I find...*oh fates.*

Wilde is stretched out on my bed, legs crossed, hands behind his head.

"What in the hell do you think you're doing?" I demand, keeping my voice low because I don't want the parents to hear.

Wilde's grin is slow and dangerous. Definitely feral. "What does it look like, Runt?"

"It looks like you're in the wrong room. This is my room now, remember?"

How's that for taking up space, dickwad?

"My room, Runt. I'm tired of sleeping on the couch. And considering what I know about your extracurricular activities, I own you now." He pulls one of the pillows out from behind his head. "You're sleeping on the floor tonight, Rayne-bow. And if you say anything, I will tell everyone—and I do mean *everyone*—how you've been making money."

My chest sinks back between my shoulders, caving with my determination to fight.

I would never, ever survive that secret getting leaked.

I grind my teeth and narrow my eyes. "I hate you, Wilde Woodward."

"Hate all you want, babygirl. I still own you."

Um...*babygirl?* I don't think so.

Definitely not his babygirl.

I harumph and stomp to the dresser, where I pull out a pair of PJs. I take them back to the bathroom to change.

When I return, the light's off. I shut the door and stand there for a minute. I'm not just waiting for my eyes to adjust. I'm pissed. Waiting for some better idea than sleeping on the hard floor to surface.

But it doesn't.

Wilde's right. He owns me now. All he ever has to do is dangle this shit over my head, and I will do anything he says.

The only thing that will end it is...

Ah. My best idea yet. I need to figure out how to get Wilde back to North Carolina.

I stalk over to the general area where he dropped the pillow and feel around in the dark until I find it. There's no blanket. No padding.

I reach up to the bed and snatch the comforter off of Wilde. He catches it, and we tug-a-war for a minute until I hear it rip and release my hold. Obviously, I will never win a strength or speed contest with this guy, so I try for sugar.

"Please, Wilde? The floor is hard, and I'm not a shifter."

It works. He releases the blanket. I fold it into vertical thirds and lie on top of it. Good thing I'm running hot these days since I have no top blanket. But it also means I will be hot in these pajama shorts. Because I can't very well sleep in my underwear like I would if there wasn't a very large male wolf in my room.

I lie curled on my side facing the bed and try to calm my racing pulse. Cool the feverish flush of heat that rushed through me the moment I came into the bedroom. I squeeze my thighs together, willing the slow, steady pulse between my legs to stop.

I don't like Wilde's scent. Why would I?

It's just having a male my age in the same room is doing funny things to my mind.

No...not my mind. Definitely, my body that's having the reaction. Waves of heat roll through me. The flesh between my legs squeezes.

For some reason, I start thinking about Wilde's dick.

I swear to fate, I've never thought about dick before in my life. Not Wilde's, not any guy's. Like I said, I've been pretty asexual.

But suddenly, I'm picturing myself on my knees, servicing him.

Which is crazy-town. I would never. Why would I even imagine that? Why would I be thinking about what it would be like to straddle his lap and sink down onto that flagpole?

Oh fates.

Flames lick over the surface of my skin. Curl in my core.

I squeeze my eyes closed tight and start to count backward from 100.

99...98...97...96...Wilde with his shirt off...95...Wilde fucking his fist in the shower...94...93...Wilde tipping me over his lap and spanking me...92...Wilde looming over me on this floor.

Wait, *is he?*

Chapter Eleven

Wilde

I had to jack off again in the shower this morning. Judging by the sound of her breath and the way she fidgeted on the floor, Rayne didn't sleep much last night. I didn't, either. Her spring scent had me agitated, and I swear, I felt blasts of heat coming off her body.

Despite the torture, I'm beyond satisfied with myself. With the new situation. Sleeping in the same room as Rayne makes my dick harder than stone.

Not that I want to fuck her. She's my *stepsister*. I just like the dominance. Making her sleep on the floor. Keeping her close, at my feet.

Tonight, the moment the parents go to their wing of the house, I forgo working on an essay that's due to barge in again.

Rayne sits cross-legged on the bed doing homework in a tank top and pajama shorts. Her hair is pulled up from her neck in a ponytail.

"What's up, Runt?" I whisper crow.

She rolls her eyes. "It's not even bedtime, asswipe."

"Ooh, language, Runt. Don't make me spank that little ass of yours."

I love the way her cheeks and neck flush pink. When I catch the scent of her arousal, I have to turn away to hide my hard-on. I cover by looking through her shit.

On the dresser is a stack of books and papers. I pull one of the school flyers out of the mix to read it.

"Wait. What in the fuck is this?" I turn it around to show her. The flier is a list of the nominees for Homecoming royalty, and somehow, incomprehensibly, Rayne made it onto the ballot.

Her jaw sets in a stubborn line. "That's Abe Oakley thinking he's funny."

I study the list again. "Who's Lauren?"

"A human. Lincoln's twin."

"Huh. I don't get the joke."

Rayne shrugs. "I don't know. I guess it's just so the entire school can have a huge laugh about how ridiculous it is that we're on the list? I don't see what's so funny, either."

I catch a whiff of hurt from Rayne, and it does something itchy to my skin.

I crush the paper in my hand and toss it in the trash can. "Yeah, it's stupid." I'm not sure what makes me agree with Rayne over Abe. Especially out loud.

I continue my search of her things, pulling open drawers. Rooting through her panties. I stop when I find a little plastic case of pills.

My body reacts with a jolt of electricity that both fries and freezes me at the same time. I click open the pills.

Yep. Birth control.

A nuclear level of rage flushes through my body. *"Who are you fucking?"* I snarl, barely remembering to keep my voice low, so the parents won't overhear us.

If it's that human, I'm going to pound him into the ground. I will break every rib in his chest.

Rayne drops her pen and stares at me, a mixture of shock and outrage in her expression. *"Excuse me?"* Her chest and neck are blotchy with a pink flush and anger shoots out of those blue eyes.

I stalk over to the bed and shake the pill pack in front of her face, careful not to actually touch her when I'm so angry. "Who. Are. You. Fucking?"

She tries to snatch the pills away, but I jerk them out of her reach.

"Who, Rayne?"

Probably realizing she can't win at the physical contest of taking back her pills, she gets sassy. "Your Daddy, Wilde."

I nearly combust, even though I know it's not true. Still, the idea of it makes me want to level the entire house.

"Who is it?"

"You really are an asshole, aren't you?"

I'm the asshole who is going to kill whoever touched Rayne.

"Tell me, Rayne, and I won't tell the parents."

She throws me off when her lips twitch. "Go ahead. Please. By all means, go tell the parents. Since my mom already knows I'm *on the pill for cramps,* they're going to love hearing how you barged in here and searched my underwear drawer."

It takes a second for the words to cut through the fog of rage around me. *On the pill for cramps.*

She's on the pill for cramps.

Oh for fuck's sake.

"You have cramps," I repeat like an absolute idiot.

"Not anymore." She folds her arms across her tits, causing them to lift and bulge against the opening of her tank top. I want to slide my dick right between them.

Because I'm still a total dickwad, I drop the pill back onto the bed and grip both her knees. She snaps them closed. "No one's been between these thighs, Rayne-bow?"

Fuck, I don't know why it matters so much to me, but it does. I can't stand the idea of anyone else touching her.

The moment is not helped in the least by the scent of her arousal, which suddenly floods my nostrils. As if my disrespectful touch gets her wet.

She tries unsuccessfully to knock one of my hands off. "None of your business, Wilde."

I bring my face closer to hers, inhaling her creosote and juniper scent, along with the sweet aroma of her arousal. "Say it, Runt. I need to know if someone's popped this cherry."

Even more of her arousal curls into my nostrils. The room starts to spin.

She clutches at both my wrists, digging her nails into my skin as she tries to pry my grip from her knees.

"Tell me the truth, and I'll let you sleep on the bed tonight."

"No! I'm a–" Her face is a deep shade of magenta.

Thank fuck. She's still a virgin. I don't have to kill anyone tonight.

"Who in this town would have sex with me, anyway?"

I narrow my eyes. "Lots of assholes, Rayne. But none of them are going to. Understand me? Not if they want to live."

She blinks up at me, her blue eyes shimmering with unshed tears.

I release her knees, my hands coming to my belt.

Her gaze tracks my movement.

I flick my brows. "Say it, Runt. I need to know you're clear on this."

Chapter Twelve

W*ilde*

Instead of taking Rayne to get her driver's license test on Saturday, I head to Tempe to watch Bo and Cole play football for ASU. My plan is to drive down to Tucson from there to sit down with Amber Green, Garrett Green's human wife, who is a lawyer. She's agreed to talk to me about my case.

I told Rayne I couldn't take her like it was her punishment to have to wait to get the license, even though I'm the one who was pushing it onto her before.

I guess I like having her beholden to me for a ride more than I want to be relieved of the burden of her. I like the chance to taunt her in the mornings as I drive her to school, reminding her I'm in charge. That I don't want her talking to those humans. That I expect her to wait in my Jeep until after practice.

She never does, but I demand it, anyway.

I love her defiance. The way she glared at me when she told me she understood I would kill any guy she had sex with.

I'm half-relieved, half-agitated to be away from Wolf Ridge. Away from my runt of a stepsister. Despite my brilliant idea to take back my bed, which now very much smells like Rayne, I couldn't sleep all week.

I spent every night listening to Rayne toss and turn and sigh.

If I had even one shred of decency, I would let her have her bed back. She clearly can't get any rest on the floor.

But each time I consider the idea of releasing her from my evil plan, everything in me balks. I'm not leaving that bedroom, even if it means I never sleep again.

Even if it means I have to jack off in the bathroom four times a day.

I don't want to fuck my stepsister. That would be wrong. I especially don't want to fuck Rayne the Runt. Why would I be attracted to a Defective?

But something about sleeping in close proximity to a female has me all riled up. A little out of control. So, yeah, the bathroom jack offs have been extremely necessary.

I've also had to get out and run every morning. In human form because I'm trying to show my dad I'm still training. I have to get up early, anyway, so the parents don't figure out I'm not sleeping on the couch.

I get to Tempe in about forty-five minutes, and go to the apartment Bailey, Cole, Sloane, Bo and Austin share to pick up my ticket to the game.

Cole and Bo's girlfriends–both human–got into Barrett, the honors college, so last year they were in a special dorm with Austin–also a brainiac, which was apart from where Bo and Cole lived. I think that was mostly to satisfy the human parents. This year, they worked it out to live together.

The guys texted earlier that they are already in the

stadium, but Bailey and Sloane would wait around to give me a ticket. Bailey comes down to the street when I text. Her dark hair is back in a high ponytail, the pink swath in the front left hanging in a frame around her face. She's not smiling.

She hands me the ticket through the window but leans her forearms on the doorframe, so I can't drive off. There's someone behind me, not that I give two shits about making them go around.

"I hear you're being a dick to Rayne."

For some reason, that bothers me. If anyone else said it, I'd buff my nails with pride. Of course, I'm giving the runt a hard time. It's my job as her stepbrother. But Bailey is Rayne's best friend.

Only friend, really, unless you count the douche-human who's tutoring her now, which I don't.

So whatever Bailey heard came from Rayne, herself. Which means I've genuinely hurt the runt. I don't like the uncomfortable twist that moves in my gut at that thought.

"What did you hear?" Not much of a comeback, but I genuinely want to know. Did she tell her I'm making her sleep on the floor? That I spanked her? That I made her get off on my fingertips?

But Bailey shakes her head, which I suspect means she hasn't heard any details at all.

It's a mixture of relief and triumph that courses through me at that deduction. Relief that Bailey doesn't know how dastardly I truly am. And triumph that what's between me and Rayne has stayed between the two of us.

I—obviously—haven't shared any of our interactions, either. Nor do I plan to. They feel private. Just between the two of us. Like there's a secret we're holding. Not keeping. Keeping would imply we both knew the secret.

117

We don't.

It's still developing. Uncracking and unfurling. A twisting and pulling, a knotting of threads between us. And that's when I realize exactly how proprietary I feel over Rayne.

Like she belongs to me, and no one else gets to see into what's between us.

I mean, I guess that's true.

She's my stepsister. My family, now. She does belong to me. It's what I've asserted from the beginning. But there's a ferocity behind my mental claim on her. Like I'd tear anyone apart who tried to keep me from her.

Hmm. Strange.

"Rayne's safe with me," I find myself saying to Bailey.

I don't even know if it's true. She's hardly physically safe. I've helped myself to manhandle her whenever I see fit. I don't even think she's emotionally safe, except that those tears of hers will make me move mountains.

But I believe what I'm saying, nonetheless.

I'm not going to let anyone harm Rayne on my watch, including our parents. And I may want her to think I'm dangerous to her, but I wouldn't actually hurt her.

Bailey doesn't buy it though. She snorts. "You're a God in that town. You could change how people treat Rayne. But you wouldn't want your own precious reputation to take a hit by a genetic misfit, right?"

"'Bye, Bailey." I take my foot off the brake and let the Jeep roll forward gently. She steps back and flips me the bird as I drive off.

As I drive to the stadium, I try to keep her words from piercing my mind.

You could change how people treat Rayne.

But do I want to?

Or do I want to keep her weakened, defenseless and *all to myself?*

All I know is when my dad texts later to tell me he's taking Leslie on a little honeymoon, and I need to get home tonight in case Rayne needs anything, my dick gets rock hard.

Screw going to Tucson to work on my legal problems.

Me and the runt home alone for the weekend.

Game. On.

* * *

Rayne

My back hurts from sleeping on the floor all week. I seriously hate my stepbrother.

I couldn't be more thrilled when Logan decides to take my mom on a belated, impromptu honeymoon. I didn't realize I was the reason he didn't take her before, but when he told me he asked Wilde to come back tonight so I wasn't home alone, I immediately texted Wilde myself.

Do not come back on my account. I don't need a babysitter.

He replies immediately: *Oh, but you do.*

I can't decide if he's actually coming back or just being a dick. It's hard to figure out his motivation for anything.

I think it's because he doesn't actually know where he is in his own head.

I'm not sure he even knows how he ended up back in Wolf Ridge. It's like it just happened to him. He seems to feel little responsibility or remorse for it. Even with getting thrown out of the pack hanging over his head, he doesn't seem to be all that motivated to solve his problems.

Yet, at the same time, he's doing everything his dad demands, like a good little wolf.

I don't get it.

I really don't.

I especially don't get what his deal is with me. Does he hate me? Is he attracted? Is this all a weird dominance game to him? Something an alpha wolf who's not quite in his power yet has to enact with the weaker pack members around him?

I enjoy the afternoon to myself and use the time alone to paint my toenails and make a bunch more foot videos. When I'm finished, I schedule them to post in my Patreon account, then I open up my schedule for privates.

Once more, Footlover352 books in.

But the sessions aren't enjoyable to me. They're something I get through, that's all. They pay the big bucks, and I need all the money I can make. I have eighty-five hundred dollars saved up already. If I keep up at this rate, I will totally have enough for room and board and the remainder of my tuition next year.

I plan to continue this work while in college to get myself through. Hey, some women strip to get through school. Some of us with cute, tiny feet make foot porn. It's still an honest days' work, no matter how much others judge.

After dinner—I was freaking ravenous again—I start the session with Footlover352. I'm wearing the Manolo's he bought me. I use an online wishlist that doesn't give out my address to my fans. The shoes ship straight to the house, which is fine, because I'm the one who's home to get the mail.

I prance around and dirty talk with Footlover352. I give him exactly thirty minutes. "Okay, time's up."

"Not yet," he says quickly. "I'll pay for another session."

Gah. I should take the money. I definitely need it. I waffle for a moment then agree. Who knows when I'll have time alone again. I need to use it while I can.

"Fine." I set the timer for another thirty minutes.

"I'll give you five hundred dollars if you mail me those shoes," he offers.

I scoff. "But then I would be out my five hundred dollar shoes. That's hardly a bargain, is it?"

"A thousand," he rushes to say. "I'll give you one thousand dollars. Upfront. I'll transfer it now. I want the shoes. *Those shoes.* The ones you wear for *me.*"

I can hardly turn down a thousand bucks, can I?

"Transfer the money," I say. I wait until I hear the ding of confirmation on my phone before I resume the session.

I do my usual prancing around the room and dancing with my feet and calves. I attempt a sort of solo Tango-style movement, twirling and jabbing one foot out to the side, then prancing around.

"Closer, Rayne," Footlover says.

I'm moving closer as it hits me. "What did you call me?"

"Rainbow. Isn't that your name?" He gives a nervous laugh. This guy is such a geek. "Why? What do you want me to call you?"

"Rainbow."

I guess maybe I heard him wrong.

"Get closer. Take off the shoes."

I do what he wants. Give him some barefoot time.

"Stand with your feet apart, facing away. Now bend over and slide your hands down your calves."

Ugh. He's getting fancy now. I have to be careful I don't get my face in the screen.

When I first started filming the videos and doing the

privates, I wore a mask, in case my face accidentally got into the screen, but I've become lazy now. I figure I know exactly where the frame begins and ends and won't mess up.

Now, as I slide my hands down the backs of my thighs, though, I'm wishing I was wearing the mask, just to be sure.

As my head gets lower than my pelvis and I can see through the window of my legs, I check out the screen.

Fuck!

He definitely saw a little face. Totally saw my hair.

Fuck this. I'm out.

"Time's up," I say, even though he still has five more minutes.

"Not yet," he whines.

"Sorry, bud. I'm short-changing you today. You're getting too needy."

"I..you're..."

I end the live before I can hear what he's going to say.

My heart pounds faster than a hummingbird's, and a weird sense of violation creeps over me, even though I'm the one selling myself.

I slam the laptop closed and head back to the kitchen in my panties. Yes, I'm hungry again. Hungry enough to eat a whole quart of ice cream as I watch television in the living room—something I never get to do when people are in the house.

It's late, and I'm curled up watching Emily in Paris on Netflix when I hear Wilde's Jeep out front.

Fuck!

I run for my bedroom and dive into the bed and under the covers. I don't care what Wilde says, I am not sleeping on the floor tonight. I was hoping he'd be staying down in Tempe with his alpha-hole buddies. Regardless, I'm sick of the floor.

He can sleep in Logan's bed tonight. Or whatever. I was looking forward to having my room to myself tonight, and I'm not giving it up.

I hear Wilde's big feet clomp down the hallway.

I locked the bedroom door, but he uses his thumbnail to open it. "Don't think I didn't see you sprinting for the bedroom in your panties, Runt. Are you pretending you're sleeping now?"

"Go away, Wilde. I'm sleeping in my own bed tonight."

He snorts, but to my relief, clomps away.

I hear him making himself a snack in the kitchen, then brushing his teeth–something I wish I'd taken the time to do.

I consider getting up to pull on some pajama shorts, but I'm too invested in staking my claim on this bed.

To my chagrin, Wilde returns to the bedroom, kicks off his shoes, pulls off his jeans, and climbs into the bed.

"On the floor, Runt." He grabs me by the waist and rolls me across his body to the outside of the bed, dangling me over the edge of the bed, so that if he lets go, I'd fall.

I throw my arms out to break my fall, but he doesn't let go.

"I'm not sleeping on the floor," I maintain.

"Are you forgetting what I know about you, Runt?"

I go for the truth. "My back hurts. I'm not a shifter. My body can't just take abuse and recover instantly. Sleeping on the floor sucks."

Wilde's quiet, like he's actually considering my argument. "Well, then go sleep on the couch."

"No. I was here first. I'm sleeping in the bed." Yes, I'm acting like I'm five years old. Sue me.

"I'm sleeping in my bed, Rayne."

"Well, so am I. So move over." I don't know what possesses me to make that statement.

I must be completely out of my freaking mind. I don't actually want to spend the night in the same bed as Wilde.

It's bad enough to sleep in the same room. I've barely slept all week!

"Oh yeah? What do you think will happen if I have to sleep next to you?" There's a threat in Wilde's voice I don't understand.

Does he mean it's so disgusting? Or...

In the next second, he's rolling me back to the inside of the bed and has me pinned on my belly. His huge form is on top of mine and—

Oh.

Um, wow.

Not disgusted.

No...Wilde is sporting an erection the size of a torpedo, and it's *right between my legs*.

"You think," he rumbles, right against the shell of my ear, "a little slip of girl like you is safe from a big bad wolf?"

I don't move. My breath comes in fast pants. My legs spread. Not as an invitation–of course not. Just to make room for his huge cock. To keep it from touching me.

But, of course, that isn't working. Because through his boxer briefs and my panties, I feel his rod pressing right up against my core.

"You think you can crawl in my bed in your panties, and I'm not going to do this?" His hand reaches under my hips to boldly cup my mons.

A shudder ripples through me, and I get wet immediately, soaking the gusset of my panties. I know he can feel it. I desperately want more of his touch, and that makes me angry. I don't like to be needy with him.

He moves his fingers as he rocks his hips to grind against my ass. "I might pop your cherry in my sleep, Runt. But no" –he lifts his hips and shifts them up a few inches, pressing his cock against the crack of my ass and undulating his fingers between my legs. "I think I'd save your virginity and just take this cute little ass. Because that's where runts take it, right, Rayne-bow? In the ass?"

I should fight him. I should howl and pitch a fit. Scratch and bite and do whatever I can to get out from under him.

But, instead, my body goes limp with submission. I want more of his obscene touches. The dirty talk. Even his cruelty. I want it all.

I let out a little whimper.

* * *

Wilde

The scent of Rayne's arousal curls into my nostrils, and suddenly, my wolf goes wild.

I've never lost control with a female before–neither wolf nor human–but something about having Rayne pinned beneath me and knowing she's turned on does something to me.

I flip her on her back and shove up her shirt to reveal the most perfect rack I've ever seen. She's small, but her breasts aren't. They are full and round. Proportional, but fucking spectacular.

What I fail to miss in my frenzy is that I've scared the shit out of Rayne.

She fights back, slapping my face and getting one leg free to kick at me.

The slap gets my wolf back under control, but because I'm still a dick, I pin her wrists down beside her head.

And that's when it happens: Rayne's eyes turn silver.

Not a glint of silver. Not a reflection of the light.

They change from blue to silver.

Rayne isn't defective.

She has a she-wolf inside her waiting to get out.

I go still.

She's still frantically wrestling beneath me, her wolf struggling to get out to help save her.

I'm so captivated by the glimpse of her wolf, I don't move for a moment, just hold her down and watch her struggle and sweat.

And then I'm jubilant. "Come here." I leap off the bed and grab her by the waist, hauling her into the air. "You have to see yourself." I carry her, kicking and fighting, over to the full-length mirror on the back of the door. When I try to drop her onto her feet, she doesn't stand, too busy flailing.

"Stand up, Rayne." I set her down in front of me, one hand around her throat, forcing her to look in the mirror.

The silver eyes are gone, though.

I close my fingers around her throat to frighten her and use my free hand to yank up her t-shirt to piss her off.

Now her eyes change.

"Look at that." I shake her until she looks.

Her eyes widen in surprise, and she sucks in a shocked breath.

Chapter Thirteen

Rayne

R "Look at you, Rayne. You've had a wolf in there all this time."

I let out a sob when I see my reflection in the mirror.

A wolf. *I am a wolf.* I have a she-wolf inside me.

Unbelievable.

I hoped and wished my entire childhood that I would eventually develop into a normal shifter, but nothing pointed in that direction for me.

I didn't have the healing abilities other pups had. I couldn't see in the dark. My hearing sucked. My nose wasn't good for much.

Even so, when I got my period and grew breasts, I'd hoped and wished and begged fate that I might also learn to shift like the other girls in the pack.

But alas. It seemed it wasn't for me. I finally accepted what everyone has suspected from the start: I was defective.

But now, as I stand restrained by my stepbrother, the bully who just won't leave me alone, she finally emerges.

And she's beautiful. At least her eyes are. Silver, like the moon we worship.

I go limp with another sob. If Wilde weren't holding me up, I would fall to my knees and weep like a baby.

"Silver eyes," he croons in my ear. There's a note of wonder in his voice like he thinks my wolf is beautiful, too.

Like he recognizes the magic and power that's present in the room. The shimmer and glow around me.

All I can do is sob, though.

"Hey." Wilde pulls down my t-shirt to cover my bared breasts, and the hand at my throat slides down to hold me up by the waist. "You're okay."

"I know that!" I sob. "I'm a wolf."

Wilde finally releases me and grins. Our gazes meet in the mirror. "You sure are."

I turn around and give him a hard shove, which doesn't move him even an inch. "What were you doing to me?" My voice is choked with tears.

I'm confused as hell about the riot of sensations in my body. The pulsing heat between my legs. The fact that my stepbrother possibly just tried to rape me.

The notion that I partly wanted him to.

For once, Wilde seems to offer me an honest response. He spreads his hands. "I don't know. I think...my wolf sensed her in there. I caught your scent, and it sort of drove me crazy. I didn't mean to try to strip you. I'm sorry about that. But then I saw your eyes..." He grins. "So I did it again in front of the mirror to show you what I saw."

I let out a wobbly exhale. "Maybe...maybe this is why I've been so hot at night. And hungry all the time."

Wilde's throat works to swallow.

I realize I can see him perfectly in the darkness.

"Maybe this is why I can't leave you alone."

128

I'm shocked by that admission.

And titillated. *Very* titillated. But I'm way too raw and confused to follow up on it. Right now I have an advantage. Wilde's being semi-respectful for a change. "Wilde." I lift my chin and point to the door. "Get out."

I'm shaking all over. I fall to my knees in front of the mirror and stare into the reflection, willing the silver-eyed wolf to return, but she's gone.

Apparently, only Wilde can summon her.

Chapter Fourteen

W*ilde*

    I have to shift and run to keep from barging back into Rayne's bedroom. My wolf doesn't like being denied, and apparently, he thought he was going to get some. After failing to get any sleep on the couch, I get up and make two huge plates full of pancakes. The kind my dad used to make for me on the day of a big game—with protein powder and nuts mixed in, and a stack of Canadian bacon slices to round it out.

Rayne's going to need her protein if she's going to shift. I remember going through puberty—I couldn't seem to eat enough. I was hangry and horny all the time.

When Rayne still hasn't emerged by ten a.m., I barge into her room.

No, I don't bother knocking. I still own her, even if I did let her sleep in the bed last night.

She's awake, leaning against her pillows, working on her ancient laptop. I see the flash of her feet on the screen.

She tries to close the cover of the laptop, but I snatch it from her before she can. It's the same stuff I saw before—her

Patreon account where she's posting photos and videos. Looks like she also has an Onlyfans account. She has a great business head, apparently.

I read the comments.

Damn, these guys are really hot for her.

"Is this safe, Runt?"

"Of course it is."

"No one knows your real name or where you live?"

"I'm not an idiot, Wilde."

"And all you show is your feet, right?" That's all I saw before. It's the only reason I didn't go apeshit when I found it. I mean, feet aren't pornographic to me. I get that they are for her patrons, but I don't feel like I have to kill anyone because they've seen them. If they were looking at her ass, I would hunt every last motherfucker down.

Even I have to admit, her feet are damn cute. In some of the pictures she wears adorable toe rings, and she changes the color of toenail polish to various vibrant colors.

"Yes, just my feet. Not that it's your business."

"Wrong. Everything about you is my business."

"Wilde, shouldn't you be worrying about your court case? And figuring out how to get the charges dropped, so you can go back to school?"

There's kindness in her tone–and genuine curiosity–and that's the only reason I don't immediately shut her down.

"I don't want to go back."

There. I admitted it to her. The thing I hadn't even quite admitted to myself.

I'm a bit surprised when I see compassion in her gaze. She rises up on her knees on the bed, and it gets my dick rock hard. "Yeah, but you'll be kicked out of the pack if you don't resolve it. It's kind of a lose-lose situation for you."

I drop her laptop on the bed and tunnel my hand through my hair. "You noticed that, too, huh?"

"Did you admit anything when you were taken into jail?"

I shake my head. "I didn't say a word."

"Were they even your drugs?"

I stare at her, surprised that of all the people who might have wondered that she's the only one who actually did. "What makes you ask that?"

"Why are you dodging the question?"

Smart girl.

I suddenly can't keep my hands off her. I wrap my hands around her upper arms and deadlift her into the air to dangle her over the floor for a moment before I drop her softly to her feet.

"Worry about your own shit, Rayne." I smack her ass. "I made pancakes."

"For me?" She twists to look at me over one shoulder. She sounds shocked.

I snort. "What, you thought I just made them for myself and ate them all?"

"Well...yeah."

I give her ass a light smack again. I might be getting slightly obsessed with the idea of spanking her.

Being in charge of her. Teaching her another lesson.

Taking care of her through her transition.

She scoots out the door, straight to the kitchen, which pleases my wolf to no end.

"You need lots of protein right now. Shifting uses a ton of calories, especially at first as your body is changing."

I pull out a chair at the kitchen table and set one of the huge plates of food in front of her with a fork.

"Um, thank you." Her big blue eyes follow me as I pick up the second plate and sit down beside her to eat it.

She eats in silence for a few minutes, shoveling food into her mouth like she was starving. "Do you really think I can shift?" she asks.

"Oh, you're going to shift," I say although I'm not certain it's true.

Now that she planted the seed of doubt, I can see that she might be right to worry. Just because she has a wolf in there somewhere doesn't mean she'll ever figure out how to get it out.

I should probably bring her to Alpha Green, so he can use the alpha command on her to get her to shift, but for some reason, I feel proprietary over Rayne's shift. Like no one else gets to know about it except me. Or at least, not until after I've groomed her. I want to be the one to teach her to shift. To help her with the transition.

And no, it's definitely not out of brotherly devotion.

My wolf craves Rayne. I don't know what that means. If it's just a reaction to living in the same house as a female going through transition or if it's something more.

All I know is that she feels like mine.

And the only way in hell this can ever come out right is if we get that wolf out of Rayne.

Because I'm not going to be the loser who fucks his defective stepsister.

"What if I can't?" she asks.

"You can. I saw your wolf. She's in there, and she wants out. So forget about driving lessons. Today you're getting shifting lessons. And we're going to keep at it until I see that silver-eyed bitch."

Rayne hides her face behind her hair, bending her head

down to her pancakes. After she devours several more, she asks, "Think she's grey?"

"Maybe. Or she might be white. That would be something, wouldn't it?"

Especially considering my wolf is black. We'd be yin and yang. Big and small. Black and white.

I don't know why I'm thinking of us as *we*. That's weird.

Rayne doesn't manage to finish more than half the plate I fixed for her, but it was still a ton of food, so I'm satisfied. I clear the plates, covering hers with plastic wrap and putting it in the refrigerator for later.

"All right. Meet me on the back deck in five."

"I..." Rayne looks like she's going to protest but then seems to change her mind. "Okay."

She meets me on the back deck wearing a pair of jeans and a t-shirt.

I cock a brow. "Clothes off, Runt, or you'll rip them."

"I'm not taking my clothes off for you, Wilde."

All my dick hears is *clothes off for you, Wilde*.

I grin and whip my shirt off over my head. "Here." I hand it to her. "Go and put this on. It's loose enough on you that it might not tear when you shift. Unless your she-wolf is huge, which would be hilarious."

Her gaze travels to my bare chest and a flush creeps up her neck. "Fine." She grabs the shirt.

"No panties!" I yell at her as she disappears inside. I chuckle when I hear her mutter something like, *fate help me*.

I yank off my jeans and stretch in the late morning sun. I'm far more pleased than I should be when Rayne returns wearing nothing but my shirt. I'm also dying to pull it up and see everything underneath.

Instead, I force myself to sit on the edge of the deck. I pat the spot beside me. "Come here, Runt."

She sits her bare ass down beside me.

"Close your eyes. Picture a wolf. I mean, don't picture it, but imagine yourself as one. Like, feel your body in a wolf form."

Rayne cracks an eye. "That's pretty hard to do when I've never been a wolf before."

"Just shut up and try it."

She closes her eyes again.

I close mine and summon a level of alpha command. "*Shift.*" I infuse my voice with the potency of an alpha.

Nothing happens.

Rayne cracks her eyes again and shakes her head. "Wilde, I don't know if this is going to wor–"

"Shift," I command again.

Nothing.

"Imagine you're in your wolf form."

"I don't know what that feels like!" she protests.

"Pretend you do."

I try to command her several more times, but each time seems to have less and less of an effect on her. Like she's giving up.

I stand and pull off my boxer briefs.

Rayne covers her eyes. "A little warning might be nice," she mutters.

I shift into wolf form and bump her knees with my giant body.

She reaches for me, burying her fingers in my fur. I let her pet me. I don't know why–it feels good, I guess.

I'm not even sure what I hope to accomplish by showing her my wolf. I guess maybe I want him to call to hers.

Instead, she gets up. "Well, I don't think this is going to work, Wilde."

I try intimidation, instead. If her wolf thinks she requires protection, she may come out. I snarl at Rayne, leaping past her to block her path to the door. I bare my teeth and growl, stalking forward.

Rayne is unimpressed. "I'm onto you, Woodward. Not scared. Nice try, though."

I lunge for her. She darts back, faster than human speed. Her reflexes are getting quicker. I wonder if she heals faster.

I probably should've thought this through before I acted, but I don't. I just lunge forward and bite her calf.

She screams. Now real fear kicks in. I can tell by her scent. By the silver glow of her eyes. I hear the crack of joints like she's about to shift, but nothing happens.

I release her from my jaws and attempt to lick the wound closed, but she's already scrambling inside.

"You bit me!" She sounds incredibly offended.

Fuck.

If she doesn't have super healing abilities my dad will throw me out of this house for good.

I follow on her heels into the house, getting past when she tries to slam the door on me.

"Get away from me! I can't believe you did that. I'm bleeding!"

I try to lick the wound again, but she kicks me in the face. "I said get away! You are fucking crazy!"

She runs for the front door, grabbing the keys to my Jeep on the way.

I shift back to human form, taking a few precious seconds to run for my boxers on the back deck.

Renee Rose

And that's when I hear the scrape and crunch of metal smashing into metal.

"*Rayne!*" I bellow as I race through the house and out the front door.

* * *

Rayne

Ohfateohfateohfateohfate.

What have I done?

I just wrecked Wilde's Jeep. I don't even know what or who I hit because my face slammed down on the steering wheel on impact.

I wrecked Wilde's Jeep. I don't even have a driver's license. I took it without his permission.

I'm so dead.

In the next moment, the door flies open and Wilde yanks at my body, fighting with the seatbelt until he gets me free.

"I'm sorry!" I squeak, thinking he's furious. "I'm so sorry. I shouldn't have taken your Jeep. Please don't kill me."

"Rayne. *Fuck.* Are you okay? Look at me." Wilde's propped me on my feet, leaned me up against the Jeep, and his hands roam all over me, checking for injuries.

I crane my neck to look around behind me to see what I hit.

Oh, God. The mailbox. I backed the Jeep at full speed right over the concrete planter and into the metal mailbox post. The back fender of the Jeep is now completely wrapped around the tilted post.

I rub my bruised forehead. It hurt a fuck-ton in the

moment, but the pain has already diminished, which seems strange.

I'm way more concerned at this point about what Wilde will do when he sees the extent of the damage. Or worse—oh fates—what Logan will do or say.

I'm so fucked.

So very fucked.

I drag in a sobbing breath and burst into tears. "I'm sorry. I'm so sorry I hurt your Jeep. I'll pay for it to be fixed. I'll give you my college money. Please don't tell your dad." I try to focus on Wilde's face through my tears. "Please? Can we figure something out?"

Wilde seems to have calmed down. "Okay, Rayne. Go inside the house. Let me get the Jeep out of the planter before someone sees what happened out here."

Relieved that Wilde at least knows what to do, I obey, walking on trembling legs into the house where I sink into the sofa. I think I'm in shock because absolutely no thoughts move through my head. I note no passage of time.

I'm not aware of anything until Wilde comes back into the house and shuts the door.

That's when the tears automatically start to flow again. "I'm so sorry. I'll pay for it. Please don't tell your dad. Please—"

Wilde holds up a hand, and I stop, mid-plea. "You can keep your college money, Rayne."

I stare up at him in surprise. When is Wilde ever magnanimous?

"I'll probably be able to work off the repair at the auto shop. And yeah, we can keep this between the two of us." He tips his head and gives me a cocky grin. "Right after I turn your ass red." He sits down beside me as I launch to my feet. Wilde catches my waist. "Or you can deal with the wrath of Logan. You may have noticed he can be a real hardass."

I go still, considering his offer.

His right-hand trails down from my waist, along the outside of my thigh to grip my calf. "Look, Rayne," he says softly.

I look down and gasp. The place where he bit me has already closed. It's still sore. I see the teeth marks, but they look a week old, rather than fresh. I have super-healing abilities now!

When I meet his gaze, I find something unfamiliar there. Appreciation? Wonder? Almost like reverence. Not for me, but for the wolf inside of me.

"Come here." He gently tugs me closer. "Your ass is way too spankable not to handle things this way."

Gah. I hate that it turns me on so much to have him humiliate me this way. I hate that I have no panties on and–

He tips me over his sturdy knees. The t-shirt I was wearing slides up my back. I clench my buttcheeks. "Yeah." I hear satisfaction in his voice. "This is how I want to handle it."

My belly flutters. I kick one heel in the air, and then he begins. He spanks me hard, slapping one cheek, then the other, warming the lower half of my ass with steady slaps. He goes for the backs of my legs, then back to my butt, concentrating on the place where I sit.

It doesn't hurt. I mean, it does, but nothing registers as pain. All I feel is heat. Tingling. A little burn. Excitement. A feverish frenzy of energy swirling in my pelvis. Pulsing between my legs.

Wilde stops and rubs away the sting. Like the first time he spanked me, his fingers wander between my legs. Only this time I'm bare. He can feel the slick of my arousal. The swelling of my lady bits.

"Don't." I scissor my legs to keep him out, and he withdraws his fingers.

"Do you ache down here, Rayne-bow?"

I let out an unintelligible sound.

"Do you want me to make it better?"

"No." I sound sulky. I think I'm pissy over the fact that I'm not going to let him get me off. Because I sort of desperately need to. But I don't want to give him that power over me.

Wilde rubs a couple more circles around my ass, then starts spanking again. I'm relieved because I needed something–more touch, more stimulation. But that isn't quite it. It was his fingers between my legs I wanted, not this.

Wilde abruptly tips me up.

"What?"

"I want you over here." He picks me up with his two hands wrapped around my waist and carries me to the end of the sofa. Then he whips the t-shirt off my head.

I cover my breasts with my forearm. "What are you doing?"

He turns me around and pushes my torso down over the arm of the sofa. "I want you bare for your spanking, Rayne-bow."

Oh, fates.

Ohhhhhhh fates.

What is happening right now?

Wilde kicks my feet wide and starts spanking me again. It's ten times more erotic in this position. I don't know why– I guess because he could easily fuck me from behind. Or maybe because my spread legs mean he can see my bare pussy peeking out between my legs. Or just the obvious reason–that I'm completely naked now.

Whatever it is, an unbearable heat starts to roll through my body. I'm moaning. Keening. Whimpering and whining. I'm lightheaded.

Wilde spanks between my legs. Light spanks that drive me even more insane. He wraps his fingers in my hair and lifts my head. His face comes down to meet mine and he peers at me. "I see your wolf," he murmurs.

I blink. His eyes glow green. "I see yours," I whisper back.

"I need to taste you." He turns me around, picks me up and sets my ass on the arm of the sofa. When he lifts one knee, I tumble backward, but his arm is there behind my shoulders. He gently lowers my upper back to the sofa seat, so I'm arched over the arm of the sofa, one knee bent up to expose my core. "Let me make you feel good, Rayne-bow." He holds my gaze.

Oh.

He's waiting for an answer. For permission.

"Yes," I whisper.

The moment I give him the green light, he turns feral, lowering his head between my legs and licking into me.

It's so crazy intense. I scream and try to kick him away. Not because I don't love it. I do. I just love it way too much.

"Enjoy it, Rayne-bow." He's sucking my labia, putting his mouth over my entire pussy. His tongue is everywhere– delving between my nether lips, penetrating me, swirling when he nips at me.

My inner thighs quiver.

"You need to come?"

"Y-yes," I warble.

"Fuck," Wilde curses, like he can barely hold back. Hearing his voice rough with desire makes me even crazier.

"*Now,* Wilde!" I'm getting bossy.

He returns his mouth to my core at the same time he starts screwing one finger into me.

I whine. He doesn't fit. It definitely doesn't feel good. Not nearly as good as his tongue felt. "No."

He slides the tip of his finger back out. "You're so tight, Rayne-bow. You *did* save this cherry for me, didn't you?"

Um, what? My mind swirls with confusion. Was that the reason Wilde was so pissed when he found my birth control? Did he want to be the one to take my virginity?

This is...crazy.

Really crazy.

It also makes me feel safe on some fundamental level. Like the buffeting winds of the storm that was Wilde have suddenly settled into a pattern I understand. All his meanness. His aggression.

It was rooted in desire.

Maybe he was angry about what he desired–especially because I should be off-limits as his stepsister–but it was still me he wanted.

"I'm going to use my pinky, instead."

Tears wet my eyes. Because I understand now. Because Wilde wants to satisfy me. He's taking care with me. I realize he wasn't angry when he pulled me out of that Jeep– he was scared. He thought I was hurt.

Wilde must scent my tears because he lifts his head in alarm. "Does it hurt?"

I blink and shake my head, trying to swallow around the lump in my throat. "No," I whisper. "Keep going."

He returns to eating me, nearly giving me seizures every time his tongue gets near my clit. Then he affixes his lips around the pulsing nubbin at the same time he slides a finger inside me. It must be his pinky because it fits a little better although it still stretches and burns a little.

"You okay?"

"Uh-huh."

"Come here, baby." He slides his finger out, and I feel the loss of it in my core. I clench around air.

But Wilde has some other idea. He tugs my wrists to sit me up, then picks me up by the waist and lifts me straight in the air. "Legs on my shoulders."

What? Oh. Um, wow.

I lift my legs to rest on his shoulders, which puts my pussy right at his face level. He palms my ass and holds me in place as his tongue returns to my folds.

I cling to his head, shrieking and giggling as he walks to the bedroom while sucking and licking me. "You're going to fall," I laugh. "You can't even see."

"I don't need to see," he rumbles.

In the bedroom, he lowers me to the bed and climbs between my legs. Then he returns to work, lapping my juices as he screws one finger into me.

I prop myself up on my elbows to see. He used his index finger this time. He lifts his head and grins, his lips glossy with my nectar. "Popping your cherry, Rayne-bow." He says it proudly like he's winning an important football game.

If you'd ever asked me who I would want to pop my cherry, or how, I never in a million years would have wished for this. And yet...

It's better than anything I could've ever imagined.

Wilde Woodward is worshiping between my legs. Taking care with me. Unlocking my secrets. The ones even I didn't know about myself or my body.

He starts to move that digit inside me slowly, a little in, a little out. Then circling it. Stretching my tight entrance, lubricating it. He presses it all the way in and strokes inside me.

My legs jerk in response like I'm a marionette, and he just pulled their strings.

"Yeah? You like that, Rayne-bow? Did I find the coveted G-spot?"

Oh. Fates.

He must have because every time he rubs there, I feel like I'm going to shoot off like a Roman candle.

"Come for me, jellybean."

Jellybean. It's a much nicer name than *Runt.* Endearing. Cute.

He touches inside me again, and I shatter–exploding in a million directions. A glitter-bomb of energy going off in my body. In my room. In the entire atmosphere above Wolf Ridge.

I sob and shudder and clench and shake, my legs kicking, my muscles drawing up tight and squeezing around his finger.

Wilde curses softly. He eases his finger out and kisses my pussy softly. Tenderly. A layer of kisses from top to bottom, making me feel cared for.

Loved, even.

The moment it's over, I roll to my belly and hide my face in a pillow.

Chapter Fifteen

Wilde

Rayne hides her face from me after she comes.

For a moment, I'm horrified. Did I do something she didn't want? Take something that wasn't given?

But no. She asked me for it. She told me she wanted more.

So she's just embarrassed now. Or feeling vulnerable. Well, that's no surprise considering we have zero trust built between us.

So I don't give her space because I'm afraid if I do, she'll shut me out forever. Instead, I stroke my palm over her reddened ass. Grab a handful and squeeze roughly. I climb over her. "You look so pretty when you've been spanked by me," I murmur darkly in her ear. My cock is thick and heavy for her, but I'm not going to try anything more. Rayne is a virgin. I've already pushed her enough.

She stays prone.

I nip her shoulder. Suck her earlobe. Stroke my hand up

and down her slender back. When she still doesn't roll over, I massage the back of her head. "Does it hurt?"

She shakes her head, her face still in the pillow.

"No, your healing abilities kicked into full gear, didn't they? Let me see that bump on your head." I gently roll her over.

There's so much uncertainty in her expression, and I want to punch my own face for putting it there. I lightly trace the bruise she got in the car accident. "It's better already." I press my lips to it.

I haven't kissed this girl on the lips. She just came all over my fingers, but I haven't tasted that mouth.

I grip her jaw. "May I kiss you, Rayne?" There. Finally, the respect Coach Jamison drilled into us with women surfaces.

She swallows, those blue eyes trained on me, forehead wrinkled like she's searching for the catch.

I'm so fucking relieved when she gives a tiny nod. I go slowly, lowering my mouth to hers, hovering over her body, so she won't feel how big an erection I have for her. She doesn't move at first. Receives my kiss but doesn't kiss me back. I slant my lips over hers in one direction, then the other. I press my tongue into her mouth, fucking her with it, still slowly. It's not a chaste kiss, by any means, but it's not aggressive either. It's just boldly exploratory.

After a few moments, she starts to return the kiss, her tongue tangling with mine, her lips moving. She groans.

She's completely naked beneath me, her nipples beaded up into points, her hips starting to roll. The scent of her arousal still fills the room. Coats my fingers. It's driving my wolf mad. If I don't pull back soon, I'm going to lose control.

I force myself away from her. "Are you hungry, Rayne-bow?"

She chuffs out a laugh. "Yeah."

I reluctantly climb off her. "You need a ton of protein right now. I'll make some lunch."

Rayne yanks the edge of the blanket up to cover herself. I hate that she needs to hide from me. I want to march back, snatch that blanket away and tell her she's never allowed to cover what's mine.

But that's crazy.

She's not mine. She can't be mine.

Except the idea has caught hold. What if...

What if *Rayne* is the reason I felt so determined to come back to Wolf Ridge? I mean, it doesn't really make sense. There's no logic to my choice to get myself here, yet I *had* to come. Being in Durham was literally killing me.

What if...*fuck!* What if she's my fated mate, and my wolf brought me back here for her transition?

Rayne the Runt, *my mate!*

I haven't had the urge to mark her, but she hasn't shifted yet. Her new scent hasn't fully come in.

I need to know for sure. I've got to figure out how to get her to shift.

And no, I'm still not willing to get outside help. Rayne is my project. I'm hoarding her all to myself. No one else gets to know the transformation she's undergoing.

I walk to the kitchen and pull out a package of bacon, turkey slices, a loaf of bread, and mustard and mayo. I make us each a pair of giant turkey, bacon and avocado sandwiches.

Rayne comes in wearing...a dress. It's a casual dress—made out of black t-shirt material–with a short, flared skirt and long sleeves that also flare and yank over her wrists.

I guess it's sort of a call-back to her goth phase, but it's also fun and flirty. I'm utterly captivated.

"Did you wear that for me, Rayne-bow?"

She ignores the question and picks up the plate of food, carrying it to the front window to look out. "How bad is it?"

She's still worrying about the accident.

"I'll handle the Jeep." I make my voice firm. "Eat your sandwich, and then we'll go for a drive."

She groans. "No more driving."

"That's why we're going. I don't want you spooked about it now. What happened in the driveway wasn't your fault. I bit you, and you freaked out. You weren't paying attention to what you were doing. It's not going to happen again."

"Is that your form of apology?"

I grin but shake my head. "I'm not sorry at all, Runt." Realizing–I know, way too late–that the name *Runt* is cruel, I make a mental note not to call her that again.

She cocks a hip. She's still holding her plate of uneaten sandwiches, which bothers my wolf. He wants to feed her. "You're not sorry?"

"Not even remotely. For one thing, I almost made you shift, so that was a win. Also, your healing abilities kicked in. And most importantly, I got to spank your cute ass red and then make you come all over my finger and face."

The scent of Rayne's arousal fills the room.

I shake my head slowly. "You're going to have to stop getting wet like that, or I'm going to carry you back to the bedroom and go for a second round."

A choked sound comes out of Rayne's mouth, and her knees go slack, causing her to stumble like the earth just moved.

"Now sit down and eat those sandwiches." When she still doesn't move, just stares at me with those giant blue eyes, I put a little alpha command in my voice. *"Now, jellybean."*

"Okay, okay." She drops onto the couch and eats from the plate there. Satisfied, I bring my plate over and join her.

"You're not in charge of me, Wilde Woodward," she asserts while chewing her sandwich.

"Keep telling yourself that, Rayne-bow. We'll see who makes you scream again tonight."

Rayne's knees slap together, and a shiver runs through her body.

I lean over and bite her neck. "I love making you wet," I murmur against her hair.

Rayne leans away from me. "I'm not your plaything, Wilde."

My lids droop. "Oh, but you are, Rayne-bow. And the sooner you surrender, the more fun we can have."

* * *

Rayne

I've never been so off-balance in my life.

I don't know what to make of it.

Wilde is actually showing kindness. Attraction to me–*shocker!*

But, of course, he's still a cocky alpha-hole at heart, so everything that comes out of his mouth is still dick-speak. Which, sadly, makes his attention all the more addictive.

I would love to be the girl here who flips him the bird and says, *go fuck yourself. You've been a dick to me from the start, and I'm not going to relent because you gave me one measly orgasm.*

But I'm not that strong, confident girl.

I'm Rayne the Runt. A reject who has been shunned her entire life by the pack.

And one of the members of pack royalty has suddenly shown interest in me. Wilde's acceptance of me could change my entire existence.

Part of me keeps looking for the trick.

Like Abe putting me on the ballot for Homecoming Queen, I feel like Wilde must be screwing with me here. Making me fall for him only to have the whole school laughing at me.

Or maybe this is to punish his dad for marrying my mom.

Like a *fuck the stepsister* revenge. Or even a *fuck the stepsister* fetish.

And yet, even with that terrible danger hanging over me, I'm not strong enough to tell him no.

I crave his attention like I crave my next breath. He's making me feel special. Worthy, for the first time in my life.

Dangerous feelings, I'm sure.

Devastating, probably. But worth the risk. I can't turn away from this offering.

Wilde taking care of me. Making me sandwiches. Buying me birthday cakes. Kissing me. Getting me off. Staking some kind of claim on my body.

I love it way too much.

I finish both sandwiches and lick my fingers. Wilde's already mowed through his food, and he watches me now then reaches out to snag my wrist. He pulls my fingers to his mouth and sucks each one.

Every time he does, my pelvic floor lifts and squeezes.

I'm helpless with this guy. My body responds no matter what he does.

He takes the plate from my hand. "Time to drive, jelly-bean. Why don't we go and see your human friend?"

"Who, Lincoln?"

Wilde's scowl makes me draw back. "Bailey," he snarls. "I thought Lincoln was just your tutor."

Oh.

Oh.

All this time I thought Wilde didn't like me hanging out with a human because it hurt his reputation. Suddenly, a new thought enters my mind.

He's jealous.

That's why he freaked out over the birth control pills, too. Wilde can't stand the idea of me being with any other guy.

The thought leaves me breathless.

"I'm not interested in Lincoln," I assure him. Not that he deserves my reassurance. It's more for Lincoln's safety. "We're *friends*. Lincoln's not interested in me, either."

"What makes you think that?"

I shrug. "He just doesn't give off the vibe. We're firmly in the friend zone. Nothing more."

"I will kill that kid if he touches you."

I would laugh at the ridiculousness of Wilde's possessiveness, except I know it's no joke. Male wolves can get hella territorial.

So I lean forward and give him my most defiant stare. "You will be nice to him because he and Lauren are my only friends."

Shockingly, it works.

Wilde sits back. Blinks a couple of times. Seems to absorb my request.

"Fine." He stands from the sofa. "As long as he doesn't touch you. Now get your shoes on. We're going driving."

I put on my shoes and go out to the Jeep. I'm utterly devastated about what I did to the back fender, but Wilde won't let me stop and examine it.

"I'm taking care of that," he says firmly as he takes me by the elbow and pulls me to the driver's seat. He lifts me into it, buckles me in and shuts the door.

I let out a little scoff. Except I'm not finding much outrage at his controlling behavior. It's based more in pleasure this time. Now that I understand it better, I'm starting to love Wilde's obsession with me.

That doesn't change my PTSD around driving, though. My hands shake when I start up the Jeep, the crunch of metal still fresh in my ears.

"You got this. Just drive, Rayne."

I back up and get on the road.

"We're going to Tempe?" I'm nervous. Highway driving in traffic intimidates me.

"Actually, let me make a phone call."

Wilde pulls out his phone and dials a number. "Garrett? Wilde Woodward. Yeah, I'm sorry I didn't make it down yesterday. I had to get home to look after my stepsister." He shoots me a look that's more devious than mean, and it makes my pulse race. "Anyway, I was wondering if there's any chance we could drive down now? Yeah? Cool. Okay, I'll meet you there. Thank you."

Wilde ends the call and looks at me. "We're going to Tucson."

"Um..." I don't want to say no because I realize the meeting's important. If he doesn't solve his legal problems, he'll be banned from the pack. But Tucson is two and a half hours away, and then we'd be driving back at night.

Wilde seems to read my thoughts. "You got this, Ru–jellybean. I'll drive home."

I suck in a long, slow breath. "Okay, but I don't know where to go."

"I'll navigate. You just relax and drive. This will be good practice for you."

I nod, but my shoulders are up to my ears with tension. Even if I don't wreck again, I'm going to exhaust my nervous system with all the flight or fight hormones dumping into my system.

But then Wilde drops his big paw on my nape and squeezes. "Rayne," he murmurs. "You got this."

* * *

Wilde

The runt (I shouldn't call her that anymore) does a decent job driving. She's nervous and a little jumpy about lane changes and navigating in heavy traffic, but she settles in.

We meet Garrett and Amber at Club Eclipse, Garrett's nightclub on Congress Street in downtown Tucson. I've never been in it before.

I shake Garrett's hand. "Garrett. Do you know Rayne?"

"No." He extends a hand, taking her in. He seems to actually see her. There's none of the dismissiveness the pack in Wolf Ridge has for her. His nostrils flare as he takes in her scent. "You're in my father's pack?"

"Um, yeah. Sort of." Rayne shrugs dismissively, her eyes dropping away.

Garrett makes a huh or hmm sound in his throat that sounds like he understands what that means and doesn't necessarily approve. Of course, he and his father don't see eye to eye on many things. Pack leadership may be one of them.

"This is my mate, Amber."

We shake hands with the human. Amber is a slender female. She's not tiny like Rayne but definitely strikes me as fragile. I don't know how Garrett can live knowing his mate is human and might die at any moment in any number of horrible ways.

Rayne may be small, but she has shifter blood. She has a wolf inside her that makes her powerful. A she-wolf I intend to bring out.

Because I have to know if she's mine.

We sit down at the bar and Amber asks exactly what happened at my arrest.

I give her my paperwork and the short and dirty version. "There was a party in my hotel room, and the drugs were out. My roommate went out for beer. My wolf got prickly, so I looked out the window and saw two cop cars outside. I told everyone to leave. The cops showed up as the last people were walking out. They saw the drugs and put me in cuffs. I said nothing at the time and pleaded not guilty the next day. That's it."

"And we're talking about cocaine?"

"Yes, ma'am."

"You can call me Amber. What amount was found?"

"I don't know. More than ten grams, I guess. That's what makes it a trafficking charge."

"They found it on your person or in the room?"

"The room."

"Did they give you a drug test?"

"Yes. I was clean."

"Okay. Sounds circumstantial to me. It might be possible to get the charges dropped. Depends on what other evidence they collected at the time. I can call your public defender and ask to be admitted as your counsel *pro hac vice.*"

I look at her blankly.

"I'm not licensed to practice in South Carolina, but I can be admitted as part of your team. Chances are good your defender can handle this, though. He or she will know the judges and the arresting officers."

I bow my head. "Thank you. I, um, don't have any money to pay you right now, but–"

Amber waves a hand. "It's all right. I'm happy to help."

I glance at Garrett. "You could put me in to fight at the next shifter fight club?"

Garrett let Bo fight a couple years ago for cash when he and his girlfriend Sloane were in trouble.

"No. That's not necessary. Let's get you back to school."

Right.

Back to school.

That sick feeling that was in the pit of my stomach the entire year and a quarter I was at Duke returns full force.

"Yeah. I, uh...I'm not in a rush to go back."

I feel Rayne's big blue gaze on me, and it makes me itchy. "But he'll be kicked out of the pack if he doesn't get the charges dropped."

I'm warmed by her interest in the case. I didn't know she'd even paid attention to my situation.

Garrett's eyes narrow. "So you're banished if you don't get it resolved, but you don't actually care about going back."

I don't answer. This is the same thing his father picked up about me that pissed him off.

"Well, what do you want, Wilde? Because I'm not going to have Amber waste her time on you if you're going to sabotage the results."

For a moment, I can't breathe.

"You felt out of place there," Rayne guesses.

Garrett waits for me to speak.

I don't really know what to say.

Rayne's right, of course. I fucking *hated* living with humans. Pretending to be one. I was homesick every day of my life there. I couldn't run as a wolf. I never shifted. Hell, I was afraid I'd forget how.

I clear my throat. "I won't sabotage it. I don't want to be banished." That much is true.

"Well, you can come to me if you are. I'm sure you know that."

My chest tightens, and I nod. "Yeah. Thank you, Garrett."

Garrett looks at Rayne. "You, too. We have all kinds here." I remember that the Tucson pack isn't all comprised of wolves. There are bears and foxes and even some misfits. Defectives, but not like Rayne. Some creatures made in a lab, I heard.

She pales. "Oh. Um...thanks."

I wrap my hand around her nape. "Rayne's a late bloomer, that's all. She has a silver-eyed wolf that's about to come out."

Rayne flicks an indecipherable glance at me.

"Regardless," Garrett says firmly. "You're both welcome in my pack."

"Thank you, Alpha," Rayne says softly.

"I'm not your alpha. But the door is open." Garrett gets up from the bar stool, indicating the meeting is over. "Are you two driving back tonight?"

"Yep. Rayne has school in the morning."

"I'll be in touch, Wilde," Amber says as we do another round of handshakes.

"Thank you so much. I really appreciate your help."

"I'm happy to help."

We walk out to the Jeep, and instead of unlocking the passenger side door for Rayne, I pin her against it facing me and brush her hair out of her eyes. "Did that offend you?"

She flushes. "No. I mean–" She shakes her head. "No. I...wonder what his pack is like. They seem cool."

"Right?"

Rayne's stomach rumbles.

I ease away from her. "Let's get you some more meat. That wolf needs to be fed." As I lift her into the Jeep, she averts her face. I don't know what's eating her, but I'm going to figure this out.

Now.

Chapter Sixteen

ayne

R   I shower when we get home. My stomach is in knots although I can't quite dissect what has me anxious. It's something about Wilde and my wolf.

Does he only like me now that he knows I have a wolf? And is his affection conditional on bringing out the wolf?

Because I think it's completely possible I will never shift. Just because my eyes changed color doesn't mean I will ever actually transform. And, honestly, considering how weak my shifter genes are, I'm terrified of shifting. What if I only partially shift? Or shift and can't turn back? In both instances, they'd have to put me down with a silver bullet.

Maybe I'm being a wimp, but I almost feel like it's better not to try. I've lived this long as a Defective. I might as well continue. It's not like I'll have any fewer friends.

But, see, Wilde needs me to be presentable as his stepsister.

Or his mate.

That comes as a tiny whisper in my ear. A thought I dare not even think.

Wilde definitely doesn't want to mate me. That's crazy.

He's just attracted to me for whatever reason. I guess because we're both under the same roof or something.

I guess some of the knots in my belly are about what's going to happen tonight. The parents are still away. Is Wilde going to be in my bedroom when I get out of the shower?

Somehow, I'm sure he is.

I turn off the water and towel dry. I was careful to bring my pajamas into the bathroom with me this time, so I won't have to change in the closet if he's there.

Not that he hasn't seen me fully naked. It's just... all this confusion welling up in me has me on edge.

Oh fates.

He's seen me *fully naked*. Just twelve hours ago.

I walk into the bedroom, not surprised to find him lounging on my bed with my laptop open. He's watching my foot fetish videos.

"Wilde! Would you leave it?"

"What?" He flashes me a bad-boy grin. A lazy, cocky, beautiful grin that ties me up in knots and makes my knees go weak. "I kind of like watching you strut around in your high heels. I'm not a foot guy, but your legs are fucking hot."

I gape at him.

He thinks my legs are hot? Um...wow.

He flips the laptop closed and sits up on the bed. "Come here, Rayne-bow." He crooks a finger at me.

I stall. Is this what I want? Doing this thing–whatever the hell we're doing–with Wilde is going to open my heart up to be savaged.

It's one thing to live with constant friction with my stepbrother. It's a totally different thing to climb into bed with him, let him call all the shots, start to like it, and then have him decide I'm yesterday's news.

Even if he didn't do that, he's destined to go back to Duke.

Yeah, but he doesn't want to.

That's the naughty little voice that wants something more. That wants to explore this with him.

"You were right," he says, suddenly serious.

"About what?"

"I hate Duke because I don't fit in. I mean, I totally fake it. I have a whole fraternity and team who think I'm the best guy ever, but no one even knows who I really am. I can't shift there. I can't run. I have to be careful not to get mad or horny and show my wolf. I don't like living with humans."

I find myself walking over to him, forgetting all hesitation. I rest a hand lightly on his arm. "That sucks."

He takes my hand and loops his fingers over mine. "Come here, Rayne-bow." He spins me, so our joined hands are now wrapped around my waist, and I'm sitting on his lap. "I'd rather stay here and torture you." The words are soft in my ear.

"Wh-what if I don't want to be tortured?" My voice has a quaver in it.

"Oh, but I think you do." He nips my shoulder, which sends a powerful shiver running through me.

Wolves mark their mates with a bite to the neck, so it feels extra-intimate. Very personal.

"M-maybe you could transfer to ASU. Play ball with Bo and Cole?"

"Yeah," Wilde says softly. "I'd give anything for that."

I twist to look at him, surprised to hear some form of

clarity out of him about what he wants. "Then make it happen."

His expression shutters, and he flicks a glance in the direction of his father's room.

Right. He's living Logan's dream right now. He probably had no choice in going to Duke to begin with.

He doesn't answer. Instead, he says, "I'm sleeping in your bed tonight, jellybean. Are you going on the floor or taking your chances with me?"

My heart thuds. Wilde is asking me something instead of throwing his weight around.

"I'm not sleeping on the floor," I find myself saying with defiance before I've even had a chance to think it through. Before my wiser self would've thrown on the brakes.

I'm not ready to sleep next to Wilde Woodward. Especially not after what happened last night.

Except that must be a lie because the idea of sleeping–or even just lying–beside him again sends tremors of excitement zipping up my spine and down my limbs.

Wilde releases me and tips me gently onto my feet, then gets up and heads to the bathroom. I use the time alone to turn off the light and dive under the covers. The moment I do, my body flushes with fever. My legs kick and stretch beneath the blankets. I'm dying of heat. Literally. Dying.

I throw back the covers to get some fresh air on my skin. I want to take the pajamas off, but that's obviously the wrong message to send to Wilde.

Or was that message already sent the moment I agreed to get in this bed with him?

Why did I do that? Do I want a repeat of last night?

Oh, who am I kidding? I definitely do. I might have a touch of stepbrother kink here. The forbidden, unattainable alpha-hole doing dirty things to me in my own bed.

Wilde comes back to the bedroom and strips down to his boxer shorts. I can see him in the darkness—I think my night vision is improving—and his body is perfection.

There's also something completely different about him right now. The cockiness is absent. He's just...Wilde.

A guy climbing in bed with me.

Oh, fates. *He's climbing in bed with me!*

I tug the blanket back up to my chin at the same time Wilde picks up the other end to climb in. His leg brushes against mine.

"Fuck, you're burning up." He throws the blankets down to our feet. "It's the transition." He glances toward the window. "And the moon is waxing."

"Oh. I guess that makes sense. I thought I was having empathetic reactions to my mom's pregnancy."

Wilde snorts. "Nope. The heat is part of it. And the hunger. And the horniness." Suddenly he's above me, pinning my wrists down the way he did last night. "Are you going to show me that wolf again, jellybean?"

I don't fight him this time. Instead, my knees bend up like I'm making a cradle for him.

He lowers them, obligingly, giving me one slow roll of his hips before lifting away again. "Hmm. Looks like you're not scared of me anymore. That could be a problem."

"Problem for whom?"

He holds my gaze as he slowly and deliberately shifts one of his hands from my wrist to wrap around my throat. "Where is she?" he murmurs just before he starts to squeeze.

He's right, though.

I'm not scared. I don't completely know what Wilde's about, but I know more than I did. I know he finds me desirable. And maybe his hate for me has been mitigated by the fact that he's seen a wolf inside me. That I might not be as defective as people believe.

And while it's a relief to not face the full blast of his resentment now, I hate the fact that his approbation is conditional. He doesn't care about me–the real me. The me I am now. He's only interested in the she-wolf he believes I can be.

He cuts my breath off, watching me intently. I hold his gaze with defiance. I refuse to play this game. He's not going to scare me into fighting him.

My resolve lasts until my head gets thick and darkness closes in. Then I can't help it anymore. I start to thrash beneath Wilde, my feet hooking onto his hips to push him away.

"There she is," Wilde whispers. He releases his hold on my throat, and I gasp in my breath.

I drag in several long inhales, and the moment I can speak, I yell, "Fuck you, Wilde!"

He chuckles. "With pleasure, Rayne-bow."

I kick him again, as hard as I can, the heel of my foot landing against his hard abs. "It's not funny." Tears form in my eyes and spill past my lashes.

He catches my ankle and holds it. "Shh." He strokes up my calf. "You're right. I'm sorry. I went too far." He continues stroking his large hand up and down my calf, soothing me. "You're okay, baby."

I'm somewhat shocked by his apology. Even more by his use of the term *baby*.

"You're okay." He murmurs it again. He shifts the hand gripping my ankle to massage the sole of my foot.

"That was a nice kick, Rayne-bow." It sounds like true admiration. "You had some power behind it." He nods knowingly. "Shifter power."

"Fuck you," I grumble again. I refuse to be admired for anything shifter-related.

He uses both his thumbs to rub my foot now, and I start to melt despite my anger. "Are *you* into feet, Rayne?"

I let out a puff of surprised laughter. "No. It's just a way to earn money."

"Well, I guess I kind of get it. You *do* have the cutest feet ever." He lifts my foot to his mouth and sucks on my big toe.

I try to jerk it away, shocked by the heat of his tongue, the unexpected sensuality of it, but of course, he holds tight.

I whimper when his tongue swirls between my toes, and he sucks the next toe into his mouth.

This shouldn't be erotic. I mean, I get that it is to my customers, but I had no idea how incredible it would feel. I scent my arousal at the same moment Wilde's nostrils flare, taking it in.

His eyes take on a green glow in the darkness as he takes my third toe into his mouth and gives it the same treatment. At the same time, he strokes a hand up my leg to the apex. The closer he gets to my lady parts, the more my inner thighs quiver. My belly flutters. The anticipation of his touch there has every nerve ending activated and alive.

He starts with just a brush—the backs of his fingers sliding across the crotch of my sleep shorts.

My hips buck off the bed. He takes my fourth toe into his mouth. His next swipe over my crotch is firmer, and I chase the touch, following his hand with my hips for more.

He moves to my pinky toe, swirling his tongue between the toes. "It's so tiny, baby. So fucking cute."

There.

His thumb presses against my clit, and I moan out loud. He sucks my toe into his mouth and strokes firmly across my pussy, right where I need it.

"So you have to tell me." His voice is thick and rough like he's as turned on by this as I am. "Do you prefer my tongue on your toes or between your legs?"

I let out a whimper. It's me conceding that Wilde's going to get everything he wants from me. Anything he asks of me. His touch is too intoxicating to refuse.

"Hmm, baby?"

"B-between my legs...please."

In a flash, Wilde drops my foot and yanks down my shorts and panties, tossing them over his shoulder. His eyes are a brilliant, glowing green now, beautiful and frightening. He slides his hands under my ass, then lifts my entire pelvis up to his mouth instead of lowering down to me.

"Wilde." There's a note of alarm in my voice when I say his name although I'm not sure what I'm afraid of. The intensity of pleasure he's about to deliver?

"Mmm hmm. That's right, baby. I want you saying my name when my tongue is inside you." He licks into me, not with delicate, nuanced strokes, but wild and wet. Aggressive and rough. He sucks at my labia, and takes my whole pussy into his mouth at once. He spears me with his tongue, penetrating me.

"P-please." I'm panting. Begging. Needy.

Wilde lowers my hips to the bed. "Are you going to take my fingers like a good girl, Rayne-bow?"

I have no idea what he means. I'm not even sure what he said. All I know is that my hips are lifting and lowering, desperate for more of his touch.

He screws one finger into my tight opening. "Still tight as fuck, baby. Does it hurt?"

I moan and shake my head as he gets deeper.

"No? You're okay?"

"Yeah," I pant. "I'm good."

"That's what I want to hear." He screws a second finger inside me. I squirm and whine a little at the thickness. "Take them, Rayne. Like a good girl."

I don't know what he means, but the words turn me on. His digits stretch me, and there's a burn, and it feels like he hits a block.

He lowers down over me and claims my mouth with a searing kiss. His tongue sweeps between my lips with a long, slow roll, and at the same time, he thrusts his fingers past the barrier.

I jerk and gasp.

Wilde smiles against my lips. "I just popped your cherry, Rayne." He sounds proud of himself. "It will feel better in a minute, baby. I promise."

He starts a slow thrusting of his fingers inside me, and he's right. It feels incredible. Especially when he starts to stroke my inner wall.

I let out a sound. A cry of pleasure. Of need. "Yes."

"Is that it, baby? Right there?" Wilde keeps pumping, his fingertips hitting the place that makes me writhe and squeal and reach for the headboard.

"Wilde, yes. Please! Wilde, oh fates...oh fates...oh, *oh*!"

My internal walls squeeze up. My feet point like a ballerina's. My brain short-circuits. Time might be passing. It might be standing still. I'm not quite sure.

Wilde slips his fingers out of me and rubs my clit, and I go off again–another spasm of my internal walls, clenching and squeezing on air.

I let out a contented whimper.

"Better, baby?" He strokes slowly over my pussy.

I'm not sure what he's asking me. My brain still hasn't returned to the room.

He rolls me to my side and arranges himself behind me,

his much larger body spooned around mine. "See? The fever's gone now." He pulls the blankets up around us. "I'm gonna fuck you to sleep every night you need it."

I register his dark promise right in my core where it causes a squeezing and tingling and buzzing.

"Maybe even the nights you don't."

Another clench.

He bites my neck. "Maybe having a stepsister isn't the worst thing in the world."

I send my elbow backward to catch him in the ribs. "Fuck off, Woodward."

His teeth sink so deep into my shoulder they almost break the skin, but I hardly notice the pain. It's his hardened cock pressing against my ass that makes me freeze.

What now...

Chapter Seventeen

Wilde

W I blow the whistle and wave my hand in the predetermined signal, and the Wolf Ridge High players divide and coalesce exactly as instructed. It's odd but not dissatisfying to be watching the team instead of playing.

The autumn sun is warm but not scorching, most of its rays blocked by the mountain at this hour. I glance over to the parking lot and receive a shot of pleasure when I spot Rayne sitting in my Jeep.

She texted me after school to say she was going to the library for tutoring with Lincoln and that she would wait for me in the Jeep afterward.

He touches you, he's a dead man, I texted back.

She sent me an eye roll emoji that made me smile.

This morning, I made sure Rayne ate a huge breakfast of the leftover pancakes and Canadian bacon from yesterday, then I opened a window in her room and stripped the bed. Our parents will be back sometime today, and they would definitely scent everything that went down between the runt–I mean, Rayne–and I.

I threw the sheets in the washing machine and started it up before I drove her to school, then I took the damaged Jeep to the auto shop to see what Greg had to say about repairing it. As I suspected, he will help me repair it at very little cost. I just have to go to the salvage yard to find a fender, and he'll help me repair the dent and replace it.

I give three short blows of my whistle, and the team switches into the next play.

I love assisting Coach Jamison. Maybe it's lame, but I feel like the Wolf Ridge High field is where I belong. Where I became a wolf. Where I became a man. Where I learned about the brotherhood of pack and the glory of youth.

Coach asked me to teach the team something new I learned at Duke, so I went through some formations and plays on the whiteboard first, and then we go out to practice them.

It took the team only an hour to master what it took the human team at Duke months to perfect.

"What do you think?" Jamison asks me.

"They look great."

"Agreed. Run them through the strength and agility and then make them stretch out before they go." He walks away, leaving me completely in charge.

It's a strange feeling to have his trust like this. To know that he thinks I'm worthy of leading a team I only left a year and a quarter ago.

He disappears, showing the team his faith in me, only reappearing when it's all over.

"You obviously won't see much of this out on the field

this weekend," Coach warns. "But these skills will definitely come in handy when you're old enough to compete in the shifter games." He refers to the regional competitions that serve as matchmaking functions. A chance for all the shifters in the region to gather and sniff each other out. See if they can find their fated mate.

"This weekend I want to see you excel at losing until the final quarter. That's the game. Look good while screwing up. Make it all seem like bad luck. Then sweep it at the end. Got it?"

This is how Wolf Ridge ballers play. We can't look too good, so we make games out of fumbling and recovering. Appearing human.

"Yes, Coach," the team chants.

"Okay, go get in the showers. Practice is over."

I head into the showers for a quick clean-up, too, then I find Abe. I've been mulling over what Bailey said to me about changing Rayne's status here and decided she's right.

"Oakley, what's this?" I wave the Homecoming ballot in his face.

He gives me a cocky grin. "What?"

"You put Rayne on the ballot. Why?"

His grin grows wider. "I dunno. I thought it would be funny to have a human and the ru–" he breaks off when he sees my upper lip lift in a snarl. "Sorry, bro." He throws his hand up in surrender.

I fist his shirt and flatten him against the gym lockers. Every guy in there was listening already, but now they get dead quiet.

"Well, you put her on the ballot, you'd better make sure she wins."

Abe's brows pop in surprise. "What?"

"Make. Her. Queen."

Abe lets out a surprised laugh. "Why?" He draws back at something he sees in my face. I don't know—maybe my eyes changed color. "Okay. Okay, man. Absolutely." He does his best to crane his neck and look around at the other guys, which is difficult because I still have him pinned to the metal. "You hear that, everyone? Rayne the– Rayne for homecoming queen."

I slowly release him and nod. "Good. You fuck with her again, and *I will end you.*"

"I'm sorry, Wilde," Abe says immediately. He may be alpha at Wolf Ridge High, but he knows I'm far superior to him. His wolf defers to mine.

"Good. I expect to hear she's being treated with respect."

With that, I walk out of the lockers, my wolf already frisky to get in that sun-soaked Jeep. It will be a veritable hot box of Rayne's scent.

And yes, her scent is unlocking new notes every single day. Notes that make my pulse race and my dick get hard.

I cannot fucking wait until she learns to shift.

I hop in the Jeep and arrange my face into a glower. "Did he touch you?"

Rayne ignores me, looking straight ahead and shaking her head with exasperation. "Don't be ridiculous."

I grin and start up the Jeep. "He'd better not have."

"Wilde. I told you. Not a problem. Okay? Chill out."

I don't know why, but I absolutely love her reassurances. That she thinks I deserve them. We both know I don't. I have absolutely no right to lay claim to Rayne, but of course, I have. And now she's responding as if she accepts that claim. So I'm reveling in the win.

We drive home to find my dad's SUV in the garage.

"Oh," Rayne says as if she's as disappointed as I am that they're back.

"Yeah." We walk in through the side door. "The sheets still need to go in the dryer," I murmur because obviously, it would look weird if I took care of them.

"'Kay," she murmurs.

I touch her back lightly as we part. One last secret message about what we shared. That we forged and became something clandestine and new. Something just between the two of us. Just *for* the two of us.

But, of course, the secret shared pleasure can't last.

"What in the fuck did you do to your Jeep?" my dad bellows from the living room.

Rayne flashes me a horrified look.

I shake my head at her and shoo her away to her room. I told her I'd take the fall for it, and I will.

"I'm taking care of it," I say in a bored voice as I walk to the living room to greet my dad. "Greg will help me repair it at no cost."

"What did you do?"

"I was texting and driving. I hit the mailbox. I will fix that, too. Tonight." I'm kicking myself for not fixing it yesterday. My mistake, for sure.

My dad looks like his head is going to spin around and pop off. He narrows his eyes at me. "You–" He waves his hands in the air. "You hit the mailbox? How fast were you going to do that kind of damage?"

I nod. "Probably too fast."

"You think?"

I keep my throat exposed in a sign of wolf submission.

"Were drugs and alcohol involved?"

"No, sir."

"Then why were you backing out that fast?"

Lying to a shifter is tricky business. If anything in your scent changes, if there's any sign of fear, they will detect it. So I go with what's closest to the truth. The reason Rayne was backing out so quickly.

"I was pissed off."

"You were pissed off," he repeats in a condemning tone. "About what?"

"About having to come back here to babysit Rayne."

Wait. Fuck. Very big mistake.

My dad's eyes flash gold, and his upper lip curls in a snarl. "I've had it with you. *Get your shit and leave this house.*"

* * *

Rayne

No.

Fates, no. What have I done? My cowardice could cost Wilde everything.

I bolt out of the bedroom at the same time my mom emerges from the master suite. Score two points for shifter hearing.

"Logan," my mom says.

"No." Logan throws his hands in the air. His eyes glow amber. "If Wilde can't show some basic respect for his new family, he does not deserve to live under my roof."

"This is so stupid!" I cry, forgetting my fear of the man. Forgetting to be respectful.

Wilde shakes his head at me in warning. "Rayne."

"No. *I* wrecked the Jeep. Okay?"

"I'm handling it," Wilde cuts in, voice firm.

"Shut up!" I'm close to tears. I whirl on Logan, my hands closed into fists. "Wilde is just taking the bullet for me. Same as he did for whoever was buying and selling drugs on his team."

Shock visibly ripples through Wilde at my words. "How did you–"

I throw my hands out in exasperation. "Because I know you!" Turning back to Logan, I say, "And you should know him, too. If you're so blind you can't see the hero your son is, or the fact that he was suffering living halfway across the country completely apart from all wolf culture, you don't deserve to ride his success."

"Enough, Rayne," my mom cuts in sharply.

"No, it's true. That's what he's doing. He doesn't care about what Wilde wants. Or his happiness."

"Is that true?" Logan's voice has calmed. His eyes have returned to normal.

"Of course it's true!" I exclaim.

"Rayne." My mom makes a move toward me, but Wilde steps in front of her, blocking her path.

Her brows shoot up, but not in an angry way. More surprise. "Huh," she says thoughtfully then looks at me.

I'm still desperate to fix my screw-up. "*I* drove Wilde's Jeep. I was pissed at him for being bossy, and I started too fast. I hit the mailbox. Wilde came running out to rescue me. He was" –I flap a hand in the air– "more worried about my safety than he was about me wrecking the Jeep." Tears spill down my cheeks.

Wilde makes a tiny growling sound in his throat, his nostrils flaring like he's picking up their scent. He reaches an arm out to me. I guess we're not going to pretend there's distance between us. I step under it and let him pull me against his side protectively.

My mom and Logan both stare at us like they're seeing us for the first time. Rewriting in their brains whatever they thought our relationship was before.

"Can we forget about the Jeep?" Weariness threads Wilde's voice. "It was an accident, and I'm going to take care of it."

Logan rubs a hand across his face. "Yeah." His gaze slides to me, and I show my throat in wolf submission. "Obviously I would've preferred that you both be honest with me, but I guess I have a clear picture of what happened." He pauses, then adds, "Thank you, Wilde, for taking responsibility for it."

Wilde swallows and nods.

"Now do you want to tell me what really went down in South Carolina?"

"Rayne," my mom says. "Come on. Let's give them some privacy."

Wilde squeezes my shoulder before he releases me, and I follow my mom out of the house and into her car.

"Where are we going?"

"To get fast food for dinner. I'm too starving to wait for them to finish to make something."

A surreal sense of reality settles around me. Some shifting and reshaping of the patterns of our lives. Like I've just now realized that this is our new existence. Me and my mom living with Logan and Wilde–for as long as he and I are here, that is. We really are a new family, as Logan said. A fucked-up and weird but maybe semi-functional family.

I mean, until they find out Wilde and I have been fooling around in our bedroom.

"How was your honeymoon?" I ask, my thoughts finally pulling away from the drama we just left.

My mom smiles. She looks beautiful pregnant. Part of it

is that she's taking care of herself now. She used to just look worn down and tired. Before she got pregnant, she was too thin and she smoked like a chimney because cigarettes can't hurt a shifter. But the moment she got knocked up with Logan's pup, she quit smoking. She started to take an interest in her appearance. All her hard edges softened along with her body.

"It was wonderful."

"Where did you go?"

She grins. "To a resort in Scottsdale. We didn't leave the bedroom the whole–"

"Ew, Mom. Please. No TMI."

We both laugh.

I realize my mom and I haven't had a conversation that was just between the two of us since Wilde got here. I've missed her. But I also love this new version of her.

I believed she had worked on her appearance and made herself into something she wasn't to please Logan–to make herself worthy, but suddenly a different thought occurs to me. Maybe the changes are a result of being cared for. Being loved.

I had an intense dislike for Logan at first, but I have to admit that he's pretty damn sweet to my mom. I'm watching her come alive with him.

I feel left out and sometimes jealous of the loss of her attention, but at least she seems happy. I can't begrudge her that, can I?

Maybe my mom was just starved for attention and kindness by this community. All she needed was a little bit of affection to bloom.

"Rayne," my mom says softly. "I know this has been a rough transition."

"It's fine, Mom." I try to head her off.

"Let me talk, honey. It's a big change for you. For all of us. And you've been an absolute trooper. I appreciate it, and I'm sorry if I haven't been there for–"

"*Mom*. It's fine."

My mom's eyes fill with tears. "I still can't believe I missed your birthday," she chokes.

Now my vision grows wavy, too. Dammit. I drop my head and hold in a sob.

"Sweetheart." My mom swerves the Subaru to the side of the road and pulls me into a hug. The two of us cry together for a minute.

"It's okay, Mom," I promise. "I love you."

"I love you so much, baby. And this new pup will never take your pla–"

"Mom. I'm eighteen. I'll be leaving next year. Hopefully. I'm not jealous of the pup."

"Sweetie, I don't know if we can afford to send you to college."

"I know." I pull away and swallow. "But I'm going to get scholarships. I'm going to figure it out."

"Well, you don't have to. I mean, I'll need help with the pup. You could stay and–"

"No." I interrupt before I realize how sharp I sound.

I may have told my mom I'm not jealous of the pup and that may be true, but I'm also not strong enough to hang out in a town where I've been ostracized my whole life and raise my mom's perfect, non-defective pup. Because I'm sure this one will be special. Logan's genes are perfect alpha stock.

Nope. No, thank you.

"I just mean–"

"It's okay. I understand." My mom's disappointment hits me right in the gut. "It just would've been nice to have

180

the pup looked after by family, you know? But it's fine. We'll find a sitter or something."

"Don't you think you could stay home with the baby? I mean, Logan makes enough money, right?"

My mom nibbles her lip. "I don't know. We haven't talked about it yet. I mean, we talked about you staying..."

Ugh. I flop my head back against the headrest. Fresh tears spear my eyes.

"Nevermind, sweetie. We'll figure something else out. We just thought it might be a good fit."

Of course, Logan would want me to be the one to stay home and watch his pup. That's all a misfit like me is good for, right? No scholarships to Duke for me.

Of course, that particular scholarship was not a gift, but a curse to Wilde...

As if my mom guesses at my thoughts, she changes the subject. "What's going on with you and Wilde?"

I hold my breath.

I can't tell her what's happening. I really can't. Wilde is my *stepbrother*.

What we've done is inappropriate at best.

"Um...it's a bit of a love-hate situation," I admit. "He's a dick, and then he's nice, and I'm not really sure what to do with it."

"Huh," my mom says for the second time tonight.

"Well, he's going through a lot right now. I almost wonder if the whole arrest was him acting out over Logan marrying me."

That thought has a queasy note of truth to it. Wilde almost seemed like he'd come home to wage war.

With me.

I know hating school and taking one for the team was also a huge part of it, but my mom might be right.

Once again, my very existence rubs people the wrong way.

"Because of me, you mean," I say.

"*Not* because of you," my mom says firmly. "Because of his parents' recent divorce. He might resent Logan moving on."

My stomach rumbles audibly.

My mom sends me a sympathetic smile. "I'm starving, too. Let's get the food."

I agree, relieved to be off the topic of Wilde. Or Logan. Or me becoming their permanent nanny.

We pick up a dozen Wendy's hamburgers and french fries and head back to the house.

"We're home with dinner," my mom calls when we come in, but the guys are nowhere to be found.

"Mom." I point to two piles of clothes laying by the back door.

"Fates." My mom frowns. "Let's hope that means they're bonding as wolves."

"Versus what?"

"Versus Wilde deciding to challenge his dad for pack dominance."

I gasp and cover my mouth with my hand.

"Fates. You don't think...?"

Wilde

I wait until after ten and the music is on in the master suite, and then I creep into Rayne's room.

I can't believe she went to bat for me. *Against my dad.* Whom I'm quite certain she fears. I know the alpha-holes have my back, but there was something different about it coming from Rayne.

The pipsqueak I've been nothing but mean to.

The girl who owes me absolutely nothing but a few swift kicks to the balls.

The adorable little runt of a wolf I can't wait to spend the night with.

She has one leg out from the covers like she's having another one of her fever-fits.

"Hey, Rayne-bow." I crawl in beside her, and she scoots toward the wall. "Where are you going?" I reach for her and pull her back against my front.

"Nowhere," she says softly.

"Thanks for sticking up for me, jellybean."

"I'm sorry, Wilde." She turns to face me. With my night vision, I see her forehead is scrunched up in concern. "I didn't mean to cause so much trouble."

"Fuck that," I mutter. "That wasn't your trouble. That was just my dad being a dick."

"When my mom and I came home and saw your clothes by the back door we were afraid you'd challenged for rank." Rayne props up on one elbow. Her breasts shift beneath her tank top, making my dick punch out against my boxers.

I let out a soft scoff. "I'd probably win." I brush the backs of my knuckles over one of her nipples. It stiffens to a peak under the fabric of her top.

"But you're still the good son," Rayne says.

"Hardly."

"You are. What happened with your dad?"

"Eh. I told him how much I hate Duke. He argued about why it's in my best interest to go back. We didn't really get anywhere. He wants me to call Coach Granview and tell him I'm innocent tomorrow."

"Will you?"

"I dunno."

"So how did you end up on four paws?"

"My dad suggested we go for a run. That's his form of bonding."

"Did he apologize?"

I snort. "Of course not. He never does–which is a big part of why my mom left the moment I went off to school." I listen for any kind of ache or wound from their parting but find none. "They're both happier now. That's all that matters. I'm just sorry they stayed together so long for me."

"Oh. I wondered."

"Yeah. Too many unforgiven events must've gone down between them. Who knows? My dad can be a real prick sometimes."

"Mmm," Rayne agrees.

"But I guess the apple doesn't fall far from the tree, right, jellybean?" I tweak her nipple.

She squirms, and the scent of her arousal fills the room.

I let out a low growl. "Don't make that sweet nectar between your legs. I don't think I can get away with licking your pussy without you making a whole lot of noise."

Rayne makes a strangled sound and rolls away from me, giving me her back.

I chuckle. "On second thought, maybe I can figure out a way. I drag her back against me and slide my lower arm under her head to clap around her mouth. With my top arm, I cup her mons. "This should work. Right, Rayne-bow?"

She moans against my palm.

"Shh." I slide my hand inside her sleep shorts to get at her bare pussy. My fingers coast over her slick folds, into the valley below. I take my time, softly exploring, learning all the tiny nooks and curves to her sweet pussy. "I like touching you, Rayne," I murmur against the back of her head.

Like is an understatement. There are energy bombs exploding from my center outward, waves of lust and pleasure just at having her small body tucked up against mine, at owning her orgasms.

I stroke her until she's sopping wet, then screw my middle finger inside her.

She scissors her legs around my hand, her muffled whimpers growing more insistent.

"You like that, Rayne-bow?"

She nods. "Mmmh hmmph."

I love controlling her mouth. Keeping those gasps and moans as restrained as this little body of hers.

I fuck her with my finger, pressing in slowly and easing out, letting her neediness build, working her up into a desperate frenzy. When her hips are thrashing and she's clawing at my wrist between her legs, I pick up the pace, thrusting faster. She grinds her mons down on the heel of my hand, stimulating her clit.

"That's it, jellybean." I keep working her. She squirms and mewls. "Come for me."

A few more snaps of her hips, and she gasps and tightens around my finger in the sweetest, tightest pulsing I've ever felt.

My dick is about to explode, but I shift my hips back from her juicy ass, afraid I'll actually try something.

I need to be sure Rayne's ready before I try to get my own satisfaction. This is about giving her relief. Helping her through her transition.

That's what I tell myself, anyway.

It's the justification in my head for what I'm doing,

which I know deep down is highly reproachable. But all of my behavior toward Rayne has been reproachable.

And for some reason, every interaction I have with her just makes me hungry for more.

She will end up giving everything to me–every inch of that body, mind, and soul. Soon.

Chapter Eighteen

Rayne

J.J., this year's senior class president stands in front of my English class. "I'm passing out the ballots for Homecoming royalty. Mark your favorite king and queen and pass them back in."

Great. The ballot my name is on. Just another day of humiliation for me at Wolf Ridge High.

To make matters worse, Casey Muchmore's in this class. She's been notably absent from my fan club since I got a peek inside her proverbial closet. If only I had dirt on every alpha hole in this school. I shrink in my seat. Still, I shudder to think what she might do to me in retaliation for my name daring to be on the same ballot as hers.

Yep. Everyone is sending me their glances as they pick up their ballots. Like they're wondering if she's going to kick my ass.

I pick up my ballot and boldly check Lauren's name, then abstain from the king vote. Abe doesn't need any more votes. These guys think they're so funny. I would seriously laugh my butt off if Lauren won queen, and Abe has to share the first Homecoming dance with a human.

I'll bet nothing would irritate him more.

These things are so stupid, anyway. Why do we have to vote to prove what everyone in a pack already knows?

Just so they can wear a crown? I sort of doubt Casey Muchmore cares about a stupid princess crown. She already knows she's alpha.

I smile remembering Bailey joking that she was going to steal the Homecoming crown and give it to me after Cole and his creepy ex won it their senior year. I guess I was bitter then, too, about the whole dumb process.

Casey looks at me as she turns her ballot in and gives me a flick of her brows.

My stomach twists into a big knot. I have no idea what that look means. Probably something like *Dream on, bitch.* Or maybe, *You're dead meat, Runt.*

After school, Lincoln finds me at my locker for tutoring. We've been hanging out after school in the library almost every day after school this week. I don't know if I actually still need his help with math. We go over the problems and do the homework together, but mostly, it's turned into a social date. It works for me because Wilde likes me waiting in his Jeep when he gets out of practice, so it gives me something to do.

Wilde...my extremely hot and devious stepbrother. The guy who makes me ride his fingers every night in bed.

I'm using *makes* loosely since I'm a more than willing participant.

I have to say, I feel like a different person. The nightly orgasms are changing me. Even though nothing at school has changed, I'm more relaxed. Confident. I feel prettier. I don't care as much what everyone thinks of me.

Lincoln leads his shoulder against the locker beside me. "Hey, do you want to go to Homecoming with me? Just as friends?"

I hesitate.

Fuck.

Wilde would kill Lincoln. I mean, really–I would fear for his safety.

But it's not like *he* can take me. Or *would* take me. And I've never been to a school dance. Not one. No one's ever asked me. I didn't even have a group of friends to go with.

Lincoln flashes a grin when I don't answer. "No? That's cool. I get it. I'm low status at this school."

"It's not that." I reach out and grab his shirt to stop him from walking away. He turns back in that slouchy-casual way of his. This guy has confidence in spades. I love how unruffled he is about my perceived rejection.

"Well?" he prompts when I still can't find words. "Like I said, it's just as friends. I'm not looking for a date-date if that's what you're worried about."

"I'd love to," I burst out, surprising myself.

Wait, *what?*

I'm actually going to do this? Go to the Homecoming dance with a guy? A *human* guy? A guy who is *not Wilde?*

Ugh. Just my luck. Abe, J J., and Markley walk by right when I say it.

Abe stops. "What's this? The runt and the new kid are going to the dance?"

J.J. drops a hand on Abe's shoulder. "*Abe.*" He says it like a warning, which I don't understand.

Abe turns his attention directly on Lincoln. "Is it a double-date?"

Lincoln and I both stare at him in confusion.

"Who's bringing your sister?" he persists.

Lincoln allows his distaste for Abe to show on his face. "Her boyfriend."

My own surprise takes a backseat to my interest in Abe's response.

Pure rage. His neck gets red, and his fingers close into fists. "Oh yeah? Who is that?"

"None of your business, Abe." I slam my locker shut and grab Lincoln's arm to walk away with me.

"Watch it, Ru...Rayne," I hear him mutter behind me. Why he corrected himself with my name, I can't fathom.

All I know is I probably just jumped headfirst into a pile of quicksand. I don't know how I'm ever going to manage to go to Homecoming with Lincoln without Wilde burning the school down to prevent it.

But I guess that should show me how wrong my relationship with Wilde is. Why would I be wasting thought on someone who not only can't show his interest in me but *wouldn't*? Not unless I manifest a she-wolf and prove to the town I'm not defective after all.

Well, fuck him.

I go hang out with Lincoln for an hour then head to the parking lot to wait in Wilde's Jeep.

Maybe the guys didn't tell Wilde about Lincoln and our non-date for the dance. I mean, why would they? Abe was only asking because he has some problem with Lauren, from what I can tell.

But when I see Wilde stalking toward the Jeep, I know that he knows.

His eyes flash green as he climbs behind the wheel. He says nothing to me.

Absolutely nothing. Which isn't like him. He's stewing. A bad sign.

Then, he doesn't drive home. He drives up into the

mountains, past the mesa where kids hang out and drink on weekends.

"Where are we going?" I finally dare to ask.

He doesn't answer.

Finally, he pulls up in front of a cabin. I know this place. Well, I've heard of it. It's Abe and Austin's cabin. Or their dad's. A place they use during full moon runs. Or to sneak off and have sex.

My heart starts hammering. "What are we doing?"

Wilde jumps out of the Jeep and stalks toward the cabin. I follow. He reaches for the key up above the door frame and unlocks the door.

"Wilde?"

He turns to look at me with wolf eyes and tips his head in the direction of the door he's holding open for me. "We're going inside. I'm going to smack your ass pink while you explain to me why Lincoln thinks he's taking you to Homecoming."

* * *

Wilde

I'm gonna kill that kid. I am seriously going to rip out the human's throat for asking Rayne to the dance.

I just keep praying there's some kind of explanation here. Something I can't see through the green haze of my wolf's jealous frenzy.

Why in the fuck would Rayne agree to go with him?

I don't wait for her to walk in. I wrap one arm around her waist and carry her inside, straight to the side of the couch where I place her, belly down, ass out. I'm spanking her before I can even think.

"Ow! Wilde!" She reaches a hand back to cover her ass. I twist it behind her back and continue the spanking.

I'm not sure there's much thought traveling from my brain to my hand. All I know is that it satisfies me to feel the impact. To be alone with her here. To have her pinned down, completely under my control. My dick strains at the zipper of my jeans.

I need more. I want to feel her bare skin beneath my palm. To see the bloom of my handprint on her ass.

I stop and release her. "Take them off."

She whirls, face red, chest heaving. "What?"

"Your clothes. *Take them off.* You know how you get punished by me." I flick my brows. "Naked."

Instead of fighting me or arguing, Rayne falls against my body, soothing my wolf. Her hands coast up my chest to look around my neck. My arms band around her back.

"Calm *down.*" She holds my gaze, showing me she's here with me. It's just the two of us.

No one else between us now.

"May I explain? Please?"

I give a jerky nod. I'm not sure I'm even capable of speech that doesn't consist of growls or orders. It must be the approach of the full moon and this raging case of blue balls I have from sleeping next to Rayne every night.

The moment Abe told me Lincoln asked Rayne to the dance, and she said yes, I went feral. I don't know how I even made it through the rest of practice. I definitely had to take my locker room shower ice cold.

Rayne climbs me like a tree, wrapping her sexy legs around my waist like a koala and tucking her face into my neck. Despite her offer to explain, she says nothing for a moment.

It's okay, though. Having her body melded against mine

soothes my wolf. My muscles start to relax as I breathe in her spring rain scent.

"I've never been to a school dance. Ever."

It takes a moment for the meaning of her words to filter through my brain and unscramble to make sense. Rayne hasn't been...she wants to go to a school dance.

Fuck.

Of course she does. It's her senior year. She should get to experience that. Especially since she's going to be Homecoming queen.

"Lincoln asked me as a friend. He made it clear—*twice*—it was just as friends."

My hands tighten on her at the mention of Lincoln. My lips twist into a snarl.

"Shh," she murmurs against my ear. "Just. Friends. I want to go to the dance. Obviously, you're not going to take me."

That missive hits me square in the chest.

I'm not sure what the *obvious* part is—because she's my stepsister or because she's Rayne the Runt, the girl I wouldn't have been caught dead associating with before our parents married? A sort of sick, guilty feeling fills my belly at that thought.

Either way, she's right. I'm not taking her to that dance. And she deserves to go.

But—fuck!

I don't want any guy near her.

I guess my brain still isn't fully functional because I find myself stalking to one of the bedrooms.

"Where are you going?" Rayne asks.

I should hear the nervous note to her voice, but it doesn't register. I toss her in the center of the bed and rip my t-shirt off over my head.

"What are you doing?"

"I'm going to fuck you, Rayne," I declare like she has no choice in the matter. Like this is about to get rapey fast.

Of course, I'd pull back if she showed signs of not wanting it, but the need to claim her is kinda blotting out my more gentlemanly instincts right now.

I kick off my shoes, then pull off hers.

"I'm gonna fuck you, and you're gonna take it. And afterward, we can talk about that damn dance."

She scrambles up to her feet on the mattress–fast. Her wolf reflexes are definitely coming in strong. Instead of running, though, she comes at me again. I'm not sure how she knows giving herself to me is the only solution here, but she does.

Wolf instinct, I guess.

She launches herself at me, wraps her arms around my neck again. "Wilde. I'm scared."

That's all it takes.

My wolf settles immediately. Like those words contain the same essence of her tears–something powerful enough to bring an enraged and possessive wolf to his haunches.

My hands are instantly on her, roaming up and down her back, squeezing her ass. "Baby, it's okay. You're safe. I won't hurt you." I tug her shirt up and start kissing the flat of her belly. "I'm sorry I scared you." My tongue delves into her belly button. "I didn't mean to be a dick." I unbutton her jeans and slide them down her hips. Open my jaw and take as much of panty-clad pussy into my mouth as I can, sliding my teeth over the fabric, blowing my hot breath against her core.

"But I do need to get into this tight pussy, baby. *Right now.* Are you going to let me do that?" The desire to master her completely, to have that little body under me, to make her scream with satisfaction has me tearing her jeans off. My balls are heavy, and my cock throbs painfully.

I nip her inner thigh, then pick her up and drop her onto her back to get the jeans off her ankles. I crawl over her, working hard to calm my breath. "Are you still scared?"

She shakes her head.

Fate, she's gorgeous. Her sandy blonde hair falls across her heart-shaped face. I brush it back.

I claim her mouth. It's a loud, insistent kiss. The kind intended to tell her that she belongs to me. That her lips are mine for the taking. I thrust my tongue between them. Her hips roll up against mine.

Thank fuck. Her first green light.

I'm so desperate to get between those legs.

"Are you going to take my cock like a good girl, Rayne-bow?" I slide my hand into her bra and pinch one nipple.

She moans softly.

"Hmm?" I really need an actual green light here. I may be half-crazed, but I'm not going to take something that's not willingly given.

The intoxicating scent of her arousal wraps around my head and pulls me into an even deeper haze.

"Go slow," she whispers.

I want to simultaneously fist pump and fall to my knees and thank fate. "I will," I promise, praying it will be true. Praying I can hold back.

I mean to take my time. But somehow her panties end up shredded between my two hands, and I'm licking into her like there's a fire to put out with my tongue.

Maybe there is. She's burning up, her flesh scorching against my lips. But I have no desire to extinguish those flames. Nope. I intend to stoke them higher.

It takes me less than sixty seconds to get her to the first

orgasm. One just on my tongue. Another sixty to wring one from her with two fingers inside her.

"You ready, baby?"

She moans and cups her own breasts, driving me out of my fucking mind with lust.

I end up shredding her bra. The shirt tangles around her neck. I suck the hell out of one nipple, then the other.

"I need to be in you." My voice comes out gravelly and deep. I slide off my jeans and boxer briefs.

Rayne's gaze is on my cock, her big blue eyes glazed with pleasure, pupils blown wide.

I crawl over her and rub the head of my cock along her slit, parting her. "Take me, baby." I press forward at her entrance, just a nudge.

She rolls her hips a little to encourage me.

"You want that? Want it deeper?"

She gives me a tiny nod, gaze trained on the place where our bodies join.

I ease in, centimeter by centimeter. She's tight as fuck. Incredible. Delicious. I can tell my eyes have changed color because my vision domes up and sharpens. The animal within me grows restless. The moment's charged. It's like the space between inhale and exhale. Zero point. The moment just after you've finished one life and are about to start the next.

Somehow I know that everything's about to change.

I just don't know how.

"Can't...hold...back...any longer," I grit between clenched teeth.

Wilde. Rayne sounds alarmed, but it's too late. I'm thrusting.

Deep.

Fuck. She's so tiny, I probably split her in two.

She cries out, reaching for my shoulders. Her legs wrap around my waist, which keeps me from moving in her. Lets her follow my hips up and down without the friction. I fucking love it. I get her tight, wet heat gripping me like a fist and work a little deeper every time I rock my hips against hers.

"Wilde."

I like her saying my name in that breathy, panicked little voice. I like it way too much.

"Who do you belong to?"

"Wilde–"

"That's right. Say my name."

"Wilde, please."

Somehow, I force myself to dial back the power of my thrusts. "Are you okay, baby?"

"I'm good," she pants. "I need..."

"What do you need?" Some of the fog clears from my brain. My female needs satisfying, and it's my job to do it. I slow my roll.

"No," she whines.

I bring the pad of my thumb to her clit and rub.

"Oh!" Her hips pop off the bed, thrusting up over my dick, which of course, makes me lose it again.

Bracing on one arm beside her head, I pound in, caressing her lovely face with my free hand as I demolish her sweet little pussy.

Her eyes roll back in her head. She arches her back. "Wilde...Wilde...please."

"Take it, baby. Take all of me."

"Yes...yes....oh!" Rayne's internal muscles squeeze around my dick–like she wasn't already tight enough–and an inhuman growl rips from my throat.

The tether on the last of my control snaps. I pound into

Rayne as the room spins. My balls draw up tight. I'm as feverish as she is now and desperate for release.

"Fuck, Rayne, fuck!" I shove in deep and come inside her, filling her with streams and streams of my hot seed.

Gratitude crashes all around me, sending me nuzzling into Rayne, cupping her nape and kissing her temple, her forehead, her nose, finally landing on her lips where I move my mouth lazily against hers while rocking slowly in and out.

"Does it hurt, baby?"

"Mmm."

I lift my face to examine hers. "Hmm?"

Her gaze is full heavy-lidded. "I like the hurt," she murmurs.

I rock a little deeper. "Yeah?"

Her eyes flicker to silver.

"Your wolf is showing," I whisper.

Rayne's whole body stiffens.

* * *

Rayne

"What is it?" Wilde slowly eases out of me. "Too sore?"

I shake my head. "I'm okay." I attempt to roll away from him. The topic of my wolf is the real sore spot, but I don't feel like talking about it.

Wilde gets up from the bed and returns with a warm washcloth which he strokes between my legs, cleaning me up. The intimacy of it is almost more than our act of sex. Because this is the gentle Wilde. The one I suspect most people never see.

Not that I mind the nearly feral version of Wilde. It was

incredible to know I affected him that way. That his jealousy and possessiveness were driving him to claim me.

I mean, not *claim me*, claim me. Not like a mating bite. But still, he was definitely out to prove I belonged to him.

I swear, receiving his cum inside me felt like a baptism. Like it somehow changed me.

Wilde climbs back up beside me and rolls me to my side, so he can mold his body around to spoon me. I absolutely adore the feeling.

This is how we slept last night. Wilde's giant arm draped across my middle, a heavy weight I never want to escape.

"Let's talk about this dance, Rayne-bow." He murmurs the words against my ear, making me feel safe from his habitual fuckery. There's affection in his body and his voice.

"Okay."

"You can let that little dickwad take you, on three conditions."

"What are they?"

"One: you tell him about us."

"What?" I turn to look over my shoulder in surprise.

Wilde nods. "I need him to know who you belong to. And that I'm granting permission for you to go."

I chuff at the *granting permission* part, but I'm secretly thrilled. About the whole thing–Wilde being okay with me going. And wanting to claim me publicly. Of course, telling a human doesn't really count as publicly in this town.

And I guess I know he won't claim me in front of others until I transition. *If* I transition. That's the part that really stings.

"Do it now." Wilde nudges me away from him.

"Okay, bossy."

He slaps my ass as I get up to prove my point.

I get my phone out of my pocket and text Lincoln as Wilde looks over my shoulder.

I need to tell you something. The reason I hesitated when you asked me to the dance, I type.

"Damn straight," Wilde mutters behind me.

It's because there's actually something between me and my stepbrother. Obvs that's on the DL. But I wanted you to know. And I talked to him, and he's cool with you taking me <smiley emoji>

"Happy?" I ask Wilde.

He takes the phone from me and pulls me on top of him. "I wouldn't say happy," he grumbles. His hands stroke up and down the sides of my body. "Actually, I take that back. I am happy."

It's true. He looks happy. There's a lazy smile on his face, and the thought that it might be because of me makes my heart pound.

"What are the other two conditions?"

"Two: After the dance I get to spank his scent off you."

"I'm not sure that's how smells work."

Wilde arches a stern brow.

I flush. This guy really likes to spank me. It's kinda daunting, kinda hot. "Okay. And the third?

"Third condition is I fuck you before and after you go."

I let out a shaky laugh. "You're crazy."

"I'm dead serious. Do we have a deal?"

I nod and smile. "Deal."

He kisses the bridge of my nose. It's a surprisingly tender move, and it sends flutters through me.

"We should get back. I have to make dinner."

Wilde groans. "I don't want to wash your scent off."

I realize, with a flip of my belly, that I don't want that, either. His scent soothes me. Grounds me. I feel changed.

I'm not sure I ever bought the idea that a female was changed by losing her virginity. I mean, that's just some patriarchal bullshit put in place to ensure the transfer of property to heirs. But I do feel different.

Stronger. Invigorated. Enlivened.

Maybe that has nothing to do with virginity and everything to do with the orgasm?

No, wait. I've orgasmed before—by myself and with Wilde. It's just that this was my first P in V sex.

Could it be...his cum?

"Come on, jellybean." Wilde scoops me up, lifting me into the air at the same time he crawls off the bed. He carries me to the bathroom where he sets me down and turns on the shower.

"I'd better keep my hair dry." I pull my hair off my nape and hold it off my shoulders as I step in. "It will be hard to explain why it's wet."

Wilde soaps me down, then sends me out of the shower while he quickly rinses off. "Let's pick up some rotisserie chickens," he suggests as we both quickly get dressed. "Also, I hate that you're in charge of making dinner. What in the hell is that about? Like you're some kind of fucking Cinderella or something?"

I work hard not to smile, absurdly pleased by his assessment. "I'm trying to contribute to the household."

Wilde's face contorts into a look of scorn. "Fuck that, Rayne. Take up space."

I give his huge, immovable body a shove. "It's hard when there's literally this huge wolf always crowding me. In my bedroom, in my bed..."

"*My* bed." He picks me up by the waist and smacks my ass. "But I don't mind sharing." He drops me back to my feet. "Let's go, jellybean."

Outside, the nearly full moon is rising from behind the peak. We both stop to honor her with our awe.

"Hunter's moon," Wilde murmurs in appreciation. Even ballers have reverence for the power and beauty of the pale goddess in the sky.

I swear I feel the energy of it enter me. A charge of electricity runs through my spine, making every nerve-ending tingle. It feels like...recognition. That I'm a part of something much, much bigger than I ever imagined. Of fate, nature, and the tapestry of our species as a whole.

For one sliver of a moment, I'm able to access some kind of deeper wisdom.

And with it, I know something significant just happened to me in there. Something that goes far beyond getting my V-card punched.

Chapter Nineteen

Wilde

I wake up cranky after spending the night on the couch. Now that I've had Rayne, I don't think I can lie in the same bed as her at night and not fuck her senseless, and our parents would certainly catch the scent or hear the pounding.

I told Rayne last night why I was staying away, but she seems cranky with me, too.

Maybe my sweet stepsister needed me.

That thought makes me harder than stone.

"Can we stop at the post office on the way to school?" Rayne has a brown paper-wrapped shoebox with a printed address taped to the front tucked under her arm as she climbs into the Jeep.

"What is that?"

"None of your business."

There's a prickle at the back of my neck. My wolf senses are telling me something. An irrational rage simmers beneath the surface.

"Try again." I refuse to start the vehicle.

She huffs and rolls her eyes skyward. "Fine. They're shoes. Used shoes. I'm getting a thousand bucks for them."

"Uh. Wow. That's a lot of money."

"You see? This is a lucrative business."

The prickle of warning returns. "I still don't like it. Is your name and address on the box?"

"Wilde. I'm not an idiot. I used a fake PO box."

"But he'll know what state you live in. What town, even."

"Yeah, and I live in a town full of shifters. You think a stranger looking for trouble would survive five minutes in this town?"

It's a valid point. We don't like outsiders here, and we do keep track of anyone who shows up and seems out of place.

"Next time, ship it from Phoenix," I concede.

"Are you going to drive me?"

I look over at her, bemused. "You've got a lot of attitude this morning, jellybean. Are you looking for punishment?"

"Shut up and drive, Wilde, or I'll be late."

I check the time on my phone. She's right. I start the Jeep and pull out. "I'll mail the package after I drop you off."

She turns to look at me with surprise. "Thank you." Her gaze goes soft on my face, and it gives me a rush of satisfaction so strong I almost want to shift.

Maybe it's the moon, which will be full this weekend for Homecoming. Or maybe it's something about Rayne's scent. It's changing. I scent more of her wolf. And the more I scent, the more I want her.

I have to get her to shift. I feel certain if I do, I'll find out she's my mate.

And if she's not?

Well, then, we're fucked. Or, I should say I'm fucked. Because her being my mate is the only excuse I could possibly offer for screwing around with my new stepsister.

If anyone finds out I took her virginity without that excuse?

I'll be out of the pack for good.

I drop her off in front of the school, and she does her usual thing of quickly slinking out of the Jeep. like she doesn't want anyone to see her. I might have appreciated it at first because I didn't like being associated with her, but now I fucking hate it.

"Rayne." I stop her as she shuts the door.

"Yeah?"

"Have a good day."

A slow smile blooms on her face, and it takes my breath away. She's beautiful in the morning sunlight. Radiant, even. And the way she's looking at me makes me feel like a king. "You too, Wilde. See you after school."

A strange lightness overtakes me as I drive to the post office before I head to the auto shop. It's something like happiness, but a kind I haven't experienced before. A weird, bubbly sensation. Like everything is new and different.

Like I'm someone new and different.

Not busted Wilde, the no-good fuck-up who got arrested on drug charges and will fail out of Duke. Not angry Wilde, who's living his life for his father and pack instead of figuring out what in the hell he wants to do for himself.

Not the fish out of water Wilde living halfway across the country with humans he can't relate to.

I feel more like myself, except it's a self I barely know.

Fuck, I know that doesn't make any sense, but that's the sensation.

At the post office, I wait at the counter to mail Rayne's shoes. They're going to someone else's PO Box. No name, just a set of initials, but the post office box is in Chandler. Right down the hill.

I don't like it. Something about it makes the hairs on the back of my neck stand up again.

Rayne's logic is sound, I don't see how this could bite her, and I'm sure as hell not going to stop her from earning a thousand bucks, but something about it feels wrong to me.

Helping her out felt right, though, and I loved that look of gratitude on her face, so I go through with it.

When I get back in the Jeep, my phone rings.

It's the head coach from Duke.

I pick up his call. Time to stop dodging.

"Woodward."

"Coach Granview."

"Son, I have been calling you for three weeks now."

"Yes, sir."

"Why didn't you call me back?"

"Honestly?" I tunnel my fingers through my hair. "I don't know. Self-sabotage, I guess."

"Self-sabotage." He gives a humorless laugh. "Yeah, that sounds about right."

"Yeah. Nothing to say, really."

"Fifteen of them failed the drug test I administered when we got back."

"Another test?"

"Yeah. I guess you fellas thought you were safe since we'd just tested."

I don't bother answering.

"Heard your drug test the police gave you came back clean, though."

I'm surprised. Not that my drug test was clean, but that

he had access to that information. "How did you find that out?"

"I've been working to get the damn charges against you dropped, son! What in the hell did you think I was calling you about?"

"Oh."

I'm humbled. And shocked.

A stab of guilt pierces my chest. Coach Granview having my back comes as a shock.

I mean, my own dad didn't believe in me.

If you're so blind you can't see the hero your son is...

Rayne's impassioned defense of me comes rushing back, and I'm humbled a second time by the memory.

"There's no evidence that the drugs belonged to you, other than the fact that they were in your room, where a large party was being held, as can be attested to by the hotel staff, who called the police and sent them to your room. I'm trying to find out if your prints were on the bag, but I suspect they weren't. Am I right, son?"

"Yes, sir."

"Yes, I'm right or yes they were on the bag?"

"Yes, you're right."

"Well, Wilde, we should be able to get the charges dropped. I want you back on the team by next week's game if we can swing it. So if I call this phone number, are you going to pick up?"

My wolf doesn't like it.

For some reason, he can't fucking stand the idea of going back to Duke.

I get it. He never got to run there. I had to hide what I was.

But it's Rayne's creosote and juniper scent crawling into

207

my nostrils that makes me clench my fist so hard around the phone I crack the screen.

My wolf doesn't want to leave Rayne.

She has to be my mate.

There's no other answer.

Still, I can't say no. Not when I face being kicked out of the pack if I do. Not when Coach Granview and the team are counting on me.

They may not be my pack, but I still know loyalty.

"Yes, sir."

"Good. I'll be in touch." He ends the call.

Fuck.

Fuck. Fuck. Fuck.

I have to get Rayne to turn during the full moon. I need to know if she's really mine.

Leaving now before we've figured things out wouldn't be fair to her. It wouldn't be fair to me. Something I probably should start paying more attention to. I keep telling Rayne to take up more space. Maybe it's time I follow my own advice.

I'm not leaving Wolf Ridge until I know for sure if my sweet stepsister truly belongs to me.

* * *

Rayne

On Wednesday, Wilde texts me during sixth period to tell me to meet him right after school instead of after practice.

He doesn't say why.

Simply receiving a text from him sends my belly into flutters. He doesn't normally text me. All I've had to go on the past few days is the times we're in the Jeep alone together.

Wilde has spent every night on the couch this week, which is probably good, but I'm restless and irritable and rather desperate for release.

I used the extra time alone in my room to make a bunch of foot videos. It's amazing how different it all feels now.

You wouldn't think having sex could change a person so much, but it truly has. I'm not the same female I was before Wilde took my V-card.

Now I feel sensual. Sexual. Awakened. When I dirty-talk to the camera, I sort of actually mean it. At least, I'm drawing from a genuine well, not just making stuff up.

I describe to my viewers how I want my toes sucked, drawing on everything Wilde did. Telling them how I'm touching myself as they do it. I imagine I'm talking to Wilde, not that I'm the dominant one in the relationship. But still, pretending he's the one watching gives me confidence.

I trust that he finds me hot. I can't wait until I can see it in his glowing green eyes again.

At least I know we're having sex this weekend. *Twice.* Once before the dance and once after. My mom and I went shopping for a dress for Homecoming. Logan even offered up the money for it. I picked out a silver one to match my wolf eyes. A secret only Wilde and I know.

Every time I think of our pre and post-Homecoming dance date I smile.

I think the approaching full moon is starting to get to me.

I've never had that before. I've observed its effect on everyone around me, but I usually remain grounded. Only minorly changed by the wax and wan of the sky goddess.

But this one is intense.

I'm feverish all night, and it's crazy, but when I saw Wilde leaving for his morning run, I had the urge to join him.

Me.

I don't run. I don't do anything athletic. But I suddenly understood why wolves have that urge to shift and run. That letting off steam thing makes sense to me now.

I find Wilde's Jeep idling right out the door I normally exit, which secretly thrills me. I didn't even know that he knew which class I had or where I come out.

I hop in the Jeep, and he takes off right away. This is no different than any other time he's driven me to or from school. I get it—it's not like he can give me a kiss when I get in.

But not even a smile? Or some kind of greeting?

Wilde is not just pretending he's not sleeping with his stepsister, he's still acting like I'm not worth his time in front of others.

I'd love to say it doesn't hurt. That I'm used to this behavior since I've experienced it my entire life.

But this guy just took my virginity and is making rules like I belong to him, so I guess I want...more.

"Where are we going?"

"To get your driver's license."

Ouch. That hurts even more.

Wilde's nostrils flare, and he looks over me. "What's wrong?"

I shrug. "Why? Nothing."

"Don't lie to me. I scented pain."

"Are you sick of driving me around?"

Wilde shocks me by swerving sharply to pull over. "Hey." It's a command of sorts.

I give him my gaze, and he holds it.

"Rayne-bow, I'm gonna keep driving you every fucking day. It's my job. As far as I'm concerned, no one needs to know you got your license. I just want you to have all the empowerment you need." He shrugs. "You should have a license. And I'm sorry I haven't taken you yet."

Oh damn. Everything in my chest goes soft and gooey.

Wilde's being sweet.

"Oh. Thank you."

He flashes me a grin. "We good?" He waits for me to nod then puts the Jeep back in gear and climbs back on the road.

"Why today? Are you missing practice for this?"

"Yeah. I have plans for you afterward."

"What plans?"

"You'll have to wait and see."

Oh.

My insides fizz and pop with excitement. I hope it's sex. I really need more sex.

Wilde takes me to the DMV, and I pass the driver's test. Afterward, he takes me to celebrate at a gelato place.

"Were these your plans?" I ask as I scoop the last spoonful of double dark chocolate gelato into my mouth.

"Nope."

"What are they?"

"No questions, Rayne-bow. Come on, let's go."

"Are we going to Abe and Austin's cabin?" I persist.

Of course, he doesn't answer. He drives us back to Wolf Ridge and then winds back up into the mountains. He parks on the side of the road in the middle of nowhere and throws open his door.

"Come on."

I follow him out, looking around. "I don't understand."

"We're going to take a little walk," Wilde says.

I look around again. There's not even a path. We're going to be bush-whacking through the wilderness. I don't think the surprise is sex.

How sad for me.

I follow Wilde through the brush for a solid twenty minutes. I'm confused as hell, but I don't try to ask any more questions, since he's obviously not going to answer them.

Eventually, we come out to a cliff's edge, and then I understand. Wilde knows this place from his full moon runs. He doesn't usually park a Jeep and hike in. He's running here on four paws from below.

I mean, it's cool and everything. I don't know if he thinks it's romantic. I definitely would've preferred a repeat of the cabin experience.

"What is this?"

"We call it 'the ledge'. It's a meeting spot for the full moon runs."

Right. Something I've never experienced and never will.

"Oh." I'm still not getting it. Not at all.

Wilde tugs my shirt off over my head.

Um...okay? Why here? And how? I mean...there are prickly things around. And the ground looks hard and rocky. I'm not sure I'm into it at this moment.

"Take off your jeans," he commands.

"Why?" I demand.

He ignores the question and unbuttons the jeans himself. I comply with his efforts to get my jeans off, which of course, requires kicking off my shoes and getting my socks all dirty.

And then Wilde picks me up and tosses me up into the air.

Over the side of the cliff.

I scream on the way down.

Wilde plunges down next to me, yelling, "Shift. Rayne–*shift!*"

Betrayal takes a back seat to downright terror. My vision tunnels and then goes dark.

I pass out completely before I hit the ground.

Wilde

Fuck!

It failed.

Rayne doesn't shift mid-air as I'd hoped, and I can't risk her hitting the ground. She may have healing abilities, but I don't know if they're complete.

I contort my body to land on my feet and catch Rayne before she hits the ground.

She's passed out cold.

Well, I fucked this up royally.

"Rayne, baby. *Rayne.* Wake up, jellybean. You're okay."

I don't breathe until her eyelids flutter open.

"You're okay, baby. I'm sorry. I thought you would shift."

Rayne wriggles as if to get out of my arms.

I set her feet down on the ground, and she gives me a shove that has more power behind it than I would expect. "I hate you, Wilde Woodward."

I laugh. She's damn cute when she's mad. "I'm *sorry.* I really thought you would shift. But I caught you, baby. No harm, no foul."

"No harm...total foul!" she stomps her socked foot.

"What is your problem, Wilde? You just can't handle that I can't shift?"

I rub my hand across my face. Shit. This isn't going well. "The moon's almost full. Your scent seems like it's changing every day. I just thought..."

"Maybe I don't *want* to shift." Her eyes flash silver with anger, contradicting her words.

"It's not a matter of want. It's who you are." I reach for her, and she jerks away, but I persist. I snatch her up and hold her with my arms wrapped tightly around her middle, trapping her arms to her sides. "I'm sorry I scared you. I did mean to, but it was for a good reason."

She doesn't stop leaning away from me, trying to get free. She's in a sky blue bra and panty set that matches her eyes and is making my dick hard.

"I'm sorry for the damage I inflicted. I didn't mean to fuck things up with you Rayne. I really didn't."

She goes quiet at that.

I kiss her temple.

"Will you forgive me?" I ask softly.

"No." There's a sulkiness to her voice, though, that tells me she's getting closer.

I turn her around to face me and lift her up to straddle my waist. "What would it take for you to forgive me?" I ask as I turn to start hiking us out, looking for her clothes.

"It would take you not being a dick."

I chuckle. "That's a tough one. Dick is my middle name."

"First, middle, and last," she grumbles, but I hear her tone lightening up.

"I know what might help." I break into a run up the steep incline because my flash of an idea gives me a superhuman burst of energy–I grab Rayne's clothes without setting her down, then run up the incline.

"What?"

"I'm going to make you feel better, Rayne-bow."

Her arms have twined around my neck–more for stability than out of affection–but I love it all the same. Her ripe tits are close to my mouth, and I nip at the soft flesh through her bra.

She tightens her hold on me, legs squeezing my waist, and I increase my speed. When I get to the top, I run all the way to the Jeep.

Rayne's laughing by the time we get there, the bouncing and closeness shaking her out of her ire.

I open the Jeep and lay her down on the backseat. "You need some relief, jellybean? I've hated sleeping away from you. Last night, I had to shift and run at three a.m. just to get some sleep." As I speak, I slide her panties off and position myself between her legs.

Rayne reaches for my head, bringing it down to meet her delicate pussy.

I inhale her scent, loving how it drugs me.

She urges me forward, and I chuckle. "Is that a *yes*, baby? You want my tongue on your clit?"

"Yes."

I give her one swipe. "Is this how I earn your forgiveness?" I give a slow roll of my tongue. "Hmm?"

"Forgiven," she pants, rocking her hips.

I laugh. "Good." I treat her to every trick I know, sucking on her nether lips, penetrating her with my tongue. "You have such a sweet pussy," I praise her as I work. "It tastes so good, Rayne-bow."

She moans.

"I could eat this pussy every night for the rest of my life and never get tired of it."

She lifts her head, rising up on her elbows to watch me.

I work her clit with my tongue and slide two fingers inside. She's already soaking wet. I stroke inside her with my fingers. She's tight and beautiful and all mine. I take my time, removing my fingers to give her my tongue alone, then thrusting inside her again. After two more rounds, she's chanting my name, begging and pleading for release.

"Come for me, Rayne-bow." I pump in faster, harder.

She kicks her legs, squeals, and comes hard, soaking my hand with female ejaculate. I keep my fingers inside her to feel the way her muscles clench and tighten around them when I flick her clit one more time.

She shudders and moans and then flops across the seat like a beautiful rag doll.

I help her dress and lift her into the passenger seat. "Better, baby?"

Her gaze on my face is moony. "Yes."

I take her jaw in an overhand grip and kiss her mouth, hard. My tongue plunges into her mouth, and I thrust it in and out, fucking her with it.

When I break the kiss, her eyes are glazed, unable to focus, and her lips are puffy and pink.

"I'll figure out a way to take care of your needs, baby. I just can't risk sleeping beside you with the full moon approaching. I'd be pounding into you all night long."

Rayne gives me a secret smile.

"Tomorrow night is the Homecoming game. You're coming, right?"

She nods.

"Cool. I'll figure out somewhere we can meet afterward. Somewhere private."

She doesn't say anything, but I know I'm forgiven.

I also know there's nothing in the world I wouldn't do for this girl.

She has to be my mate.

And there has to be a way to get her to shift.

Chapter Twenty

R *ayne*
Thursday night, Lauren, Lincoln, and I sit on the back bleacher for the Homecoming game. We're five rows behind Casey Muchmore and her volleyball girls. The stands are packed. I'm wearing my silver and blue Wolf Ridge High t-shirt, like most everyone in the stands.

Lauren and Lincoln abstained from the practice, choosing to not even wear school colors. Instead, Lauren looks like she stepped off a New York runway in designer jeans with holes ripped at the knees and an off-the-shoulder sweater.

I watch Wilde's broad shoulders on the sidelines. He looks natural coaching–like it's a job he was born to do. Unfortunately, this will probably be his last game. His coach from Duke called before the game to let him know the charges against him in South Carolina had been dropped due to lack of evidence, and some good-old-boys' pressure on the District Attorney. He's now free to go back to Duke. Able to stay a member of this pack.

I should be happy for him. I mean, I am.

219

But I'd be lying if I didn't say that a sizable piece of my heart is breaking over him leaving. Of course, I knew this thing wouldn't last. Couldn't last. He's my stepbrother, for fates' sake! A real relationship was an impossibility.

But I can't help thinking about how incredible it was to have Wilde's attention and focus these past few weeks. To realize that despite his dickish ways, he's actually in my corner. An alpha-hole who wants *me*.

I watch Wilde signaling the team with a slash of his hand, and they instantly score a touchdown.

The thing about Wolf Ridge High Homecoming games is that you know we're always going to win. There are a few games throughout the season when we lose. They're predetermined by Coach Jamison, and only he and the players know. A lot of the finesse of our players is showmanship. They entertain us with their play-acting. Pretending to be human players who suddenly pull out a few spectacular moves. The Wolf Ridge audience marvels more at the choreographed misses. It's like theater.

So far, they've kept the scores even. We're at 21 to 21 by halftime. The cheerleaders do handsprings along the sidelines.

Our very lame marching band–because Wolf Ridge is all sports and no arts–heads out to the field for the halftime event, and then J.J. gets out there and takes the mic. "All right, folks, it's the moment you've all been waiting for. Time to reveal this year's Homecoming royalty."

I roll my eyes at Lincoln and Lauren. "As if there's any mystery. It's always the same people." I touch Lauren's arm. "I threw in my vote for you though, of course. Not that it will mean anything here."

Lauren shrugs her shoulders. "As if I care. I voted for you, too, girl."

"So what's the scoop with your date to Homecoming?"

"My boyfriend is flying in from New York tonight." She shrugs. "I don't know, I think we're about to break up, but at least I have a date."

"Oh no, I'm sorry."

"No, it's okay. We're in different states, and we're changing. We've grown apart. It makes sense to break up. And if we get back together when I move back East for college, that's cool."

I'm starting to think Lincoln and Lauren are the most emotionally-developed people I've ever known. I guess that's what happens when you lose your mom. You get perspective on the things that really matter.

"For the junior class," J.J. announces, "Ty Wolstein is the prince." The crowd cheers. "And his princess is... Melanie James!"

More cheering.

He waits until Melanie and Ty come out and receive their crowns, scepters, and sashes.

"For the senior class, this year's Homecoming king is... Abe Oakley!"

"Big surprise," I mutter.

"And the Homecoming queen for the senior class this year is Rayne Lansing."

I slump lower in my seat. "Fuck."

"Ra-ayne!" One of the volleyball players calls out in a sing-song tone twisting to look at me.

"What the fuck is happening?" I feel the heat surging to my cheeks. This is the most humiliating moment of my life, and I've had a lot of humiliation, let me tell you.

Lincoln and Lauren meet my horrified stare with confusion. "What is it?" Lincoln asks.

"I - I don't know! They're fucking with me. This is some big mind fuck to embarrass me."

"Well, maybe you just won?" Lauren offers.

I shake my head. "There's no way in hell I won."

Five rows ahead, I see Casey Muchmore stand up and look at me.

Oh, shit.

She marches up the stairs toward me. I would love to say that I puffed up my chest and stood up to her, but the shock of the announcement was too much. I literally cower in my seat. She takes my elbow and urges me to my feet. What throws me completely off is the smile on her face.

"It's you, Runt. Didn't you hear?"

"I'm sorry, Casey." I shake my head. My legs are trembling. "I don't know what this is about."

"Come here." She tugs me. "I do."

I don't know what's about to happen to me, but I am sure it's awful.

"No," I whimper.

That whimper throws Lincoln into action. He surges to his feet and grabs Casey's arm. "Hey, let her go."

For a moment, I think there's going to be a fight. And it's going to be the worst thing ever. Because if Casey swings on Lincoln, it's a lose-lose for him. Either he swings back on a girl, and will be destroyed by everyone in these stands. Or he looks like a wimp getting knocked around by a girl who doesn't look nearly as strong as she is.

But Casey just holds her hands in the air, palms out as if to show she has no weapons.

"There's no trick, Rayne. You won Homecoming queen."

"Rayne Lansing. Get down here. Where is our tiny queen?" J.J. says over the loudspeaker.

Everyone turns to look at me.

I literally want to bomb the entire stadium right now, even if it means me going up in flames as well.

"I gotta get out of here," I mutter more to myself than anyone else.

Casey frowns. "No, Rayne. You need to go down there and get your crown. You really don't know why this happened?" She has a smirk on her face like she's in on some kind of joke I'm not getting. "Your new stepbrother did this. I guess he decided to elevate your rank around here."

That hits me like a punch in the gut.

In fact, I fall back on the bleachers as if I've been socked.

Wilde did this. Wilde humiliated me in front of all the school. No, not just the whole school, the entire fucking town is here tonight.

I know it wasn't to play a joke on me or to hurt me. I'm sure he thought he was doing me a favor, but this is the absolute worst thing ever.

How will I ever hold my head up around here knowing my stepbrother bullied the students into voting for me when everyone knows I'm the lowest in the pack?

And why would he think it was a good idea?

And then, suddenly, I know.

I know exactly why, and I have to clap a hand over my mouth to keep in a sob.

Because he's embarrassed to be associated with me. It's the same reason he's trying so hard to get me to shift.

He needs to elevate my status in order to be okay with having me as a stepsister. Or even, a lover–if anyone found that out.

Tears spear my eyes, and I stumble back to my feet.

"Come on, I'll walk you up so everyone knows we're cool," Casey says.

Now I get it. She's protecting her own reputation here. Showing that she allowed this vote to take place. That she was a part of it.

"No." I launch my body past hers and take off running. Not down the concrete steps to the field, but around the back of the bleachers, to the side stairs that lead out to the parking lot.

I can barely see anything through the tears, but I manage to make it down without stumbling. When I hit the pavement, I start running.

"Rayne! Hold up! You want me to drive you home?" Lincoln leans over the back of the bleachers to shout at me.

"No! I'll call my mom," I lie. "I just want to be alone." That part is true.

I take off running, away from the stadium.

"Rayne!" I hear Wilde's booming voice behind me.

I ignore him and keep on running. The moon is full, and my legs feel strong in a way they never have before.

Of course, it's not long before I hear his feet pounding behind me. I may be fast, but Wilde is a full-grown wolf and an athlete. "Rayne!"

I stop and whirl. "Leave me alone, Wilde."

He catches me and bands an arm around my torso, trying to lock me in against him.

I wriggle out of his grasp. "I said, *leave me alone!*"

"What is it? What's the matter? Everyone's waiting for you back there, Rayne-bow." When I meet his gaze, his brow furrows at my tear-streaked face. "What is it, baby?"

"No." I shake my head. I don't know where it comes from, but I finally find my strength. My sense of self. My pride. "I'm not your baby. We're not doing this anymore, Wilde."

His brows pop. "What? What's going on? Talk to me, Rayne."

"Why did you tell everyone to vote for me, Wilde?"

His shoulders drop. He's in a coach's jersey, his broad chest stretching the fabric across his muscled trunk. He looks beautiful. "I wanted you...I wanted to change things for you."

"Right!" I exclaim in outraged triumph. "You wanted me to be something different than what I am."

He spreads his hands. "Rayne, I–"

I shake my head. "Admit it. Why are you trying so hard to get me to shift? It's because you can't stand that I'm the pack omega. You need to better me to make it okay that you're having sex with me. Because fate forbid anyone find out that you dropped so low as to dip your dick in a defective runt."

He winces. "That's not true."

"It is, Wilde. You can't accept me for what I am–the lowest-ranking non-shifter in the pack. You couldn't stand that my mom married your dad and dragged me into your life, and now that you've decided I'm worth fucking, you're trying to change me.

"Well, what if I don't want to change? I was perfectly happy before you came along, Wilde Woodward. I don't need you to fix me. I don't need you to teach me how to shift. I don't need you to change my position at school. Because the truth is nothing changes that. Not you telling them to vote for me. Especially not that!

"You just made a laughing stock out of me, Wilde. And I'm done. *We're* done."

"Rayne-- " He reaches for me.

I shake him off. "We're done, Wilde. Touch me again, and I'll tell your dad you forced yourself on me. Then you'll be out of this pack for good."

Wilde's eyes round in shock, and I'm instantly sick that I even said such a thing. But I don't take it back because I need him to give me space. I need him to give me space, or I will never follow through with this breakup.

And I have to break up with him. He's my stepbrother, which means this was always going to end in heartbreak for me. I might as well have it on my own terms.

As it is, I don't know how I'll ever recover.

I take off running, away from Wilde and the school stadium.

"Rayne! Let me drive you home," Wilde calls.

"Go back to your game, Wilde. I'll call my mom," I lie for the second time that night.

I hear the huff of Wilde's exhale. His muttered curse.

But I don't look back. I just keep running because I will fall down and bawl if I don't.

I run so hard I don't notice the car pull over in front of me. I barely register the guy getting out of it. I'm dashing past him when I feel the sharp prick of a needle jabbing into my neck and then his rough hands yanking me toward the car.

I try to fight, but my muscles go limp and stop working completely. The last thing I remember is collapsing into the back seat of a small, dirty car.

* * *

Wilde

Fuck!

I want to follow Rayne.

I want everything she said to be untrue, but the fact is, on some level she's right.

I did want to change her. I wanted her to better herself. To rise up. To shift. To claim a higher status in the family, in the pack, and especially at school.

She's also probably right that my misguided Homecoming royalty coup didn't help. I don't believe anyone is laughing at her. They would know I would slaughter them for it. But, I can see that telling someone to vote for her as Homecoming queen is not the same as her earning respect or rising through the ranks. It won't make real change for her.

The need to fix this nearly drives me mad.

An inhuman snarl issues from my lips, and I punch a stop sign, busting a clean hole through the metal. The blood that runs from my knuckles looks bright under the light of the full moon. I look up at her, to see if she offers any guidance, but her pale light just feels like judgment. Like I've let her down. Fucked with fate.

The urge to shift and follow Rayne in wolf form brings another snarl to my lips. But Coach Jamison and the team will be looking for me. I'm supposed to be calling all the plays tonight.

I trudge back to the stadium. Every step I take feels like I'm dragging my feet through concrete. Feels like I'm making the biggest mistake of my life. My wolf thrashes within me, frantic to get back to Rayne.

But she made it clear to stay away. Threatened me with banishment, even though I know her too well to believe she would follow through. I could see how she horrified herself when she said it.

I wish I knew how to fix this.

Hearing the whistle blow for the first play, I jog back to

the field where Coach Jamison gives me a condemning frown.

I stand beside him. "I'm sorry."

For some reason, it feels important to own what just happened. To speak Rayne's name to Jamison and honor her that way. "Rayne didn't appreciate my interference in the Homecoming royalty," I offer, even though he didn't ask.

It takes Jamison a moment. He drags his focus from the field to my face.

"I hurt her. I didn't mean to, but I did."

He studies me with interest. "You catching feelings Wilde?"

"Caught."

I sense my entire being wobble on its axis when I admit it. Like I've been dropped into a vast ocean with no land in sight.

What does it even mean? That I care about Rayne regardless of whether she's my mate?

That was the main reason I was trying to get her to shift. Yes, I also wanted to fix her. But mostly I wanted permission to claim her.

And the only reason I would want to claim a female who doesn't trigger my mating instinct would be... *for love.*

Something we wolves think very little of. We discount the human notion of love and marriage. There are love matches all around us, even within our own community, but we only revere fated mates.

Would I still want Rayne if she wasn't my fated mate?

If you'd asked me an hour ago, I would've denied it.

But now, faced with losing her, the answer becomes a clear and resounding *yes.*

So, maybe that's the answer.

That's what I need to tell her.

I have to apologize for having my head up my ass and explain that I want her as-is. I'll take Rayne the Runt with her supposedly defective genes and her omega status.

Hanging onto that thought is the only way to make it through the game. I move robotically, call the plays, watch the game, but in my mind, I'm already with Rayne.

I'm celebrating everything she is—a small but infinitely powerful presence. Far stronger than I am. Far clearer. Far more balanced. Rayne sees things other people don't see. She's kindness and acceptance to everyone, even after the way she's been treated.

I allow the team to excel in the second half of the game, downright slaughtering the other team by the fourth quarter. The guys grin as they score touchdown after touchdown.

With two minutes left on the clock, I challenge them to get one more.

The crowd is rowdy—chanting and cheering.

I turn to scan the bleachers. I don't know why I'm looking for Rayne. She made it clear she was leaving. Said her mom would pick her up.

I spot her human friend, Lincoln, and his twin sister up in the back.

I see my buddies Austin, Cole, and Bo have come up from Tempe. Sloane and Bailey are with them, along with Slade.

The sight of Bailey makes my chest ache all over again for Rayne. She should at least be with her friend right now while she's upset, not home alo–

Suddenly, I take in two figures sitting in the middle of the crowd.

My dad and Leslie.

Which means...

Rayne didn't get a ride home.

I tip my head back, barely stopping myself from letting out a full-on wolf howl in front of the humans from the other team.

Rayne—my gorgeous, darling female—*is somewhere out there alone.*

* * *

Rayne

I wake to the smell of mold and cleaning solution and soap. It takes a huge effort to unstick my eyelids and get my eyes open. I'm in some kind of cheap motel room, with my wrists tied together above my head and high heels on my feet.

High heels?

I lift my head to squint at my feet. It takes huge effort—my muscles barely work. My head weighs as much as my mom's Subaru.

There's a large bed pillow under my calves and—yes—I'm wearing a pair of stilettos.

Not just any pair.

The *Manolo Blahniks.*

The ones I sent to Footlover352.

As things click together in my mind, a surge of adrenaline runs through me, giving me the strength to try to tug at my arms. I can't break free, though. I'm too weak. The knots are too strong.

I listen for any sound but don't detect anyone else in the room. There's no breathing or movement. I look at the clock beside me. It says twelve o'clock. Is that twelve noon or midnight? I can't tell with the blackout shades drawn.

How long was I out?

That's when I realize I'm naked.

I was so focused on the shoes, I hadn't picked up on the fact that Footlover stripped me naked before tying me up.

Oh Fates, did he...

No. I don't think so. At least, I don't feel tender or used.

I resume my effort at tugging free of the bonds, but I'm still too limp. All I succeed in doing is chafing my wrists with the rope.

The door clicks open, and an unshaven guy in a wind-breaker walks in carrying a bag from In-N-Out Burger.

He's younger than I'd pictured. Like, in his mid-twenties, with dark hair that sticks up in several directions.

"Hi, Rayne." His familiar voice seems so much more sinister now. The guy is as dorky as I pictured, but now I know he's not just shy, he's unhinged. Dangerous.

I'm nauseated by him and my situation, but the smell of the food makes my stomach rumble. It must be twelve noon based on how hungry I suddenly am. Fate, I hope it's only been a half-day since he grabbed me and not more. I know we're not in Wolf Ridge because there's no In-N-Out there.

I summon all my inner strength and glare at him. "Untie me now." I use my best domme voice.

I wouldn't exactly say it works, but it does seem to fluster him. He drops the bag of food on the floor, then scrambles to pick it up.

"Now."

"Um...no. I can't do that."

"You can't keep me here." I keep my tone brusque and confident, despite the trembling in my legs.

His gaze travels to my feet, and I see the bulge in his crotch area grow.

Fates. I need to get out of here.

Think, Rayne, think.

You need to think your way out of this.

"You're even more beautiful than I imagined." He advances slowly.

"You can't have me."

Some of his awkwardness drops away. He meets my eyes for the first time. "I do have you." There's not a threat in the words. He's not gloating. He just states the irrefutable fact.

Fuck.

"You can't keep me," I modify.

He tips his head. "Maybe not. I don't really care. This is what I wanted."

Oh, Fates. Icy cold washes across my skin. That means he's going to kill me when he's done with whatever he plans on doing with me.

I need to get free.

Food might help.

"I'm hungry." I add a strong dose of petulance to my tone.

It seems to work because he scrambles to bring the bag closer to me. He pulls out a box of french fries and puts one to my lips.

If I weren't so starving, I might try to argue for the use of my own hands. Eating from his hand disgusts me. But I simply gobble the french fry down. "Are there any burgers?"

"Yeah. Yeah, I have a burger for you, right here."

"Just one?" I use my snotty tone again.

His brows pop. "How many do you eat?"

"At least three. I may be small, but I require a lot of calories."

"Well, you'll have to wait. I just have one for you now."

He picks the burger up and peels the half-wrapper back to offer me a bite.

I go feral–wolf on it, my teeth tearing at the meat.

He jerks the burger back, staring from the giant bite I took to me in shock.

"I told you, I'm hungry," I say with my mouth full. "Bring it back."

He offers it again, and I take another giant bite. The smell of the food revives me. I'm downright ravenous. When he tries to take the burger away, I lunge for it, taking a third bite into my mouth before I've even chewed the last. My cheeks puff out with food as I chew them both down.

Footlover appears slightly disgusted.

Good. Maybe he'll be so disgusted he'll forget about whatever it is he plans to do with me.

I swallow down the food and demand more. I finish the burger in five bites, then demand the fries.

Footlover keeps his fingers out of reach, bringing the end of each fry to my mouth while staying back.

"Where are we?" I ask with my mouth full. I need a napkin. I know I have the special burger sauce all over my mouth.

"Motel."

"Yeah, I gathered that. Where?"

He doesn't answer.

"You need to take me back to Wolf Ridge."

He shakes his head. "No, I don't."

"I don't want to be here with you. I don't like this. I will never make movies for you again."

I don't know–I'm just trying anything here.

He abandons the fries beside me, forcing me to twist my neck and strain against the bonds to grab one with my teeth.

He strokes two fingertips down the top of my thigh, along my shin bone, to the ankle strap of the stiletto.

"They're even prettier in person," he says. "Your face is pretty, too, but I don't really care about that. It's these feet. They're the best I've ever seen."

My body starts to shiver. I take it as a good sign. At least there's energy running through it now. My muscles must be waking up.

Once that tranquilizer wears off, I might have enough shifter strength to get myself out of these ropes by breaking the headboard they're tied to or something. I may not have shifted, but I'm not the weakling I used to be anymore.

I'm definitely not going to lie here and take whatever this creep wants to do to me.

"Cross your legs," he orders.

"No."

He picks one ankle up and crosses it over the other. I kick him in the head.

"Ow! Fuck, bitch." He holds his hand to his head and staggers away from me.

I'm celebrating the small win until he turns with a needle in his hand.

Oh, fuck!

I bide my time, waiting until he's close enough, then I twist to deliver a kick to his head, aiming the heel of the stiletto right at his eye socket.

I miss and the needle jabs into my shoulder.

"No," I snap, twisting to knock it away, but the fast-acting tranquilizer is already taking hold. My body sinks into the bed, as if invisible weights suddenly coiled around every limb, dragging me down, deeper and deeper until the entire room goes black.

* * *

Wilde

My dad, Sheriff Gleason, and Russ, his deputy, hold me down as I struggle on the floor.

I can't even remember why I'm in this fight.

Oh yeah, I was trying to tear the sheriff's office apart.

"Enough, Wilde." Alpha Green uses alpha command in his voice, and my body goes slack.

He comes to stand over me. My limbs are still pinned to the floor by the older men. "Do you want to find your mate?"

The words *your mate* snag my wolf's attention, and I'm suddenly listening, paying attention to my alpha.

He's talking about Rayne. Finding Rayne.

He called her my mate.

How can he tell? Never mind–it doesn't matter. He's talking about getting her back.

Yes, mate, my wolf howls.

I find my tongue. "Yes, Alpha."

"Then sit in that chair and wait for instructions."

"Yes, Alpha."

The men release me, and I climb jerkily to my feet and sink into the chair opposite the Sheriff's desk.

It's been sixteen hours since Rayne left the football stadium. We've been up all night searching for her. Two of the sheriff's deputies and I shifted to try to follow her scent, but it disappeared up the hill from the football stadium, indicating Rayne got into someone's car.

They traced her phone and found it by the side of the highway that leads down the hill to Phoenix.

Rayne's mom weeps in the corner. My dad's been trying to get her to eat all day, but she's been too upset.

I don't think I've eaten, either. I can't remember.

After I spotted Leslie in the stands at the game, I went frantic. I abandoned the end of the game to race in the direction Rayne had headed. When I didn't find her, I got in the Jeep and drove up and down. I called all her friends. Then I found our parents to let them know what happened, and they called in the Sheriff and Alpha Green. Now the entire town is on alert for Rayne, but we have no clues.

"What haven't you told us?" Alpha Green asks again.

"I told you. We had a fight. She was upset with me for getting her elected as Homecoming Queen. She said she would call her mom for a ride, but she didn't. When I saw Leslie in the stands, I went looking for her but couldn't find her."

"There's something else."

I can't think. I don't know what he wants to hear from me, but I would admit anything if it helps get Rayne back. I don't give a shit what anyone thinks about me. I don't care if it gets me kicked out of the pack.

"I took her virginity."

"For fuck's sake, Wilde!" My dad growls.

Alpha Green holds his hand up to silence my dad, his gaze still firmly on my face. "Something else. You were afraid for her from the start. Why? Do you suspect self-harm?"

I sputter. "Self-harm? No! Someone has her. A Venador, maybe." I reference the sinister group of wealthy humans who enjoy hunting shifters for sport. Word is, they've been targeting shifter teens through online chats.

But then my brain clicks back into full gear, and I know what he's picked up on. What I haven't yet said. "Okay. Okay. I'll tell you." I swallow. I hate to reveal Rayne's secret, but it has to be done. She's in danger. "Rayne's been selling photos and videos of her feet to save money for college. She sold this guy her shoes, and I had a bad feeling about it."

The sheriff surges to his feet. "And you just now think to tell us this? She's been missing for sixteen hours, Wilde."

I draw back my fist to punch the desk but Alpha Green gives the command, "*No*," and my arm slackens.

"Where does she sell them? What sites? Are there emails? Messages? I need everything." the sheriff says.

"Patreon and OnlyFans." I nod. "It's all on her laptop."

My dad pulls out his keys. "In her bedroom?"

"Yes. On the shelf above the bed."

"I'll be right back."

"Okay, I'll get Kylie or Jackson King on the phone," Alpha Green says, referring to a pair of shifters from Tucson whose billion-dollar company specializes in cyber security.

"The shoes she mailed–where did they go? Do you remember the name or address?"

"Yeah. The name was just initials– F. L.--and the address was a post office box in Chandler."

"Put out an Amber Alert on Rayne for the entire Phoenix, Tucson, Flagstaff area," Sheriff Gleason barks at Russ, his deputy.

Russ nods and leaves.

Alpha Green is talking to someone on the phone, but my brain is too addled to follow the conversation.

I stand. "I'm going to Chandler."

"Hold up, son," Sheriff Gleason says. "Wait until we have more information."

"I want to be there when you get the information."

"What if she's in the opposite direction?"

I know my brain isn't functioning, but I trust my wolf.

He wants me there. Now. I shake my head. "She's there. Call me when you get the info."

The sheriff shakes his head as I stalk out, but I don't care. I'm already running for the Jeep, grateful to finally have something to do.

I drive to Chandler and just start winding through the streets. I'm not stupid enough to think I'll spot her on the street, but I'm hoping my wolf might feel her. That I'll get a nudge in one direction or another. I end up in a shitty part of town, along the freeway.

I pull over and get out of the Jeep. Drag the surrounding scents in through my nostrils. It smells like misery. Carbon dioxide and concrete.

I start walking up the frontage road, begging my wolf to guide me, but he's as frantic as I am. Together, we're barely functioning.

I look up at the nearly full moon and send up a silent prayer.

Keep Rayne safe. Please, goddess. I will do anything if you just keep her safe.

* * *

Rayne

I fight to regain consciousness.

Someone is stroking my feet. I try to kick, but find my ankles have been restrained now.

I manage to open my eyes and find Footlover at the foot of the bed, one hand stroking my bare foot, the other his dick. The stilettos are off, lying on the bed beside me.

"Rayne," he moans when he sees I'm awake. He rubs his junk over my other bare foot.

The sight gives me a surge of adrenaline, which helps me get some feeling back into my fingers and toes.

"Get off me!" I snarl.

My indignation only seems to excite him, though. He pumps his fist harder over his cock, rolling his hips to stay in contact with my foot. He crushes my foot in his other hand.

"Ow! You're hurting me," I try.

"Use your toes," he commands. "Use your toes on my balls."

I don't know if it's terror or rage that makes my heat spike, but I'm suddenly burning up. I feel like puking and screaming at the same time.

Footlover pushes his finger in and out of the crevice between my big toe and second toe, and I nearly weep remembering Wilde. The way he'd sucked my toes. His tenderness with my feet.

Wilde, the guy I just broke up with.

If you would even consider us together to begin with.

Wilde, the guy I may never see again. It's that thought that brings on a flush of grief and desperation so heavy, I'm blinded.

I fight to come back to consciousness. I fight and I fight. Somewhere, I hear a splintering pounding.

The tranquilizer must've had a second phase.

I don't know how long I'm out or what I do to come back. All I know is that when I can finally see again—when objects and shapes come into focus, when I can see light and shadow and a human form—what I see doesn't make sense. Because everything is washed in blood.

Chapter Twenty-One

Wilde

Something makes me break into a run. I trust the urge, bolting as fast as my human form can take me. I end up circling a motel. My phone is ringing, and I'm torn between answering it and–

No. No time.

Rayne is here.

I catch her scent faintly. Or maybe it's just the memory of her scent, but I trust the sensation.

I want to shift, so I can follow the trail, but then my ears detect a sound.

A wolf snarl.

I hurl my body in its direction, slamming my shoulder against a motel door until it breaks from the frame and falls in.

It only takes me a second to understand what's happened.

Rayne–my beautiful, sweet female–stands naked on a bloodied carpet, broken tethers around her wrists and ankles. Blood covers her face and chest. Her blue eyes are wide and frightened as she stares at the dismembered man on the floor.

The scent of blood overpowers the room but under it– oh fates. Under it is Rayne's scent. Her new shifter scent.

And my wolf *fucking howls* with recognition.

I nearly drop to my knees with the awe of it, except my precious mate's fear takes all precedence.

"Wilde?" There's shock in her breathy voice. *"What happened?"*

I force myself to move slowly, to touch her gently. "You don't know, baby?" I take her shoulders and rub them. "You don't remember what happened?"

"No," she wails. "I...I...did *you* do that?" She gestures in the direction of the body.

"You shifted, baby. Your wolf got free to defend you. You're safe now. Your wolf took care of it."

She shivers, and I pull her against me and wrap my arms around her. "Did I...Wilde, did I–"

"Yeah, you killed him. It's okay, baby. You had no choice."

My phone rings again, and I pull it out and answer Alpha Green. "I found her. She's safe. She shifted and killed her captor. Um, we'll need some major cleanup, though."

"Where are you?"

"He had her at a motel."

"Okay, get Rayne home. We'll take care of the clean-up. Text me the address and room number."

"Thank you, Alpha."

I end the call. "We're going to get you out of here. Were you wearing your clothes when you shifted?"

"Um...what?" She's totally in shock.

I don't see fragments of clothing hanging off her the way

they do if you shift while dressed, which means she was probably naked.

That thought nearly makes me shift, the desire to further mangle the asshole on the floor's body is so strong.

When I spot her clothes folded on the dresser, I grab them and help Rayne into them. Then I steal a wet washcloth from the motel bathroom and scoop Rayne into my arms, wiping the blood from her chin as we walk.

"What about—" She looks back over her shoulder at the body.

I set her down to lift the door and prop it back in place. "It's okay, baby. Alpha Green wants me to get you home. They're going to take care of the rest."

The Jeep is a few blocks away, and I carry her there, unwilling to leave her alone even for the few moments it would take me to get it. I set her in the passenger seat and take off before the scene is discovered by anyone we'd have to answer to.

It's over an hour from Chandler to home, though, and I need Rayne in my arms, so I pull over a few miles away and get out.

"What's going on?"

I walk around to her door, open it, and use the washcloth to finish cleaning her face, chest, and hands.

Her eyes fill with tears. "I thought I'd never see you again."

"Rayne." My voice breaks. "I was so scared about losing you."

She searches my face, and there's so much vulnerability in her gaze that it nearly knocks me to my ass.

Fuck. I still have to explain. To heal this rift between us.

"Listen, baby. I'm so sorry about Homecoming."

She drops her face and looks away like she doesn't want to talk about it.

My touch is tender as I cradle her chin between my thumb and forefinger. "You were right, I was trying to fix you. And I need you to know that I've pulled my head out of my ass.

"Rayne, I was trying to get you to shift because I suspected you were my fated mate. But after you left, I realized I don't care whether you are or aren't. I don't care if you shift. I don't care if you become popular or stay on the sidelines. Baby, all I care about is being with you. I think you're the reason I'm back in Arizona. Not because I hated school or was homesick. I think my wolf was telling me to get back here, to you. He's the one who led me to get arrested."

Water swims in Rayne's beautiful eyes, and I lean in to give her a soft kiss on the forehead.

"But I did shift. So, I mean..."

My lips quirk. I bring my wrist to her nostrils. "What do you think?"

She draws a deep breath of my scent, and her eyes change to silver.

My smile grows.

Two tears simultaneously cascade down her cheeks.

"Well?"

"I-I don't know."

I'm full-on grinning now. "I think you do. I see your wolf, baby. She's looking right back at me now."

Rayne lets out a watery laugh. "You think I'm your mate?"

I smile and slowly shake my head, making her eyes round. "I don't *think*, Rayne-bow. I'm fucking *sure*. I'm claiming you. You belong to me, sweet girl. Whether you want me or not."

She lets out a breathy laugh, then sobers.

"Wilde, I don't even remember shifting. I don't know if I can do it again."

I cradle her face in both my hands. "Rayne, sweetheart. I told you–I don't care if you shift. I don't care if you dye your hair green or bark like a fucking seal. You're mine. And even if you weren't–even if I never got this clarity–" I hold her wrist to my nose and breathe deeply– "I would want you. I would want you because you're smart and kind, and you pay attention to people. And you're fucking adorable when you're mad. And you have the cutest little feet–but you are never selling videos of them online again."

Rayne shivers, and I'm instantly sorry for reminding her.

"Baby, are you okay? Will you tell me what happened?"

She reaches for me, wrapping her hands behind my head and tugging me to her. "I just want to be with you right now."

I pick her up from the seat to straddle my waist, so I can hold her tight. "I just want to be with you, too, Rayne-bow. That's all I want. You're the only thing that matters to me in this world."

Rayne breaks into a sob, and I hold her, rocking from foot to foot.

"Are you going to mark me?"

I let out a humorous laugh. "Are you still not sure?"

"I mean...now? Or tonight?"

I have to fight back the surge of lust that rockets through me. "Oh fuck, baby. Are you ready?"

"Yes."

"Shouldn't I get you home? You probably want to see your mom and get cleaned up."

She doesn't answer.

"Or I can get us a hotel for the night."

Rayne relaxes some more. "Hotel. Definitely."

"Okay." I tuck her back into her seat and fasten the seatbelt.

"You know what this means." My wolf is full-on gloating now.

"What?"

"I get to take you to the Homecoming dance."

"Oh. Um. I don't know."

I pull back, laughing. "You don't know? I don't get to publicly show you off to the entire fucking school as my mate?"

She blushes.

"Hmm?"

"Well...okay." Her smile is warm enough to light the night sky. "That does sound nice."

My wolf spikes the ball in a touchdown celebration.

Suddenly, everything in my life feels right. All the broken parts, the missing pieces, the dissociations are gone. Everything has aligned. The pieces fit together—not in the old configuration but in something beautiful and new.

I search my phone map for the closest, fanciest hotel and drive Rayne there. I have the cash Greg paid me from working at the auto shop, and I'm happy to blow the entire wad on making tonight perfect for Rayne.

Tonight, I will make her mine.

* * *

Rayne

Wilde checks us into a luxury hotel in downtown Phoenix and draws me a bath while he orders room service.

"They think I'm having a party up here with the seventeen burgers I just ordered." He grins.

I smile back. The giddiness that's taken over me is completely foreign. I'm trembly and light.

Wilde called my mom on the way to the hotel to let her know I was safe but he had to claim his mate, and we wouldn't be back until morning. I heard her laugh-crying as he ended the call.

He strips my clothes off and lifts me into the full bathtub. Using a washcloth, he cleans every inch of me.

The food comes, and he brings it into the bathroom, crouching beside the tub to feed me from his own hand, his watchful gaze never leaving my face.

He strokes my hair back. "I wish I'd seen your wolf. I'll bet she's magnificent."

This time, it doesn't hurt to hear he's interested in my wolf. He's also told me he doesn't care if I never shift again.

"You're going back to Duke," I tell him. I don't want him to throw away his future to stay here while I finish high school. It doesn't make sense.

He hesitates. "I'll finish football season. Then I'm transferring to ASU. That's where you're going, right?"

I melt a little more. "Yes." I finish the last burger and stand from the tub. "That sounds like a good plan."

Wilde wraps a towel around me and dries me off. In the bedroom, a champagne bucket stands beside the bed.

"Ooh. Fancy. How did you manage? You're not even twenty-one."

"Fake I.D., baby." He winks and crooks a finger at me. "Come here." He pours the champagne and hands me one glass, wrapping an arm behind my back. "I love you, Rayne Lansing." He tugs the towel wrapped under my armpits open and kisses between my breasts. "I love how small you are."

I brace for it, but his mention of my size doesn't hurt. I feel only love from him and for him. I sense his adoration of my body. I do believe that he finds me perfect, just as I am.

He kisses a circle around my nipple. "I love how soft you are." He sucks one nipple into his mouth. "I love how sweet you taste."

I pull his shirt off over his head. I want to taste him, too. I straddle his lap and nibble his neck.

"You want to mark me, little she-wolf?" Wilde chuckles. "Go ahead. I can take it."

Of course, female wolves don't mark their mates. We don't have the serum that coats our teeth to permanently embed our scent in another. I nip Wilde anyway, and my pussy gets wet picturing his claiming of me.

"Oh, fuck, Rayne." Suddenly, I'm on my back, Wilde on top of me, pinning me down. "You think I can't smell that sweet nectar of yours?" His eyes glow green, the muscles in his chest flex, making me dizzy with lust.

He crawls down between my legs, cupping my ass in his large hands, and licks into me.

I surrender to the sensation. The heat of his wet tongue, the delicious stroking of my most delicate parts.

"Wilde," I moan.

"That's right, baby. I want to hear my name while I'm eating you."

I repeat it. A lot. Because he gives me the tonguing of the century, licking and lapping at my folds, sucking and nibbling, bringing me to orgasm after orgasm.

"Wilde, I need more," I cry out.

He lifts his head, his lips glossy with my juices. "I thought I *was* giving you more."

"I need you. Your cock. *Please.*"

His grin is so cocky. "Say no more, baby. My mate will be satisfied." He shucks his jeans and boxers and climbs up over me.

I can hardly breathe. I'm so excited. My body trembles everywhere. I just came five times on Wilde's tongue, but he didn't use his fingers at all, and the anticipation for penetration has me out of my mind with need.

I reach for him as he climbs up over me, but he grins and rolls me to my belly. "Spread your legs, beautiful."

I part my legs wide, and he kneels between them and rubs the head of his cock over my sopping entrance.

"Lift your hips." Wilde tucks a pillow under my pelvis to lift my ass, then gives it a slap.

"Mmm," I moan.

He squeezes my cheek roughly and then eases into my tight entrance. I love the sensation of him snug inside me. Filling me. Taking me.

And now, soon, *claiming me.*

Wilde goes slowly, filling me, pulling back, filling me again. Every time he presses in, I groan in satisfaction. He fists my hair and lifts my head to give me a searing kiss from the side. He starts to thrust a little harder, snapping his hips to get in deep. When the force pushes me up on the bed, he catches my nape to hold me in place.

"You gonna take it hard tonight, Rayne-bow?"

"Yes, please," I whimper. Because despite the pleasure, it's not enough. I want more. I want to feel Wilde in every cell of my body. I want him to be rough and wild. To show me how much he desires me. I want to feel fully claimed by him, forever.

"Good," he growls, thrusting in even harder.

I arch my low back to offer my ass up to him even more,

to get him where I need him. He plows into me, his loins slapping against my ass. I brace my hands against the headboard. It's way too much, but I absolutely love it. Crave it. Need it.

My cries grow louder, higher in pitch. I'm sure if there's someone in the hotel room beside us, they're calling the lobby right now.

I don't care. I wouldn't stop if they were beating down the door right now. All I care about is riding this incredible wave with Wilde.

"Rayne." Wilde's voice sounds ragged. His thrusts grow jerky. "Rayne. Baby. Rayne...it's you." He thrusts into me and comes.

I orgasm, my body convulsing with ecstatic release. It's so much more than a physical experience. It's beyond even a spiritual one.

It's cosmic.

An aligning of who I am—who I've always been but never trusted—with the one, perfect mate for me. All of the so-called problems in my life and his life suddenly seem inconsequential. The Homecoming debacle. The kidnapping. The fact that I killed a man. That Wilde's going back to Duke. Not remembering that I shifted.

None of it matters. All that matters is my mate.

Wilde's teeth sink into my shoulder, breaking the skin to embed his scent in my flesh. The pain is eclipsed by pleasure. Glorious, mind-altering pleasure.

The serum coursing into my bloodstream sends me into a state of euphoria. My entire body relaxes, beyond sated.

Metamorphosed.

That's when I know for certain that I'll be able to shift. That I am a she-wolf now.

I also realize it was Wilde's semen in me that first time

that kicked my transition fully into gear, just as it's his essence in me now that makes me feel whole. Like I'm finally the being I kept hidden from the world for some dark and mysterious reason.

Wilde rocks his cock in and out slowly as he eases his teeth from my shoulder and licks the wounds closed. He strokes my hair, petting my head like a cat's. "Are you okay, "Rayne-bow? Does it hurt?"

I turn my face to the side to smile dreamily up at him. "I'm perfect." The words don't even express how incredible I feel.

He grins back and pulls out to roll me over. "You're mine now." He hovers over me, braced on one arm. I lift my legs to wrap around his waist and pull his cock down to the notch between my legs where it belongs.

"I'm yours," I murmur.

* * *

Wilde

Saturday night, I sit on the couch in my best, er only, suit waiting for Rayne to emerge from her–our–bedroom for the Homecoming dance.

We got home this afternoon after making love in the hotel all night and all morning.

I wasn't sure if my dad would kick my ass for not bringing Rayne home the minute I found her, but he and Leslie both seemed overjoyed.

"I can't believe it," Leslie kept saying over and over again, tears streaming down her face. "You both found your fated mate, right here, under our roof. It's incredible."

Rayne called her human friend and told him we were out as a couple, and she wanted to go to the dance with me.

Of course, I had to eavesdrop, and the guy was surprisingly gracious about it. I guess it was true that he didn't have designs on her.

At long last, the door opens and Rayne steps out. She's in a little silver halter dress that hugs her hips and draws her breasts together into the most alluring cleavage I've ever seen.

My hands close into fists. "You were going to wear that for him?" I snarl.

It's wrong, but I can't help myself. I know I should be telling her how amazing she looks, how honored I am to take her, but all I can think—

Rayne can reach my shoulders in her sexy heels. She leans into me and lifts her face. Her scent instantly calms me. Getting my hands on her helps more. "I wore this for you," she murmurs.

I slide my hands down her sides to her ass and squeeze. "You look beautiful. Beautiful enough to eat."

"It matches my eyes," she murmurs.

My cock stirs. "Yes, your beautiful wolf eyes." I want to see her wolf, want to teach her how to shift without the post-traumatic amnesia from it, but I'm not going to push. I made that mistake once, and I will never hurt her with it again.

"Oh, let me see!" Leslie chirps, rushing down the hall with her phone out to take photos. She gasps. "You two look incredible."

We stand and pose for her, inside and outside, under a tree. Then I pick Rayne up and carry her to the Jeep.

She loops her arms around my neck. "I can walk, you know."

"I need to hold you." I settle her in the seat and buckle the seatbelt around her.

"Yeah?" She sounds breathless. Pleased.

"All the fucking time. I don't know how I'll make it through football season without you."

"We'll Facetime. Every day. And I can always sell more photos of my feet to buy a plane–" Rayne breaks off and grins at my growl of disapproval.

"Tell me you're joking?"

Her smile is fond. She's absolutely glowing with a radiance that comes from below the skin. "Mostly."

"Come here." I cradle her face and urge her closer. "I love you."

"I love you, Wilde Woodward."

"We should get married."

She laughs. "Why?" She's right. Wolves don't require the human construct of marriage. Mating goes so far beyond that.

"I don't know. Insurance or something? I just want to do it all with you."

"Mmm," she murmurs. "I thought we did that last night. And this morning."

"Oh, baby. We haven't even scratched the surface of the things I'm going to do to you in bed." I give her a claiming kiss, the kind aimed to curl her toes in those sexy stilettos she's wearing. Then I shut the door and walk around to my side.

I can't wait to take Rayne to this dance. Everyone there will catch her new scent. Not just the one that says she's a shifter now, but my scent embedded in her skin. My claim on her.

No one will ever fuck with or demean Rayne again. She belongs to me, and she will be respected. I think that will go without saying, but I will make sure everyone understands it tonight if it's not clear.

Renee Rose

The dance is over at the brewery in their banquet hall. This town is so small and enmeshed that at least half of the kids' parents work at the brewery. It's pack-owned, and the school is predominantly pack kids, so that means they roll out the red carpet for the students at events like this.

I park in the brewery lot. Even though we're late, there's a place right up front. Almost like it was reserved for us. I take Rayne's hand, and we walk under the archway of balloons and streamers to get inside.

There are double-takes left and right as people catch sight of us together. The fact that tonight we're an actual couple, not new stepsiblings. Or maybe they're just admiring how beautiful Rayne looks because she is truly stunning. Especially in the high heels no other female her age even knows how to walk in.

Abe is the first–or perhaps the only one with balls big enough–to approach us. "Hey, guys. There's my Home-coming queen." He flashes a pirate smile at us.

I pull Rayne closer to my side. "She's not *your* anything, Oakley. Rayne is all mine now."

Abe's nostrils flare as he takes in her scent, and he raises his brows in appreciation. "*Mates.* Wow. What did your parents say?"

Of course, everyone hears Abe's words and openly stares at us.

"They're cool with it." I massage the back of Rayne's neck, letting her know I'm here. Her champion. Her mate.

"Good for you both."

"Rayne!" A girl named River walks over, a cheerleader, I think. Casey walks behind her in an oddly protective way. The cheerleader holds out the homecoming queen crown. "Here's your crown, Rayne."

I tense, but I don't sense any upset coming from Rayne

other than flushed cheeks from the attention. I think she's pleased.

Instead of handing it to Rayne, the cheerleader sets it on her head, adjusting it until she deems it perfect. "You look beautiful." She gives Rayne a quick peck on the cheek. "Thanks for what you said to Casey," she whispers in her ear. Then, in a normal voice, she says, "Congratulations. On the mating, too." There's genuine warmth in the girl's words.

Behind her, Casey gives us both an approving nod. "You mated your stepsister. I like it. Forbidden love."

That's when I get it. *Casey and the cheerleader.* Not exactly forbidden in Wolf Ridge, but out of the norm, for sure. Shifters are not a homophobic society, but certainly heteronormative. Our species can be strongly gendered.

"You gotta do you, Casey," I tell her. "The pack will follow." She's an alpha female. She can make new rules for herself at Wolf Ridge High.

"That's pretty much what your mate told me, too." Casey gives Rayne a rueful smile before the two of them walk away.

"Come on, let's say hi to Lincoln." Rayne tugs me toward a wall where Lincoln stands surrounded by a bunch of human females.

He looks bored, but not uncomfortable.

"Hey, Lincoln." Rayne gives the guy a hug, and I don't even want to smash him into a pancake.

I hold out my hand. "Hey, man. Thanks for being cool about the change in plan."

Lincoln shrugs. "It's cool. I'm glad you two found a way to make things happen."

Rayne beams at him. She looks every inch the Homecoming Queen. Beautiful. Goddess-like. Ready to rule her court with love and grace.

"And now will the Homecoming royalty come out to the dance floor?" J.J. requests from the stage.

The crowd claps and whistles.

"Are you ready for this, your majesty?" I wink at Rayne, holding out my hand with a bow.

She flushes and smiles. Her eyes glow a radiant silver as she gazes up at me. "With you? Always."

She gives Lincoln a quick peck on the cheek then gives me her hand, so I can lead her out to the floor.

Abe's smart enough to grab a random girl to be his dance partner as we take the floor with the junior royalty couple. For some reason, he's glaring at a human couple standing in the corner. The girl looks like Lincoln–must be his twin.

I pull Rayne into my arms where she fits. Her small body against my large one. Her softness against my muscles. Right here, where she was always meant to be. She tips her face up to me, looking absolutely beautiful in her crown.

"You're perfection, my queen," I murmur.

She flushes. "I love you."

My grin turns wicked. "Doesn't matter if you do or don't, Rayne-bow. You belong to me now."

Her eyes turn liquid silver under the spotlights. "How long until we can ditch this dance?"

I laugh out loud. "It's your night, sweetheart. I'm at your service."

* * *

Rayne

"You're my mate," Wilde growls as he slams me up

against the wall in Abe Oakley's cabin. His eyes glow green in the darkness. My legs are around his waist, the short dress I'm wearing is ruched up my hips.

After the first dance, he informed Abe we were using his cabin, and he should keep everyone away until we emerged.

Now, he's carried me inside, but we haven't made it to a bedroom. We're just inside the door in the dark cabin. Amazingly, even without the light of the full moon shining through the window, I could see perfectly in the dark now.

"You haven't been fucked up against a wall, yet, have you, Rayne-bow?" Wilde grinds the bulge of his erection between my parted legs.

"Not yet," I purr. My arms loop around his neck.

"I'm your first. I get all your firsts," he claims.

"First and only."

That sends him into a frenzy. He yanks at my panties, ripping them in half to get them off my legs without putting me down.

I don't complain. I love this savage side of Wilde. The idea that he's so desperate to take my body that he can't control himself intoxicates me.

Keeping me pinned against the wall, he uses one hand to unbutton his pants and free his erection. His lips meld against mine at the same time the head of his cock rubs over my slit.

I moan my assent. It feels so good. So smooth and satisfying. So delicious.

His tongue thrusts in my mouth at the same time he pushes inside me, a simultaneous claiming. One hand slides into my Homecoming gown to cup my bare breast. Wilde devours me, his strong, athletic body in control of every part of my small one. He's rougher now that my wolf has emerged. It's okay, because the fleeting pain of his commanding touch is infinitely satisfying. Like my wolf wants it as wild and feral as he can give it.

Wilde's hips snap as he drives into me, his lips still locked on mine, his fingers pinching and twisting my nipple, making me gasp into his mouth. He swallows my cries. Thrusts harder.

"This is your first time against the wall, baby," he says in a rough voice. "And then you're going to have your first time bent over a couch." He plows into me, driving me up the wall and down again. "And then your first time on your hands and knees. First time in the ass."

I lose my mind. My nails score the back of Wilde's neck, drawing blood. I think I'm screaming, I'm not sure. My ears are ringing too loudly to know what that sound is.

There's a moment of no time. The space between seconds. The vast expanse of a zero point.

And then I come, my channel tightening around Wilde's dick. "That's it, baby. Come all over my cock," he commands, and I convulse against the wall, my middle shaking and trembling, my inner thighs squeezing like a vise around his hips.

As soon as I finish, he makes good on his promise, carrying me to the arm of the sofa, where he bends me over, spanks me, and takes me again.

Five incredible positions later, it's past midnight, and I'm as limp as a rag doll, but we hear the howling of wolves in the near distance.

"Come on." Wilde grabs my hand and tugs me off the bed where he'd just taken my anal virginity. He pulls me outside where we stand naked under the moonlight. He looks at me with wolf eyes. "Want to run?"

My insecurities pop up. My fears. I don't know how to shift. Last time I shifted, I killed a man.

But Wilde's standing beside me. My lover. My mate. My sexy, sinful stepbrother. He will take care of me. He's everything.

I nod. In a blink of an eye, he's on all fours, an enormous, beautiful black wolf. He licks my calf.

I don't know what happens. I don't know how I do it. All I know is I have this intense feeling in my body that I want to run with him, and suddenly I'm looking down at two delicate snow white paws.

I bound forward in surprise, my unfamiliar body twisting with joy in the air.

Somehow, I can tell Wilde's laughing. His wolf's mouth is open wide in a crocodile grin. I run to him, bumping my shoulder against his much larger one.

He lifts one mighty paw and throws me to my side, pinning me on my back for a tongue-lapping. I yip and whine in pleasure. In fact, I've never felt such ecstasy.

Wilde releases me and nips my flank to get me back on my feet, and then he's chasing me in the direction of the wolf howls.

We find the kids from Wolf Ridge on the mesa. Some are in their human form, sitting around the fire. Some are naked, like they just shifted back. Others still run and chase each other in wolf form.

Everyone stops when we come into the clearing.

"Is that..."

"It must be Rayne."

"Yeah, that's Wilde and Rayne. Holy shit. She's a white wolf."

"Black and white. Yin and yang. So cool."

Suddenly everyone's in wolf form, gathered around me,

sniffing, licking, welcoming me to the pack.

It's almost too much joy to take. I feel like my heart might explode from the pleasure of it. I want to cry and laugh all at the same time. I lift my nose to the moon and yip and howl with joy.

The pack kids mimic me. Join me. We are one. Joined together by the moon and our blood and rules of this tight-knit community.

And then Wilde nudges me out of the circle. At first, I'm not sure what he wants, but then I realize.

He wants me to run. Tonight, I lead the pack on the full moon run.

I take off and everyone follows, Wilde pacing right alongside me. There are yips and cries of pleasure all around me as we spill down the side of the mountain, chasing our own wildness. Exploring thes sense of freedom. Communion with each other and nature.

I love it all so much, and yet it's just icing on the cake.

I have Wilde now. I'm one of the lucky few to find her fated mate.

And even more than that–I have myself. My wolf self and my human form. Neither is defective. Both are a miracle to behold.

We run and play and run some more.

At sunrise, I find myself standing naked again, nestled in Wilde's arms, watching the soft glow traveling across the mountain. Around me, stand my classmates. Shifters who never accepted me before, now in complete oneness with me.

"I love you, baby," Wilde murmurs as he strokes the back of my head.

"I love you, too," I whisper, happy tears blurring my vision.

Epilogue

Wilde

I slam the football into the turf and backflip as the stadium and my teammates go wild.

"Touchdown! And that's the game! An incredible score by Sophomore Wide Receiver Wilde Woodward, Duke just won the bowl game!"

Confetti flies. My teammates pick me up and carry me down the field. I pump my fist in the air, but I'm looking to the stands where the most incredible little blonde is on her feet cheering for me. The one I haven't seen in person since Christmas break.

The only way I made it through was lots and lots of video chats, frequent mailings of clothes with her scent and the knowledge that next year we'll be at ASU together.

I contacted their coach about transferring, and they offered me a full ride next year including money from boosters and endorsements. It also comes with a primo dorm I can share with Rayne. After the struggle and strife of being apart this school year, we'll never have to do it again. I need to wake up every morning with her in my bed. Have her scent all over my pillow. Have the taste of her on my

261

tongue. I need to protect her, care for her, honor her in all the ways I failed to in the beginning.

I catch sight of her–how, I'm not sure, considering she's tiny, and the stadium is packed with jostling fans, but a wolf knows his mate. Her fists are in the air, and she's jumping up and down.

The moment my buddies drop me to my feet, I break into a run for the stands, leaping up the wall to get to the bleachers, causing the crowd to scream in delight. I get to Rayne and scoop her into my arms.

And then I'm home. Not in Arizona, but exactly where I need to be. With my beautiful, sweet stepsister's legs wrapped around my waist.

"You were perfect," she says.

I know what she means. It's not the athleticism she admires, but my ability to make it look hard, when it's actually all too easy for me.

I drop kisses all over her face.

I don't even have words for how happy I am to see her. To hold her. "Baby," is all I can croak over and over again.

"Look," she points at the stadium video screen–the one that shows replays and close-ups of fans. On it is a close-up of a baby wrapped up in a blanket.

"What?" I don't get it.

The video camera pans back from the baby to show my dad and Leslie waving at a camera.

"Duke star Wilde Woodward became a big brother today. His parents sent this video to congratulate him on the game," the announcer says. "Eleven pounds, twelve ounces. Looks like there will be another football player in the family."

"Oh. *Oh!* Oh, wow. Did you know?"

Rayne laughs. "Yeah. They texted me just as the game

started. His name is Nathanial. He and my mom are doing great."

I grin. "It's so weird, right? That we're both siblings to him?"

"We're the new measure of weird, for sure." Rayne lifts her smiling face to me for more kisses.

I make this one slow and deep, stroking my tongue between her lips, exploring her.

I'm so taken by the moment, that it feels as if the stadiums are going wild, once more. Oh wait, they are.

Rayne pulls away, laughing, and points once more to the screen, where the close-up is on us, this time. Our kiss. Our love.

I wave and return to kissing the living daylights out of my mate. Showing her she's mine forever. Everything I need.

Everything I live for.

* * *

Thank you for reading Step Alpha! If you enjoyed it, **I would so appreciate your review.** They make a huge difference for indie authors.

For **a special bonus scene and for news on the release of Abe and Lauren's story**, subscribe to my newsletter: https://subscribepage.com/alphastemp

Want Another FREE Renee Rose book?

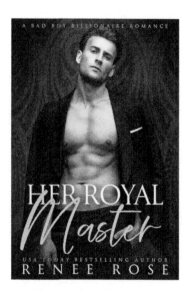

Read Her Royal Master for free here: https://hyzr.app.link/
herroyalmaster

Want Another FREE Renee Rose book?

Other Titles by Renee Rose

Paranormal

Wolf Ridge High Series

Alpha Bully

Alpha Knight

Step Alpha

Two Marks Series

Untamed

Tempted

Desired

Enticed

Wolf Ranch Series

Rough

Wild

Feral

Savage

Fierce

Ruthless

Bad Boy Alphas Series

Alpha's Temptation

Alpha's Danger

Alpha's Prize

Alpha's Challenge

Alpha's Obsession

Alpha's Desire

Alpha's War

Alpha's Mission

Alpha's Bane

Alpha's Secret

Alpha's Prey

Alpha's Sun

Shifter Ops

Alpha's Moon

Alpha's Vow

Alpha's Revenge

Alpha's Fire

Alpha's Rescue

Alpha's Command

Midnight Doms

Alpha's Blood

His Captive Mortal

All Souls Night

Alpha Doms Series

The Alpha's Hunger

The Alpha's Promise

The Alpha's Punishment

The Alpha's Protection (Dirty Daddies)

Other Paranormal

The Winter Storm: An Ever After Chronicle

Made Men Series

Don't Tease Me

Don't Tempt Me

Don't Make Me

Chicago Bratva

"Prelude" in Black Light: Roulette War

The Director

The Fixer

"Owned" in Black Light: Roulette Rematch

The Enforcer

The Soldier

The Hacker

The Bookie

The Cleaner

The Player

The Gatekeeper

Alpha Mountain

Hero

Rebel

Warrior

Vegas Underground Mafia Romance

King of Diamonds

Mafia Daddy

Jack of Spades

Ace of Hearts

Joker's Wild

His Queen of Clubs

Dead Man's Hand

Wild Card

Contemporary

Daddy Rules Series

Fire Daddy

Hollywood Daddy

Stepbrother Daddy

Master Me Series

Her Royal Master

Her Russian Master

Her Marine Master

Yes, Doctor

Double Doms Series

Theirs to Punish

Theirs to Protect

Holiday Feel-Good

Scoring with Santa

Saved

Other Contemporary

Black Light: Valentine Roulette

Black Light: Roulette Redux

Black Light: Celebrity Roulette

Black Light: Roulette War

Black Light: Roulette Rematch

Punishing Portia (written as Darling Adams)

The Professor's Girl

Safe in his Arms

Sci-Fi

Zandian Masters Series

His Human Slave

His Human Prisoner

Training His Human

His Human Rebel

His Human Vessel

His Mate and Master

Zandian Pet

Their Zandian Mate

His Human Possession

Zandian Brides

Night of the Zandians

About Renee Rose

USA TODAY BESTSELLING AUTHOR RENEE ROSE loves a dominant, dirty-talking alpha hero! She's sold over two million copies of steamy romance with varying levels of kink. Her books have been featured in USA Today's *Happily Ever After* and *Popsugar*. Named Eroticon USA's Next Top Erotic Author in 2013, she has also won *Spunky and Sassy's* Favorite Sci-Fi and Anthology author, *The Romance Reviews* Best Historical Romance, and *has* hit the *USA Today* list over a dozen times with her Chicago Bratva, Bad Boy Alpha and Wolf Ranch series, as well as various anthologies.

Renee loves to connect with readers!
www.reneeroseromance.com
renee@reneeroseromance.com

- facebook.com/reneeroseromance
- twitter.com/reneeroseauthor
- instagram.com/reneeroseromance
- amazon.com/Renee-Rose/e/B008AS0FT0
- bookbub.com/authors/renee-rose
- tiktok.com/@authorreneerose